T0018650

Titles by Jenn McKinlay

Cupcake Bakery Mysteries

SPRINKLE WITH MURDER
BUTTERCREAM BUMP OFF
DEATH BY THE DOZEN
RED VELVET REVENGE
GOING, GOING, GANACHE
SUGAR AND ICED
DARK CHOCOLATE DEMISE
VANILLA BEANED

CARAMEL CRUSH
WEDDING CAKE CRUMBLE
DYING FOR DEVIL'S FOOD
PUMPKIN SPICE PERIL
FOR BATTER OR WORSE
STRAWBERRIED ALIVE
SUGAR PLUM POISONED
FONDANT FUMBLE

Library Lover's Mysteries

BOOKS CAN BE DECEIVING
DUE OR DIE
BOOK, LINE, AND SINKER
READ IT AND WEEP
ON BORROWED TIME
A LIKELY STORY
BETTER LATE THAN NEVER

DEATH IN THE STACKS
HITTING THE BOOKS
WORD TO THE WISE
ONE FOR THE BOOKS
KILLER RESEARCH
THE PLOT AND THE PENDULUM
FATAL FIRST EDITION

Hat Shop Mysteries

CLOCHE AND DAGGER
DEATH OF A MAD HATTER
AT THE DROP OF A HAT
COPY CAP MURDER

ASSAULT AND BERET
BURIED TO THE BRIM
FATAL FASCINATOR

Bluff Point Romances

ABOUT A DOG
BARKING UP THE WRONG TREE
EVERY DOG HAS HIS DAY

Happily Ever After Romances

THE GOOD ONES
THE CHRISTMAS KEEPER

Standalone Novels

PARIS IS ALWAYS A GOOD IDEA
WAIT FOR IT

SUMMER READING
LOVE AT FIRST BOOK

Fondant Fumble

Jenn McKinlay

BERKLEY PRIME CRIME
New York

BERKLEY PRIME CRIME
Published by Berkley
An imprint of Penguin Random House LLC
penguinrandomhouse.com

Copyright © 2024 by Jennifer McKinlay
Excerpt from *A Merry Little Murder Plot* by Jenn McKinlay
copyright © 2024 by Jennifer McKinlay
Penguin Random House supports copyright. Copyright fuels creativity, encourages
diverse voices, promotes free speech, and creates a vibrant culture. Thank you for buying
an authorized edition of this book and for complying with copyright laws by not
reproducing, scanning, or distributing any part of it in any form without permission.
You are supporting writers and allowing Penguin Random House to continue to
publish books for every reader.

BERKLEY and the BERKLEY & B colophon are registered trademarks and
BERKLEY PRIME CRIME is a trademark of Penguin Random House LLC.

ISBN: 9780593549148

First Edition: June 2024

Printed in the United States of America
1 3 5 7 9 10 8 6 4 2

This is a work of fiction. Names, characters, places, and incidents either are the product
of the author's imagination or are used fictitiously, and any resemblance to actual persons,
living or dead, business establishments, events, or locales is entirely coincidental.

PUBLISHER'S NOTE: The recipes contained in this book are to be followed exactly as
written. The publisher is not responsible for your specific health or allergy needs that may
require medical supervision. The publisher is not responsible for any adverse reactions to
the recipes contained in this book.

For Paige Shelton and Kate Carlisle,
brilliant writers and even better friends

One

"Tyler Matthews and Keogh Graham are buying a franchise," Tate Harper, the financial wizard behind the bakery Fairy Tale Cupcakes, announced at the weekly staff meeting.

Melanie DeLaura and Angie Harper exchanged an amused glance and burst out laughing. The three of them had been best friends since middle school. When Mel had quit a high-stress marketing job to become a professional cupcake baker, both Angie and Tate had joined her. Now Angie and Tate were married with an adorable daughter, Emari, while Mel had married her childhood crush, Joe DeLaura, who also happened to be the middle of Angie's seven older brothers.

"Oh, honey, that's hilarious," Angie said. She reached

up to tighten the messy bun she'd twisted her long dark hair into as her laughter had shaken it loose.

"I'm not joking," Tate said.

"Right, because the two best players on the Arizona Scorpions NFL team are suddenly going to become cupcake bakers?" Mel asked. She rolled her eyes then studied the plate of cupcakes on the table between them.

It was ten o'clock in the morning, and while she never let the time of day dictate her cupcake consumption, she did wonder if it was too early to have one right now. She glanced at the flavors and decided on a strawberry cupcake, which, loaded with chunks of real strawberry, had a very high fruit-to-cake ratio. So it was more of a fruit salad than a cake, really, and that was healthy. Right? Right. She reached for one of the pink confections, feeling very virtuous.

"I'm not kidding. I have the paperwork right here," Tate insisted. He gestured to the stack of papers beside him.

The three of them were seated in the front of the bakery in one of the booths beside the large picture window that looked out onto the street. The bakery's pink interior with black accents embraced the 1950s heyday of Old Town Scottsdale, the neighborhood where they'd all grown up and subsequently opened their first bakery.

The shop hadn't yet opened for the day, and every Monday morning they took advantage of the quiet to go over the business particulars. Tate was in charge of the finances and the franchises, Melanie was the executive chef in charge of creating their cupcake flavors, and Angie was Mel's assistant, keeping the flagship bakery in Scottsdale leading the way for all of their franchises.

"You're just teasing me because you know Keogh Graham is my NFL husband," Mel said. "Not nice."

Tate shoved a hand through his wavy light brown hair, looking exasperated. "I'm being honest. Why does no one believe me?"

"'I admire that honesty. That's a noble quality. Never lose that,'" Angie said. She gave Mel a side-eye.

"*Mrs. Doubtfire*," Mel identified the movie quote. It was a game the three of them had played since they were middle school movie buffs. She and Angie exchanged a high five and turned back to Tate.

There was a knock on the front door just as Marty Zelaznik, their octogenarian counter help, pushed through the swinging door from the kitchen into the front of the bakery. Scrawny and bald, Marty strode forward with his usual take-charge attitude, and Mel wondered what he'd been like as a younger man. She had a feeling he'd been a force of nature.

"You want me to get rid of them?" Marty asked. "We're not open for another ten minutes."

Tate glanced past Mel and Angie, who had their backs to the window. "No, go ahead and let them in," Tate said.

Mel powered down her tablet since it was clear the meeting was over. "Thanks for the update on everything, Tate, and nice try on the football player franchise. Ha! That was a good one."

Tate glanced at the door as Marty turned the dead bolt. A small smile curved Tate's lips as he slid out of his side of the booth. Marty pulled the door open, greeting the customers in his usual exuberant Marty way.

"Welcome to Fairy Tale Cupca . . ." Marty staggered

3

back from the door. His mouth dropped open as two of the largest men Mel had ever seen entered the bakery.

It took her only a moment to recognize Keogh Graham. Tall, dark, and handsome, with his trademark braids that reached his shoulders and his wide grin, it was as if he'd stepped right out of *Monday Night Football* and into the bakery. Mel clutched the bib of her apron and looked at Tate.

"That's Keogh Graham," she said.

"I know," Tate said. And while he didn't use those words, his tone reeked of *I told you so.*

Angie grabbed Mel's forearm and squeezed it hard. In a shriek-whisper, she said, "And Tyler Matthews is with him."

Not only were the two NFL football players massive, they were both ridiculously good-looking. As in movie star gorgeous, despite Keogh's broken nose and the deep scar on Tyler's chin. If anything, those flaws made them even more handsome.

"Good morning, Tate, ladies," Keogh said. His voice was deep, and he glanced at Marty, who stood frozen, and said, "Sir . . . er . . . are you all right?"

Marty's head bobbled on his skinny neck in the affirmative but it was clear he had lost his powers of speech.

"Can I get you a glass of water or something?" Tyler asked him. He ran a hand through his pale brown hair while his blue eyes narrowed with concern.

Marty shook his head from side to side.

Tate stepped forward with his hand outstretched. "Come on in, guys. I think my colleagues are a bit starstruck. Just give them a sec."

"Mel," Angie hissed as Keogh and Tyler shook Tate's hand and then walked towards them.

"Yeah?" Mel answered.

"Is this real? Is your NFL boyfriend actually here in the building or am I hallucinating?"

"Um, that's NFL husband," Mel corrected her. "And if you're delusional then so am I."

"Oh, goody, a mass hallucination," Angie said. "I always wanted one of those . . . said no one ever."

Tate gestured for the men to sit and Tyler and Keogh slid onto the bench seat opposite Mel and Angie. They had to adjust themselves, sitting a bit sideways to accommodate their large frames in the booth. Mel wanted to reach across the table and poke Keogh's hand just to see if he was real, but she was aware that this might be considered rude so she decided against it.

Tate grabbed a chair from a nearby table and sat at the end of the booth. He grinned at Keogh and Tyler. "Your timing is perfect. I just told the girls you were going to buy a franchise but they didn't believe me."

Tyler and Keogh glanced at Angie and Mel. Their expressions were earnest and Mel thought she might be having an out-of-body experience. These guys wanted to buy a cupcake bakery? She couldn't wrap her brain around it.

Correctly reading her expression, Keogh said, "It's no joke. We want in."

"Key has convinced me that owning a small business is a sound investment," Tyler said.

"It is," Keogh insisted. "We need to have something to do after we retire, like how George Foreman took up barbecuing after he hung up his gloves at the end of his boxing career."

"Barbecue feels a bit more masculine," Tyler said. He flexed as he turned to study the bakery, and the muscles under his T-shirt rippled. "There's an awful lot of pink in here. Not that there's anything wrong with that."

It was true. Even Tate had balked about the level of pink Mel had insisted upon when they first opened their doors. She tried to see it through the football players' eyes. Pink vinyl upholstery in the booths, pink trim on the windows and walls, and pink accents everywhere. Okay, sure, it was a lot of pink, but Mel thought it was cheerful. She also thought people wouldn't balk at the color pink if it was called light red.

"We can tone it down in your franchise," Tate said. "Maybe skew a little more aqua than pink."

"Or we could do it up in the team colors," Tyler said. "The Arizona Scorpions' trademark orange and black."

That slapped Mel right out of her stupor. "No."

Tyler looked surprised as if he wasn't accustomed to hearing that word and had to process its meaning for a beat. Tate shot Mel an exasperated look.

"What I mean." Mel paused to clear her throat. "Orange and black are really a seasonal color combo, you know, for Halloween, so you probably want something a bit more far-reaching."

"Aqua would be cool," Keogh said.

"Right . . . sure . . . absolutely," Mel said. She felt her face get warm. Silently, she chastised herself. *You are a happily married woman, get it together.*

"Yeah, we could do that," Tyler agreed. "Although, the Seattle Booms, our rivals, have aqua as one of their colors."

"We're talking bakeries, not football," Keogh said. "Get your mind off the game for a second."

Tyler raised his hands in the air. "Sorry. Force of habit."

Both men glanced past her with their eyebrows raised. Mel turned to find Marty standing on the booth seat behind her. He had his cell phone out and was attempting to take a selfie of himself and the football players.

"Marty, get down," Angie cried. "Before you fall and break something."

Marty ignored her, shooting a peace sign and winking at the reflected image of himself and the players.

"See? That's why we need our colors," Tyler said. "Fans are going to want to buy our cupcakes in a bakery that lets people know they're in Scorpion territory."

"You can just make one wall an Instagram wall," Marty said. "Then customers can take selfies with life-size pics of you. It'll be great."

Keogh and Tyler exchanged a glance, and Keogh said, "That's not a bad idea."

Marty hopped down from his perch. "Not bad? It's genius."

Tyler looked like he was going to debate the description, but Keogh jumped in and said, "It is. We'll add it to our idea list."

"Back to the color scheme, I don't think given your desired proximity to the stadium that you have to worry about anyone mistaking your bakery for a secret Seattle fandom," Tate said. "Speaking of which, how's the location scouting going?"

"We narrowed it down to two places," Keogh said. "Both were former restaurants, so it should make for an easy transition. We were hoping you'd come out and check them out and give us your opinion."

Tate nodded. He glanced at Mel. "We can do that, right?"

"Sure." Mel nodded. Her voice came out high and squeaky. She let out a nervous laugh. This could not be happening. Keogh Graham, a man she had watched quarterback the Arizona Scorpions for five seasons, was sitting in her bakery talking about opening a franchise. Suddenly, she felt queasy. She was clearly on fangirl overload.

Tate glanced at her with a knowing look. He pushed the glass of water she'd been drinking earlier across the table so it was right in front of her and gave her a pointed look. Mel took a long sip. It helped a bit.

"Can I get you guys anything?" Angie asked. She hopped up from the booth as if suddenly remembering her manners. "Cupcakes all around?"

Keogh grinned. "I never say no to cupcakes."

"Me, neither, and milk to wash them down with if it's no trouble," Tyler said. He smiled, too, and Angie looked momentarily stunned to be on the receiving end of so much male attention.

Tate cleared his throat and Angie turned to look at her husband. As if he'd broken her trance, she gave him a quick hug, and said, "Be right back."

Mel wanted to follow her, but Tate turned to her and said, "Keogh and Tyler have never worked in a restaurant before. Do you have time to teach them the basics?"

"Teach us . . . wait . . . what?" Tyler asked. He looked wary.

"It's a requirement of all of our franchise owners that you learn how to bake the cupcakes that you sell," Tate said. "Not all of them and you don't have to do the actual baking, you can hire a chef. But it's part of our franchising qualifications that you agree to learn the basics because we've found that the owners who understood how much work it is to craft the cupcakes were much more successful than those who didn't."

"That makes sense," Keogh said.

"No." Tyler shook his head. "I am not wearing that." He pointed to Mel's hot pink apron, which sported an embroidered cupcake on the bib. "My masculinity would shrivel up and die on the spot."

"Aw, come on," Keogh cajoled him. "We wear pink in October to raise money for breast cancer."

"That's diff—" Tyler began but his words were cut off when a navy blue apron hit him square in the face. It dropped to his lap and Marty, who was standing across the bakery, said, "I hear you. We also have navy, too."

He lobbed another one that Keogh caught in the air.

"Now this I can live with," Tyler said. He pulled the bib strap over his head to try it on. Keogh did the same. They looked child-sized on these behemoths.

Mel ripped her gaze away from Keogh's muscle-hardened chest and turned to Tate. "I'm sorry, what were we talking about?"

Tate gestured for her to drink more water as if Mel wasn't tracking because she was dehydrated and not because there were two enormous football players in their bakery, talking about learning how to bake from her.

How was she supposed to teach these guys to cook? Would they even fit in her kitchen?

"Do either of you have any experience with baking?" she asked.

"I can't even boil water," Tyler confessed. "If it weren't for food delivery apps, I'd starve to death."

"It's true," Keogh said. "He tried to microwave something once and almost burned down his apartment."

"And how about you?" Tate asked. "Any experience?"

"I used to help my mom cook when I lived at home, but I haven't had much time to keep up my skills since going pro," Keogh said.

"That's all right," Tate said. "Mel will get you both cooking in no time. Right, Mel?"

"Right," Mel said. Her voice was still coming out a bit breathy so she cleared her throat and added, "No problem."

"You are in for a treat, guys." Angie returned with a tray loaded with cupcakes. "I tried to cover all of the food groups. So we have your Death by Chocolate, Orange Dreamsicle, Cookie Crumble, and Tinkerbell cupcakes. Marty, I left a couple of glasses of milk in the kitchen. Will you bring them out?"

"On it." Marty turned back to the kitchen and disappeared behind the swinging doors.

Tyler and Keogh surveyed the cupcakes in front of them. Tyler reached for an Orange Dreamsicle while Keogh chose a Tinkerbell. The cupcakes looked ridiculously small in their large hands. Tyler peeled off the wrapper and polished his off in two bites. Keogh unwrapped his and then used his fingers to separate the bottom half of the cupcake from the top. He then placed it on top of the frosting, making it a cupcake sandwich.

Mel had seen more than a few people use this cupcake hack but she was surprised Keogh knew it. Tyler was, too.

"What sorcery is that?" Tyler asked with a laugh.

"That's how Mama June taught me to eat cupcakes," Keogh said. "She said it kept the frosting off your fingers and her furniture." He chomped his in two bites as well.

"I'm impressed," Mel said. She felt herself relax. Somehow seeing Keogh know the secret way to eat a cupcake made her feel like they had some common ground. Her mother, Joyce, had also been a big fan of the cupcake sandwich and frosting-free fingers.

"I know my way around baked goods," Keogh said. "Just more from a consumable standpoint than a creator one."

"We can work with that," Angie said. "Mel is brilliant. You're going to learn so much from her."

Keogh met Mel's gaze and she felt her face get hot. She glanced down at the table. "I think Angie might be biased about my abilities."

"Nope." Tyler made a sandwich out of one of the Death by Chocolate cupcakes and took a bite. Around a mouthful, he said, "These are the best cupcakes I've ever tasted. And I've eaten a lot of cupcakes in my time." He looked at his friend. "We're going to make a fortune."

"Told you so," Keogh said. He tipped his head in Tyler's direction. "This knucklehead wanted to invest in a cryptocurrency."

Tyler laughed. "I did." He shook his head. "What was I thinking?"

Keogh shrugged. "No idea." He glanced around the bakery with approval in his eyes. "We are definitely all in, so where do we start?"

Two

"No way. Keogh Graham and Tyler Matthews were here and you didn't call me?" Ray DeLaura held a cupcake in each hand while staring at his sister Angie with a look of ultimate betrayal on his face. He'd stopped by the bakery while Mel and Angie were loading up the display case with Mel's latest creations. Naturally, Ray had immediately volunteered to taste-test them.

The bakery crew had already done several taste tests and Mel wouldn't have put them out if she didn't think they were worthy, but she was very fond of Ray and figured one more opinion couldn't hurt. She was particularly proud of her latest, a vanilla cupcake topped with bright pink watermelon-flavored buttercream frosting that she then sprinkled with mini chocolate chips. She had thought about dyeing the vanilla cupcake bright green but she tried to avoid dyes when she could.

"You're going to have to take that up with Tate," Angie said. "He's the one who knew they were coming by today."

"You mean he didn't tell you they were coming?" Ray looked outraged.

"No, he did," Angie said. She glanced away. "We just didn't believe him until they were actually standing in front of us."

Ray shook his head. "I can't believe I could have shaken the hand of the arm that got us into the play-offs last year."

"Don't you mean the hand of the man who got us into the play-offs?" Angie asked.

"No," Ray said. He shoved a cupcake in his mouth and chewed. When he swallowed, he said, "Keogh has an arm like a rocket launcher. That right arm should definitely be put in the Hall of Fame and then cloned or something."

Mel and Angie exchanged a look. "Well, you'll probably get another chance to meet him since Keogh and Tyler are opening a franchise."

"A franchise of what?" Ray asked. He ate his other cupcake.

"The bakery," Angie said. "Our bakery."

"Get outta here," Ray said. He narrowed his eyes at his sister. "Is this a prank?"

"No prank," Mel said. "Keogh wanted to invest in a small business for his retirement and Tyler went along with his idea of a bakery."

"Let me get this straight, two professional football

players are opening a cupcake bakery," he said. "Am I the only one who thinks that sentence is weird?"

Mel laughed. "Not so much weird as unexpected."

"They have to start training camp in a few weeks for next season," Ray said. "How are they going to run a bakery and play football?"

"I'm going to teach them the basics just so they know how the place operates," Mel said. "And Tate is going to help them hire qualified candidates to run the bakery in their absence. We already have a head chef, Cheri Spinelli, who studied in Paris. She's brilliant."

"Sure, she can cook, but can she run a business? Navigate the ins and outs of supply and demand?"

"She's worked in several prominent bakeries—" Mel began but Ray cut her off.

"Nah." Ray wiped the crumbs off his fingers and pointed to his chest with his thumbs. "I'm your guy."

"Excuse me?" Mel asked. She had not seen this coming.

"No you're not," Angie said. "You don't know the first thing about running a business."

"I do, too," Ray protested.

"You can't have people pay you under the table for cupcakes," Angie said. "This isn't like your other sketchy income streams."

"I think I'm offended," Ray said. He crossed his arms over his chest. He was on the short side of medium, built thick, and dressed in black leather even on the hottest Arizona days. Given that it was July in Arizona and the temperature was in the triple digits, Mel could hardly look at him in his leather vest and jeans. Per usual he had a tank top on under the vest and the thick gold chain he wore around his neck glistened in his chest hair.

Mel shook her head. She could only imagine what her husband, Joe, who was also Angie and Ray's brother, would have to say about this situation. "Tell you what, Ray, how about you come with me when I teach Keogh and Tyler the basics of cupcake baking. You can meet them and help clean up."

"Yeah, and I can give Tyler some advice about his running game," Ray said. "My man needs to be a little more knees to chest, if you know what I'm saying."

"No, no, no," Tate said as he entered the kitchen through the swinging door. "There will be no giving of football advice. These guys are buying one franchise right now but with their celebrity status, they could give the bakery a super boost and potentially buy even more." He glared at Ray. "You are not screwing that up with your 'advice.'" He made air quotes as he said the word.

Ray sent him a sour look. "You're not the boss of me."

"Which is exactly why you're not running a franchise for Keogh and Tyler," Tate said. "Following the rules does not play to your strengths."

"I consider it free thinking and I'd argue it's one of my better qualities," Ray said.

"Of course it is," Mel said. "But not when applied to running a bakery. I'm headed out there later this week. Come with me. You can meet the guys and use it as bragging rights at the Italian-American club."

Ray took a second to consider her offer, looking a little bit pouty as he did, then his face cleared and he asked, "Think I could get them to sign a bunch of stuff so I can sell it?"

"Ray!" Angie, Mel, and Tate wailed his name in stereo.

Five days later, Mel arrived in their bakery cupcake van at the football players' new location. She and Ray had driven to the address of the former sandwich shop, which Keogh and Tyler had purchased having decided it would be perfect for their bakery.

The shop was small and set in a strip mall between a karate school and a pet groomer. Mel could see the stadium a block away and, judging by the constant stream of traffic going by, she thought Keogh and Tyler had chosen well.

Tate was already there, waiting outside with Keogh and Tyler. He had driven separately since he was on his way to the airport to fly to Colorado to check on yet another franchise location in Eagle Valley. There had been a surge in franchise openings after the pandemic and Tate was traveling most weeks now, trying to keep up. Angie didn't seem to mind, but Mel suspected it was going to wear thin after a while.

"Hi, guys," Mel said. She waved and they waved back. She stepped out of the van and walked around the front of it. It was then that she realized Ray hadn't followed her. She looked back at the van and saw him sitting in the passenger seat with his mouth hanging open.

She sent him an intense look and waved him out of the vehicle. He didn't move. Mel glanced at Tate and said, "He's your brother-in-law."

"He's also yours and you brought him," Tate countered.

"Rock, paper, scissors?" Mel asked.

"No need." Tate glanced past her.

Mel turned back to the van just as Ray burst out of the passenger side. "Keogh Graham and Tyler Matthews, what a pleasure it is to have you joining the family business. I'm sure Tate and Mel have told you all about me."

Keogh and Tyler exchanged a look. "Maybe?" Keogh said. "Who are you?"

"Right, right," Ray said. "I'm not recognizable like you two. I keep my public appearances on the down-low. You can think of me as the man behind the curtain."

"He did not just say that," Tate muttered to Mel.

Trying not to laugh, she said, "Yeah, he did."

Tate ran a hand through his hair and blew out an exasperated breath. "Keogh Graham, Tyler Matthews, this is Ray DeLaura, our brother-in-law."

"Otherwise known as the brains of the operation," Ray said as he shook hands with the football players.

"'You're killing me, Smalls,'" Tate quoted a movie to Mel. She grinned. They frequently tried to trip each other up with difficult movie quotes, but this one was easy-peasy.

"*The Sandlot*," she said, identifying the film.

Tate nodded and pulled himself together. "All right. How about we unload the truck and Mel can get you started on the basics of cupcake baking?"

Keogh clapped his hands and rubbed them together, clearly eager, while Tyler shrugged as if resigned to his fate. Mel led the way to the back of the van. When she pulled the doors open, their jaws dropped.

"We need all of this to bake?" Keogh asked.

"This is just a fraction of it," Mel said. She handed him some industrial-sized cupcake tins, which held thirty-six cupcakes each, and a stack of mixing bowls. "Remember this isn't home baking, it's commercial, so you're baking on a much larger scale than you're likely used to. And if all goes well, you're going to be moving hundreds of cupcakes per day."

"Fridays are big bakery days, lots of pre-weekend traffic," Ray added. He grabbed one of Mel's extra mixers and tucked it under his arm. "And large cupcakes sell well because size matters . . . heh heh heh." He elbowed Tyler, who snort-laughed.

Mel and Tate both glanced at him in surprise.

"Did you know he knew that?" Tate asked.

"No. You?"

"Nope."

"What? Why so shocked?" Ray asked. "I pay attention." He turned back to Tyler and Keogh and said, "Also, you want to have plenty of edible glitter. It's pricey but pretty cupcakes sell and a little glitter goes a long way."

"I'm speechless," Tate said. He grabbed a box of supplies and started towards the bakery. "I am without speech."

"Ditto," Mel said as she followed him with a box of her own. "All this time and he actually learned a thing or two. It might not be a bad idea to have him helping out here."

"No." Tate shook his head. "He'll be running a bookie operation out of the kitchen if we leave him on his own."

"Fair point," Mel agreed. "Bad optics, given the bakery is owned by football players."

"To put it mildly," Tate agreed.

They strode through the front of the bakery, which had been painted a refreshing aqua with black accents, and into the kitchen. There was still a lot of work to be done to convert the place from a sandwich shop to a bakery, but Mel figured she could at least teach them a few things about baking before they had to take off for training camp up in Flagstaff.

Tate had the carpenters on a tight schedule to finish the bakery's interior and he was interviewing several people to assist Cheri Spinelli, the executive chef who would run the bakery for Keogh and Tyler. They'd gotten some terrific résumés and Mel wondered if it was the lure of working for the football players that had garnered so much attention.

She found the box with the aprons and pulled out a couple, handing them to Keogh and Tyler. Despite his apparent knowledge, Ray was not included in the lesson and had been tasked with taking the cupcake van to the car wash instead. Sure, it was a ploy to keep him from being underfoot, but that didn't mean the van didn't need it.

"You said you cooked with your mom," Mel said. "Did she do a lot of baking?"

"She did and she still does," Keogh said. "She's an amazing baker."

"She is," Tyler agreed. "Unlike Key's, my mom is not a cook. We lived on takeout, and desserts were made by Marie Callender and Pepperidge Farm."

"You can't go wrong with their coconut cake," Mel said.

"Oh, that was never allowed in our house," Keogh said. "Mama June believes in scratch cooking. Nothing premade and never frozen."

"She has a point," Tyler said. "I mean, how about that peach crumble she makes every summer? It's so good. Sometimes I dream about it."

Keogh glanced at Mel. "I'm from the South so our desserts are a lot of crumbles and fruit pies."

"And you're okay with cupcakes?" Mel asked as she unloaded her ingredients onto the steel worktable.

"Oh, yeah," he said. "I was always more of a cake person. Besides, there are loads of traditional southern cakes that would make amazing cupcakes. One of the reasons I noticed your bakery was because of your Hummingbird cupcakes."

"Hummingbird cake," Tyler sighed. "I could eat that every day."

Mel grinned. "Good thing you're going to own a bakery then." She turned back to Keogh. "What other southern cakes do you think we could craft into cupcakes?"

"So many," he said. "There's caramel cake, butter cake, brown sugar pound cake, and lemon meringue angel cake, just to name a few."

"Not that you've given it much thought," Mel teased.

He chuckled, looking sheepish. "Those are just the first ones that came to mind."

"Caramel cake," Tyler said. "Mama June makes one that's like a fluffy biscuit in caramel sauce. To. Die. For."

Mel could appreciate that. She loved caramel. Sometimes she loved it even more than chocolate, which was strange because chocolate had been her go-to flavor for most of her life. She shook her head, attempting to focus.

"I'm going to use the office, if that's okay?" Tate asked. "I need to make some calls."

"Have at it, partner," Keogh said. Tate beamed, clearly loving the idea of being partners with the football players.

"And I'm off to take the van for a wash, unless you need me?" Ray asked.

"We're good," Mel said. "We're doing the basics of chocolate and vanilla today. Chocolate cupcakes with vanilla buttercream and vice versa."

"Can't go wrong there," Ray said. "Those are the two most popular cupcake flavors."

Mel frowned. *How did he know these things?* She didn't get a chance to ask as he grabbed the keys to the van and headed out the door.

"Is that true?" Keogh asked. He wound his long braids back into a messy bun on the top of his head. There was no way this should have been an attractive look, but with his broad shoulders and wearing an apron, he looked amazing. Mel thought the team was really missing an opportunity to drum up the female fan base. More women than ever loved football, but how much more would they love a football player who cooked? *A lot.*

"It is," she said. "Which is why I figured I'd teach you those first."

She laid out the ingredients. She'd baked these cupcakes so many times, she didn't need to measure, but she still premeasured it all as if they were on a cooking show so that the guys could jump right in. She set Keogh on one cupcake while Tyler made the other. Thankfully the sandwich shop came with steel counters and a professional-grade convection oven. There were other appliances they were going to need, like a Hobart mixer, but for today, they could make do with her more portable KitchenAid.

While the cupcakes cooled, Mel showed them how to make their frosting. The vanilla cupcakes would be frosted with chocolate and the chocolate with vanilla. While seemingly plain, these were the ultimate comfort cupcakes, and even if the bakery didn't work out, Mel thought it would be handy for the guys to know how to bake them.

Tyler's knee, which he'd injured last season, started to ache, so he took a seat at the table to get the weight off it. Mel offered him an ice pack, but he waved her off.

"I'm all right," he said. "I'm doing physical therapy and all that. Have to get in top condition to be able to catch my man's passes this year."

"That's right," Keogh said. "No slacking."

They both laughed but Mel saw the wince Tyler made when he bent his knee after so much standing.

"These cupcakes will be finished as soon as we frost them, and I am positive they can cure what ails you," she said.

"Bring me a dozen then," Tyler joked.

Mel handed them each a loaded pastry bag. The distribution of frosting needed a gentle touch, but both men had more strength in their pinkies than Mel did in her entire hand. There were several splats of frosting on the table and floor, plus some gentle cursing, but the two of them finally mastered the twist-and-squeeze technique and managed to decorate their cupcakes with a healthy dollop of frosting that didn't ruin the ever-important cake-to-frosting ratio.

It was when Keogh was finishing his final cupcake that a shout sounded from the front of the bakery.

"We're not even open yet," Tyler said. "Why is someone shouting out there?"

"Maybe it's a superfan," Mel said. "Tapping into that market could make you instantly successful."

"Let's go welcome them," Keogh said. He grabbed a cupcake. "We can offer them the first of many."

"Excellent idea." Mel led Keogh and Tyler from the kitchen to the front of the bakery. She hoped it wasn't just Ray returning, being his usual loud self. It was not.

Instead, it was a man wearing a gold and black football jersey, standing in front of the bakery, chanting horrible things about the Arizona Scorpions at the top of his lungs. And as if that wasn't enough, he turned his posterior towards the window and dropped his pants, mooning the bakery.

"Ah!" Mel jumped back.

"So, not a fan then," Tyler observed.

Three

"He's a fan of our rivals," Keogh said. "The Oregon Beavers."

"That"—Mel gestured to the window—"is an insult to beavers."

"Agreed." Tyler nodded. "And no cupcakes for him."

They were about to turn away when a flash of pink caught Mel's eye. It was the cupcake van and it was headed right for them. Well, not all of them, just the mooner. It was definitely barreling down on the guy shimmying and shaking with his backside exposed.

"Uh-oh," Mel said. She leaned forward. Ray wouldn't actually run the guy over . . . would he?

The man seemed to catch on that he was in mortal peril and he quickly yanked up his pants and ran out of the way just as Ray stepped on the brakes with an earsplitting squeal, parking in the spot in front of the bakery that the man had just vacated.

"You lunatic!" the man yelled. He shook his fist at the van, which Ray responded to with a blast of his horn and a hand gesture that his mother would have smacked his fingers for.

"You want a piece of me?" Ray bellowed as he stepped out of the van. Mel wasn't sure if it was the sun glinting off the chain around Ray's neck and his black leather pants, or the eager expression on his face, but either way the Beaver fan took in the whole package and went into full retreat, holding up his pants while running across the parking lot and cursing all the way.

Mel hurriedly opened the door for Ray. She knew she sounded just like her mother, but she couldn't help it. "Ray, what were you thinking? He might have had a gun. You could have been shot and killed!"

Ray waved her off with his hand. "A gun? Where would he keep it? He sure wasn't leaving anything hidden."

Keogh and Tyler both started to laugh and Mel gave them a look. "Do not encourage him."

They both tried to be serious but it was an effort, judging by the chuckles that escaped when Mel turned back to Ray.

"Not to mention you can't drive the cupcake van that recklessly," Mel said. "It represents the business. Other drivers could film you and it could go viral. Not a good look for us. And what if you got into an accident? Tate would have a fit."

"I am an excellent driver," Ray countered. "I would never let anything happen to your pretty pink van."

."Maybe we should get an aqua one," Tyler said. "To match the interior of our shop."

Keogh nodded. "We could trick it out and give it a sweet sound system."

Mel reined in the urge to roll her eyes. "How about we get your bakery up and running first and then you can think about a van."

"Good point," Keogh said. He handed the cupcake he'd been holding to Ray. "Thanks for having our backs."

Ray looked surprised and then a bit taken aback, as if he hadn't expected to be acknowledged by the superstar. He shook his head, dismissing any show of emotion, and straightened up. "Yeah, sure, no prob."

He lifted a fist and Keogh knuckle-bumped him. Ray looked fierce but when Keogh and Tyler turned to go back to the kitchen, Mel saw the pure excitement that lit Ray's eyes. He looked like a little boy who'd just met his heroes. It was ridiculously adorable.

Ray caught her looking at him and immediately shoved the cupcake into his mouth. This did not make him look any more grown-up but Mel knew better than to tell him that. She patted his shoulder as she followed Keogh and Tyler into the kitchen, leaving Ray to follow.

"Does that sort of thing happen a lot?" she asked them.

"What? A pink cupcake truck almost running over one of our haters?" Tyler asked. "I can't say that it does . . . unfortunately." He bit into the vanilla cupcake with chocolate icing and his eyes went wide. He reached over and punched Keogh on the shoulder. "This is good. Like, really good."

Keogh laughed and punched him back. "Of course it is. Mel's a professional. She wouldn't steer us wrong."

"You're right," Tyler said through a mouthful. He reached for one of the chocolate cupcakes with vanilla icing. He looked at Mel and grinned and said, "Clearly, you're a genius."

"I've been called worse," Mel said. She took one of the chocolate cupcakes and, using Keogh's method, she made a sandwich out of it.

"There you go," Keogh said. They exchanged a smile as he grabbed a vanilla with chocolate frosting and did the same. "Mmm mmm. This is next level."

"It's mostly just chemistry with high quality ingredients thrown in," Mel said. She finished her cupcake and tossed the wrapper in the trash. "But back to our unwelcome visitor, do you think you'll get a lot of negative attention like that? I mean, could owning the bakery be dangerous for you?"

She hadn't thought about this before but now that she'd seen such a public display of stupidity, she was worried that things could escalate and Keogh and Tyler could find themselves in danger.

"It depends upon how we play," Tyler said. "When you're winning, everyone loves you."

"But when you're losing, no one does," Keogh added. "With the natural ups and downs of the season, I expect we'll get more of that and probably worse from our own fans."

"Yeah, our own fans can be really vicious when they're disappointed," Tyler said. "I remember I had one guy pee on the side of my car when I was coming out of the grocery store because he knew it was my car. That was a serious low point."

"That's disgusting!" Mel cried. "Doesn't being a fan

27

mean you root for your team no matter what? Win or lose? Good times or bad?"

"Maybe it was like that back in the day, but the world has changed a bit," Keogh said. "I mean, it's not like a marriage where fans promise to love their team through thick and thin and in sickness and in health and all that."

"Well, they should," Mel said. "I mean, where's the loyalty?"

"Like Key said, the world's changed. People are angrier and now everyone has a social media platform and they want to fill it with replays of our mistakes," Tyler said. "Pretty easy to criticize from behind a keyboard when you're not the one getting flattened by a three hundred–pound defensive lineman."

"But what about the great plays, shouldn't they be replaying those?" Mel asked.

"Good plays are never as click-baity as a spectacular fumble," Tyler said. "And great plays make for a nice highlight reel, but no one cares about that if you don't win in the end."

"And those fumbles trend even harder if you lose the game," Keogh said. "It's pretty crazy out there, and you can't even say anything because everyone points out how much money you make just to throw a ball, and they're not entirely wrong."

"Of course, they never consider that you've been concussed repeatedly and are literally putting your brain on the line for them. Every washed-up high school quarterback thinks he can do it better and, yet, they're not in the NFL." Tyler tsked.

Mel thought about the poor reviews the bakery had gotten over the years. Mercifully there were very few of them, but what if those people were out there posting about her bakery every single day? Spewing their hate and dissatisfaction and trying to hurt her business? She didn't think she could handle it.

"How do you manage it when they get in your face like that?" she asked. "I mean, I've never baked a one-star cupcake in my life and if someone hit me with a review like that, I'd want to choose violence and punch them in the face."

Tyler grinned. "I'd pay to see that. You're feisty, Mel."

"I have my moments," she conceded.

"You have to ignore them," Keogh said. "It's not always easy, but I think people who write nasty tweets, put up one-star reviews, trash teams, and go after public figures personally, well, their nastiness is really more about themselves than the person they're trying to take down."

"I'll say. Remember that one guy who boarded the team bus last year when we were about to leave for the big game? The dude was on his phone doing a live stream of himself 'coaching' us because clearly we just needed the right man on the sidelines and Coach Casella, in his opinion, wasn't it."

Mel stared at them. "You're joking."

"Nope," Keogh said. "It took three security guards to get him off the bus and then he trolled Coach so hard, he had to get a restraining order on the guy."

"How do you deal with that sort of lack of boundaries?" Mel said. "I'd have a nervous breakdown."

Keogh and Tyler both shrugged. "It comes with the job. You get used to it."

Nope. Mel knew there was no way, nohow she'd ever get used to that.

"Given your high profiles, you should probably invest in some security measures like cameras or possibly even a security guard," Mel said. "You don't want an overzealous hater to shut you down before you even get started."

"On it," Ray said. He had his phone out and was scrolling through his contacts. "I can get you a list of possible security people. I know a guy."

Tyler and Keogh glanced at Mel and she nodded. "Ray always knows a guy."

"Right on," Tyler said.

They packed up the cupcakes for Keogh and Tyler to share with the team at their training that afternoon. Mel was surprised that they were so enthusiastic about sharing their product with their teammates. She wondered how they would be received and couldn't wait to hear what the other players had to say about the two of them buying a franchise and about their baking skills.

Maybe more of the players would be interested in buying a franchise. Fairy Tale Cupcakes could become the official baked goods of the NFL. The thought made her smile.

"Ray, you like sports, right?" Mel said. They were driving back to the Old Town bakery and Mel couldn't stop thinking about the guy who'd mooned them. Not that she wanted to think about it because *ew*, but still she couldn't seem to let the hostile act go.

"I'm a guy, aren't I?"

"Women like sports, too."

"True," he said. "But men have been socialized to play

and watch sports whereas women were actively excluded from participating in athletics up until a few decades ago."

Mel nodded. It was true. "Back to my original question— being an avid sports fan, would you ever go after your favorite team just because they had an off game?"

"Oh, that's a tough one," he said. "There are a lot of factors involved."

"Such as?" Mel asked. She'd been hoping for a declaration of blind loyalty.

"Have they had a good season or a bad one? Is it a regular game or playoffs? Do I have any money riding on it?" he asked.

"What if none of those conditions exist?" Mel asked.

"Then we have to consider the science."

"Science?" She turned her head to look at him before glancing back at the road.

"Yeah, for real. Scientists have discovered that there are mirror neurons—specialized cells in the brain—that activate whether you're throwing the ball yourself or watching someone else do it. Either way, your testosterone level rises, affecting your emotions and elevating your aggression."

Mel stopped at the red light and turned to stare at Ray. He never ceased to amaze her.

"What made you learn about that?" she asked.

"Punched a hole in the wall when the Phoenix Suns blew the lead in the finals last year," he said. "Tara made me go to a counselor."

Now it was coming into focus. Tara Martinez was Ray's girlfriend but also a detective on the Scottsdale PD. She didn't tolerate any nonsense.

"It was her wall, wasn't it?" Mel asked. She drove

through the intersection and took a right onto the bakery's street, where she passed their building and turned left on a narrow service road that turned into the alley behind their shop, allowing her to park behind the bakery.

Ray nodded. "Had to call some of the brothers to help me patch it."

"That big of a hole?" Mel asked.

"Yeah, my fist went right through the drywall, which was a good thing," he said. "If I'd punched a stud, I'd probably have broken my hand."

"You got lucky," Mel said.

Ray nodded. "As I explained to my doc, I don't normally get that mad but I had a few C-notes riding on that game and there was no reason for them to lose, I mean, come on . . ."

"Breathe," Mel instructed.

Ray took a deep breath in through his nose and out through his mouth.

"You're seeing a doctor about it?" Mel asked.

"Yeah, Tara said I had to see a counselor or she was going to dump me. He's not a bad guy for a head shrinker."

Mel rolled her eyes. There he was, the Ray she knew and loved.

Together they unloaded the van of its supplies, hauling the items into the kitchen. Oscar Ruiz, a former employee who went by Oz, stepped out of his apartment above the bakery and came down the stairs to help them.

"Give it here," he said. He took the heavy container out of Mel's arms and brought it inside. Once the van was unloaded, he glanced from the steel table littered with cookware to Mel.

"What's all this? I'd ask if it was new equipment, but I recognize most of it."

"We just spent the morning with the guys who are opening a franchise on the west side," Ray said. He struck a casual stance. "You know, Keogh Graham and Tyler Matthews."

Oz's eyes went wide. He slowly turned his head in Mel's direction. "He's joking, right?"

Mel shook her head.

"It's true?" Oz gaped.

"It is," Mel said. "Keogh and Tyler wanted to start investing in small businesses for their retirement and they chose a cupcake bakery to start."

"No way." Oz looked dumbfounded for a moment but then he frowned. "Wait. Keogh can't retire. He needs to lead the Scorpions to the Super Bowl."

"Relax." Mel held up her hand. "He's planning for the future. As far as I know, he's not retiring anytime soon."

"Phew." Oz put his hand on his chest. "I was panicking there. He's the best QB we've ever had. It'd be a crime to lose him."

"Speaking of crime, did you manage to get in touch with your guy?" Mel asked Ray.

"I left him a message," he said. "As soon as he calls me back, I'll reach out to Tate with the particulars. I'm positive he can install a set of cameras that will be able to do a three-sixty monitor of the bakery and the surrounding area."

"Cameras?" Oz asked.

Mel nodded. "Because of their status, I'm afraid the bakery might become a target for haters."

"Who could hate Keogh Graham or Tyler Matthews?" Oz asked. He looked mystified. "Those guys have done so much for the children's hospital, the city libraries, and the community at large. They really give back."

"They are great guys," Mel agreed. "But that didn't stop a fan of a rival team from standing in front of their bakeshop, yelling insults, and then . . ."

Her voice trailed off. Oz waited. Mel felt her face grow warm even thinking about this morning's eyepopper of an altercation.

"He dropped trou," Ray finished for her.

"Excuse me?" Oz asked. Ray stared at him until Oz blinked. "He"—Oz pantomimed unfastening his pants—"did that?"

"Yeah," Ray said. "But he also did this." He turned his back to them and put his hands on his knees and began to twerk. It was not an attractive sight.

The door to the bakery opened and Marty stopped halfway into the kitchen. "All right. I'll bite. What's happening? Did you invent a new cupcake flavor or something?"

"No." Mel shook her head. "Ray was just demonstrating what the fan of a rival football team did in front of Keogh and Tyler's bakery this morning."

"Except that guy had his pants down," Ray said. "Which I am not prepared to do in a place where food is handled."

"Please tell me you wouldn't do it anywhere else, either," Marty said. Ray shrugged.

"Are you worried about the franchise?" Oz asked. He rubbed his eyes with his knuckles as if he was trying to expunge the image of Ray.

"Not worried so much as concerned," Mel said. "I

don't want them to be targets and I think if we could get their fans engaged in their bakery then they'd squeeze out the haters."

"I can make some calls," Oz said. "Everyone loves Keogh and if I let the morning-show people know that he's opening a bakery, I bet they'll run a piece on him and the shop."

"Look at you," Mel said. "All connected with the local media."

"Well, I am their go-to for morning baking spots," he said. He grinned, revealing a slash of white teeth and two deep dimples.

Mel marveled that the awkward teen who had arrived at her bakery from Urban Tech High School to intern at the shop was now a fully grown, handsome man and a local celebrity. For years, Oz had worn his bangs covering his eyes and most of his face, had multiple piercings, dressed all in black, and looked as if he'd be more at home in a morgue than a bakery.

But over the past few years, he'd found his way. He was now the pastry chef at a local resort. He went on the morning show every week to do a cooking demo and the viewers loved him. Mel suspected it was only a matter of time before Oz was tapped for greater things, like a food channel show of his own or maybe a job as a pastry chef at an exclusive restaurant in New York or Chicago. The thought made her unaccountably sad. She felt her throat get tight and she sniffed.

"You all right, chef?" Oz asked.

Mel nodded. She pressed her hands to her cheeks, trying to pull it together. "Yeah, I'm fine, just overthinking the new franchise."

Oz studied her for a beat as if he didn't quite believe her but he didn't press it.

"Why are you overthinking, Mel? There's no need to worry," Ray said. "Those two guys are like their own personal mountain range. What sort of nut would be dopey enough to take them on? They'd squish him like a grape."

"They do seem perfectly capable of taking care of themselves," Mel agreed.

"Exactly," Ray said. "I mean, it's a cupcake bakery. What could possibly go wrong?"

Four

True to his word, Oz did get his news station to come out to the bakery and do a feel-good piece on Tyler and Keogh. It was received so well that when ribbon-cutting day came, anyone who was anyone in the Valley of the Sun was at the opening.

Mel and Angie worked behind the counter in the bakery, along with the newly hired staff, to make certain that everything went smoothly. Tate was there in the seating area of the bakery, helping Keogh and Tyler field questions about their decision to open the franchise.

The bakery was decked out with football-themed decorations—balloons, bunting, and streamers. Several cupcake towers that featured chocolate and vanilla cupcakes decorated with chocolate footballs nestled in vanilla buttercream that had been dyed a bright green lined the top of the display counter. The overall look was very football and very festive. Even the team's mascot, the Scorpion, showed up and stood taking pictures with anyone who wanted one and took it upon himself to lead the people waiting outside in line in cupcake-themed cheers.

The reporters and their crews helped themselves to the free cupcakes, and Mel watched as they ate, making certain they all smiled. If the cupcakes made them happy, she figured they'd run nice pieces about the place. So far, so good.

Tate walked by the counter, pausing to kiss Angie's cheek as he headed into the kitchen. "Keogh and Tyler are crushing it. This might be our most successful cupcake franchise opening to date." He shot them a thumbs-up and then disappeared.

"They're certainly bringing the star power to the bakery," Angie said. She glanced around the packed room. "Look, there's a few political bigwigs, including the governor and a congresswoman, and across from them are some athletes. Man, they can sure pack away the cupcakes."

Mel glanced at the group of men and women. She recognized a few of the Phoenix Mercury, the women's basketball team, a couple of former hockey players for the Coyotes, as well as several baseball players from the Diamondbacks. The others she didn't recognize but they all carried themselves with a posture that indicated they could break into a pickup game of one sport or another at any moment.

"Oh, and over there, look." Angie grabbed Mel's forearm and squeezed. "Famous rock star and his actress wife."

Mel glanced at the couple. They looked familiar but she

couldn't place their names. She used to be so good at keeping up with who was who but owning her own business had seriously cut into her time to consume pop culture.

"And look who just arrived, the infamous assistant district attorney," Angie said. She laughed when she pointed at her brother Joe, who was also Mel's husband. He entered the bakery, spotted them across the room, and headed straight for them. Mel felt her heart lift at the sight of him.

Joe had been her schoolgirl crush. Her best friend's older brother who had seemed so unattainable to the shy and introverted Mel. After high school, she had gone to university in Los Angeles and studied marketing, forgetting all about her teenage infatuation . . . mostly.

She took a job working for a high-powered marketing company and was miserable all the way down to her soul. Her only solace was the pastry she bought every day from her local bakery. After one particularly bad day, Mel realized the bakery was her happy place. She quit her job the next day and flew to Paris to study the art of being a pastry chef.

When she arrived home, she reconnected with Angie and Tate as they wanted in on the bakery. While she and Angie were learning the ropes of baking and Tate was doing the financials for them, Joe began stopping by the bakery every day to check on his sister. It took a few months before Mel realized he was dropping by to see her, not Angie. Now he was her husband and she still couldn't believe how lucky she was to have married the first guy she'd ever loved.

"Hey, cupcake." Joe leaned over the counter and kissed her quick. "Look at this crowd. This is amazing."

"It has been nonstop for two hours," Mel said. "We gave out tickets for one free cupcake per person but customers have been buying up the stock. I had to send your brothers back to our bakery to bring some of our cupcakes because I am almost positive we're going to run out, which would be terrible."

"Does that mean I don't get a cupcake?" Joe asked. He didn't actually pout but, given his legendary sweet tooth, Mel knew his disappointment would be keenly felt.

"Of course you do," she said. "I hid one of your favorite lemon ones in the kitchen for you."

Joe grinned. "You're the best."

He started to circle the counter when the front door banged open with what the person stepping into the bakery clearly thought was a grand entrance. The force of it made Mel wince and she hoped it wasn't another bunch of haters coming to ruin the opening.

It wasn't. Instead, it was the owner of the Arizona Scorpions. Even a non–sports fan like Mel knew who Chad Dayton was. He walked with all the swagger that a man barely over five feet tall could manage when he owned a professional football team, which was to say, quite a lot.

He wore a sports coat over a dress shirt and jeans. He had on cowboy boots, which gave him a couple more inches, and his thinning silver hair was parted on the side and combed over the large bald spot on his head. On his arm was a woman, easily forty years his junior, and she was breathtakingly lovely with a thick head of black hair, a heart-shaped face, arching eyebrows, and a figure reminiscent of Marilyn Monroe. In stiletto heels and a curve-hugging red dress, she towered over Dayton, which to his credit, he didn't seem to mind.

"Oh, the owner and his wife are here," Joe said. "This could get interesting."

"Why?" Mel asked. "Isn't it nice that he's supporting his players?"

"Is he?" Joe tipped his head to the side.

Keogh and Tyler were standing at the far end of the bakery. They were mixing and mingling with customers, reporters, and the other famous attendees of the event. Dayton made a beeline for them, pulling his wife along with him.

"Keogh! Tyler!" Dayton called as he cut through the crowd like a tugboat through ocean waves. Both players turned to face him. Mel studied their faces to see if she could gauge how they felt about the guy.

Keogh looked impassive, giving away nothing, but Tyler had a big smile on his face as if welcoming a dear friend. Hmm.

"Keogh used to date Kendall," Angie whispered.

"Kendall who?" Mel asked.

"Kendall Dayton, Chad's wife."

"Oh," Mel said. Then she grasped the ramifications. "Oh."

"It was a shocking breakup," Joe said.

Mel turned to look at him and he said, "What? I follow the team. I can't help it if the team gossip gets reported with their stats."

"Uh-huh," Mel said. She had been married to Joe long enough to know he loved reality television. He was all about the true crime shows, which, given his occupation, made sense, but he also loved the over-the-top, ridiculous housewife drama shows. When Mel had asked him why, he'd shrugged and said, "I'm Italian. It comforts me."

"Who broke up with who?" Angie asked.

"I don't know," Joe said. "Does it matter?"

"Does it matter?" Angie repeated with a shake of her head. "Is water wet?"

"Oh, don't go there," Tate said, reappearing at Joe's side. He handed Joe the lemon cupcake Mel had put aside for him.

"Sorry, but I have to," Joe said. He turned back to Angie. "Technically, water is a wetting agent, it is not actually wet itself."

Angie stared at him for a few beats. Joe quickly bit into his cupcake as if afraid she'd smack it out of his hand. Angie blinked and turned to Mel. "It matters who broke up with who, don't you think?"

"Definitely." Mel nodded. "But how did Kendall end up married to Dayton?"

"He slid in on the breakup," Tate said. "For the record, Keogh broke up with her."

"Really?" Angie asked. "I wonder why. I mean, look at her."

They glanced back at the woman who could easily have been a supermodel.

"*Meh*," Mel said.

"You did not just say that." Angie's eyes went wide. "She's like the perfect female specimen."

"Is she?" Mel said. "I mean, personality and smarts should count for something, shouldn't they? Maybe Keogh was looking for more than just a pretty face. Maybe he wanted to be with someone who brought more to the table than her—"

"Uh-oh," Tate interrupted. "It looks like things are getting tense. Should I go over there?"

"You won't be welcome if it's team business. Let's see

if we can listen in." Angie jerked her head in the direction of the far end of the counter and the four of them sidled to the area closest to Keogh and Tyler.

Mel could just make out what was being said over the noise of the crowd. She glanced over her shoulder to make certain Cheri, the newly hired executive chef, could keep up with the requests from the crowd. A curvy gal, she looked good in her bright pink apron. With her thick mane of light brown hair, twisted up and held with a clip, and her wide welcoming smile, Cheri looked as if she'd been working in the bakery for months instead of mere days. She was the perfect hire.

Mel turned back to Keogh and Tyler and their conversation with Dayton.

"When you said you were going to invest in a small business, I thought you were talking about something a bit manlier than cupcakes," Chad said. He forced a laugh that came out in a wheeze as if he didn't laugh often and was doing an imitation of what he thought laughter sounded like.

"Such as?" Keogh glowered. He crossed his arms over his massive chest, and Mel noted that his chin jutted out just a little bit.

Kendall glanced between Keogh and Chad. She looked nervous. With a hair toss, she stepped in between the two men. "Chad's just teasing. Look at this turnout. You're crushing it."

She batted her false lashes at Keogh, and Mel rolled her eyes. Despite watching football with Joe and joking that Keogh was her NFL husband, she didn't know much about his personal life and she found it disappointing that he'd dated such a vapid woman as Kendall Dayton.

"I'm not teasing, Fire Starter," Chad said. He stretched so he was standing as tall as possible. He still only came up to Keogh's sternum. "I meant what I said. I thought you'd open up something cool like a strip club or, I don't know, an MMA gym or something. You know, a business you could flex like a man about. Not this . . . whatever this is."

"Flex like a man?" Keogh said. "I think I do more than enough of that on the field."

He and Chad stared at each other. Mel didn't think she was imagining the hostility between the two men.

"Ha! I see what you did there," Tyler broke in, shattering the tense moment. "Flex. On the field. Good stuff." He held out his arm and pointed to where Mel and the others were flagrantly eavesdropping. "Mr. and Mrs. Dayton, why don't you grab yourselves some cupcakes and see why we made this 'sweet' investment."

Kendall tossed her hair as she threw back her head and laughed, clearly overselling Tyler's joke. "And *I* see what *you* did there, Tyler. Isn't that funny, Chad?"

"Yeah, good one." Dayton winked and pointed his finger at Tyler as if it were a gun.

Mel had the sudden feeling that Dayton was one of those guys who had sat on the sidelines his entire life and believed owning a football franchise allowed him into the game. While Tate and Angie plated cupcakes for Dayton and Kendall, Mel and Joe moved back down the counter to help Cheri with the other customers.

In between taking orders, she asked Joe, "What's Dayton's story?"

"Meaning?"

"How long has he owned the Scorpions? Where did he make his money? Is he a good owner?" she asked.

Joe handed an eager young girl a Death by Chocolate, a chocolate cupcake with chocolate chips topped with chocolate ganache.

"He inherited his money—Texas oil, if I remember right," Joe said. "He's owned the team for about ten years. He's blown through seven general managers in that time, which is a very high turnaround for that position."

"Huh," Mel said. "Do you think it's because he thinks he can do a better job than the general managers he's hired?"

Joe shrugged. "Probably. I suspect it's a toxic combination of the desire to win and a supersized ego."

From the little she'd seen of Dayton, that seemed an accurate assessment. Mel turned back to their customers. She helped a family of four while Joe rang up their order for another half-dozen cupcakes. Mel tried not to worry about running out of product. They had clearly underestimated the appeal of the football-player-and-cupcake combo. She glanced at the people filling the bakery. There were a lot of men and women, all of whom were wearing their Arizona Scorpions jerseys and T-shirts.

"Hey there, baker." Chad Dayton approached the counter, cutting in front of the next person in line.

Mel was about to tell him to get at the end of the line, when the person said, "No, it's fine. Mr. Dayton is a busy man. He can't be expected to wait."

Mel disagreed but decided to go with it if it would make Dayton go away faster. She didn't like the vibe she got from him.

"I want to talk to you," Dayton said. Mel's eyes widened in surprise. She could think of no earthly reason why the owner of a football team had any need to speak with her. Correctly reading her expression, he added, "Yeah, I mean you, blondie."

Rude. Mel felt her jaw drop just slightly before she had the presence of mind to close her mouth. She noted Dayton's wife wasn't with him but was still talking to the players. Kendall was easy to spot because of her frequent hair tosses. She reminded Mel of a horse.

Cheri was boxing up an order while Joe was ringing up a young couple. Tate and Angie were in the kitchen bringing out more cupcakes, so there was no backup available. She was stuck with Dayton all by her lonesome.

"How can I help you?" she asked. She decided to treat him just like anyone else.

"How'd you do it?" he asked. "For that matter, why'd you do it?"

Mel glanced around as if the answer to his question would appear out of thin air. This was unlikely as she had no idea what he was talking about. She turned back to Dayton and asked, "Do what?"

"How'd you get Keogh and Tyler to buy into this?" he asked. He glanced around the bakery with a sneer curving his lips as if he found the entire concept disgusting.

"I didn't get them to do anything," Mel said. "They came to us."

"Yeah, right, sure," he said. It was obvious he didn't believe her. "What exactly are your credentials as a chef?"

"Excuse me?" Mel asked.

"What are you, like some housewife who got bored and decided to start baking cupcakes for your kid's school events and then everyone told you they were 'so great' so you decided to start a business?"

Mel's eyes went wide. "I happen to have trained at Le Cordon Bleu in Paris. Not that it's any business of yours."

Dayton waved his hand in the air. "Ooh la la, fancy."

Mel inhaled sharply through her nose. She was quite certain she'd never wanted to punch someone in the mouth as much as she wanted to serve this guy a knuckle sandwich. Instead, she leveled a stare at him and said, "Are you serious right now?"

"Deadly." He gritted the word out from between his teeth. "I don't know what sort of game you're playing, but you messed with the wrong guy."

Mel glanced around. The place was packed. She decided to point out the obvious to Dayton. "Look around you. This is a solid business investment. Keogh and Tyler did their research and chose to invest in a bakery."

"*Phthbt.* A cupcake bakery. Are you telling me a professional quarterback on Keogh's level would actively go out looking for this sort of place to invest in?" Dayton scoffed. "No, I don't believe it. You have to be working some sort of angle."

"No angle," Mel said. "Maybe you just don't know your players as well as you think you do. Keogh happens to be a really good baker. It's an untapped interest of his, so he bought a franchise. I think it's nice."

"Nice?" Dayton snapped. Then he raised his voice, mimicking her in a singsong little-girl voice that put Mel's teeth on edge. "I think it's nice." He shot her a look of disgust. "How nice do you think it's going to be when his head isn't in the game because he's dreaming up cupcake flavors? Or maybe he's fixated on what color sprinkles he wants to put on his signature cupcakes and he gets sacked like a little girl?"

Mel stared at him. In her opinion, Chad Dayton was about as misogynistic a man as she'd ever had the misfortune to meet.

"Does that really seem likely to you?" Mel asked. "Do you really think Keogh or Tyler can't have a side business and be able to give the game their full attention?"

"I've been in this biz a long time—" he began but Mel interrupted.

"A whole ten years," she said. She resisted the urge to slow-clap. "Not exactly Jerry Jones of the Dallas Cowboys, are you?"

He glowered. She raised her eyebrows. The hostility bristling off this man was palpable.

"Maybe not, but that's ten years longer than you, blondie," he snapped.

Mel clenched her jaw. "Why are you talking to me about this? What do you want?"

"You need to fire Keogh," Dayton said.

"That's not how this works," Mel said.

"I'll make it worth your while," he said. "Six figures dropped right into your personal bank account if you get it done today."

"Keogh's not my employee," Mel said. "He bought a franchise. *He's* the boss of this place."

"Then terminate the franchise agreement," Dayton said. "This isn't brain surgery." He was huffing and puffing and his face was getting red. He pounded his fist on the counter. "I can't have my quarterback thinking about anything but the game. Do you understand? Nothing. But. The. Game."

His overt aggression flipped a switch in Mel's head. She'd dealt with this sort of bullying client when she was in marketing. It was why she'd come to hate the job. She'd walked away from that career for precisely this reason and she sure wasn't about to put up with this nonsense now.

"Really? You're so worried that he'll be distracted by his side hustle that you want me to push him out of it. Huh." She held his stare and asked, "Did you care about where his head was when you married his ex-girlfriend?"

Dayton sucked in a breath as if he couldn't believe her audacity, but Mel didn't care. She had earned her money the old-fashioned way—by working her butt off—and she wasn't about to let some entitled generational-wealth-loaded blowhard belittle and berate her.

"Hey, now, there you are, boss." A tall man, built like a football player and wearing a baseball hat with the Scorpions logo on it, joined Dayton at the counter, interrupting their conversation. "Man, this place is packed. I couldn't find parking anywhere."

Dayton didn't acknowledge the man. Instead, he kept his stare trained on Mel and picked up one of the specialty football cupcakes from the tower beside her. Very slowly, he tipped it upside down and then let go. It went splat onto the counter.

"That's what I think of this place," Dayton said. "If I were you, blondie, I'd think long and hard about what I said. I won't make my offer twice."

Five

Dayton turned and shoved his way through the crowd until he was back beside his wife. Mel held her breath until he was gone, then let it out in one long whoosh.

"So, I see you've met the owner, Chad Dayton," the man in the hat said.

"Met or been harassed by? It could go either way," Mel said. She grabbed a wad of paper towels and began to clean up the mess Dayton had left behind.

"Which is standard operating procedure for Chad," the man said. He smiled and his eyes crinkled in the corners. He held out a hand and said, "I'm Pete Casella."

"Wouldn't that make you Coach Casella?" Mel asked. She shook his hand. He had a firm grip, not too tight and his palm was warm and dry.

"Yeah, I suppose it would," he said. "Call me Coach,

everyone does. And I'm guessing you must be Melanie DeLaura. I've heard a lot of great things about you from Keogh and Tyler."

"Call me Mel," she said. "They really mentioned me? Can I assume the fact that you're not yelling at me means you don't mind them owning a bakery?"

Coach glanced around the packed cupcake shop. "Looks to be a solid investment to me. Who knew? I may have to look into doing the same as I'm getting up there in years. Maybe I'll open one in my hometown of Evanston."

"Illinois?" Mel asked.

"The same," he affirmed.

"I happen to know we don't have a franchise there . . . as of yet."

"This is sounding more promising every minute," Coach said.

Mel laughed. She liked this man. He was nothing like Dayton and for Keogh's and Tyler's sakes, she was grateful.

"So, what's the story with Dayton?" she asked. "Is he really that upset about the guys owning a franchise? I mean, once all of the staff is hired and trained it really will run itself. I don't understand why he's so against it."

Pete stared at the ceiling, seeming to consider his words. "Chad considers himself very knowledgeable about the game of football both on the field and off."

"And?" Mel prodded.

"He doesn't believe they should have any interests outside of football," he said. "No friends, no family, no side hustles should ever interfere with the game."

"He is aware that they're human beings and not ro-bots, right?"

Coach shrugged. He pointed to a cupcake on the stand and Mel nodded. Those were the freebies.

"That doesn't exactly prove out, given that he married his quarterback's former girlfriend," Mel said. "Even if the breakup was amicable, there had to be some weirdness, which seems counterproductive if you're looking for your players to be solely focused on the game."

"Which you pointed out to him so very clearly," Pete said. He raised his eyebrows and bit into the cupcake. It took just a second and then a slow smile spread across his features. "Oh, wow."

"Thank you," Mel said. She let him swallow before she asked, "Did I cross a line with Dayton?"

He shook his head. "It's not like he can fire you."

"True," she said. "I'm just not sure how difficult he can make things for me."

Pete assessed her for a moment. His voice dropped and he said, "If that should happen—and I don't think it will, but if it should—feel free to call me and I'll take care of it. Keogh knows how to reach me."

Mel studied him for a moment. He looked sincere. "Okay," she said. "Thank you."

"Now how about another one of these cupcakes?" Pete asked. "And is it true that Keogh and Tyler baked them?"

Mel smiled. "They baked some of them."

Pete nodded. He took the cupcake she handed him and he glanced around the place. His voice was wistful when he said, "Yeah, I can see why they wanted a slice of this. There's a lot of positive energy in here."

"Might be the sugar," Mel said.

Pete grinned. Joe joined them, glancing between them. "Everything all right?"

"Just fine," Mel said. "Coach Casella, this is my husband, Joe DeLaura."

The men shook hands. "I was just telling your wife that I may have to look into buying one of these franchises myself."

"As something to do when you retire from coaching?" Joe asked.

Pete sent a quick glance in Dayton's direction before turning back to them with a rueful expression. "Yeah, it might happen sooner than I expect so I'd best be prepared."

Joe nodded. "I've heard professional sports can be like that."

Coach held up his cupcake. "I think my guys are smart to have a side hustle." He took a big bite of his cupcake and a smile spread across his face as he chewed. "And a delicious one at that."

He glanced at the far end of the bakery where Dayton appeared to be squaring off with Keogh. His smile vanished and he said, "Excuse me."

Joe looked at Mel. "Tension in the team?"

"Oh, yeah," she said. "Chad Dayton was just here and he was straight up mean."

"To you?" Joe asked. His eyes narrowed and his head snapped in the direction of Dayton, whom he stared at as if assessing him for weaknesses.

"Easy there," Mel said. "He was only mildly insulting . . . Okay, a little more than mild, but it's not about me."

"If he insulted you, it's about you." Joe turned back to her for confirmation. Mel knew he was seconds away from stepping out from behind the counter and taking on Dayton, but Keogh and Tyler didn't need that sort of altercation and she didn't want to be the cause of it.

"No, it's not. Not directly," she hedged. "He's very unhappy about the guys opening a franchise."

"Why?" Joe looked mystified.

"According to Coach, Dayton wants them to focus on football and football alone," she said. "Dayton thinks anything else is a distraction."

"But they're grown men with families and lives, how realistic is that?" Joe asked.

Mel glanced over his shoulder and watched as Coach stepped in between Keogh and Dayton, who were now full-on arguing. Tyler was standing by, looking like he wanted to be anywhere but there, and several of the other players who had turned up to support their teammates also looked like they'd like to slip out a side door.

They were recognizable by their sheer mass. Quinn Lancaster, a defensive lineman, stepped towards Dayton, flexing his fingers as if preparing to snatch Dayton up by the back of his collar and haul him outside to the trash. Another lineman, Trevor Hernandez, grabbed his arm and held him back.

Kendall, Dayton's wife, slipped her hand through her husband's arm and appeared to be trying to pull him away. He shrugged her off. In a voice that carried across the bakery, he barked, "You think you're so special, don't you? You strut around the stadium so full of yourself, Mr. Team Captain. Keogh Graham, Heisman Trophy winner, friend to the friendless, and all-around great guy. Everybody likes Keogh. You eat that crap up, don't you?"

Keogh's teeth were clenched so tight, Mel could see the knotted muscles in his jaw. Coach Casella was whispering something in his ear and Keogh shot him a glare.

Coach took the opportunity to step in front of his

player. "Chad, I think we can all agree that Keogh is something special. Now, let's get this party started!"

He waved his hands in the air as if that could break the silence that had blanketed the bakery as soon as Dayton had started yelling. Everyone remained silent, watching the scene unfold, wondering what was going to happen next. Coach Casella looked at his other players, clearly expecting them to step up, but they were all watching Keogh. As team captain, he carried a lot of sway with the players and they wouldn't do anything to undermine him.

Keogh stepped forward, around Coach, and addressed Dayton. "What exactly is your problem with me?"

"I'll tell you." Dayton held up his hand, putting the back of it right in Keogh's face. "Do you see a Super Bowl ring on my finger? Do you? No, you do not. How much am I paying you to win me a championship? How much?"

"You can't buy a Super Bowl championship," Keogh said. "Paying athletes high salaries doesn't guarantee a win. You have to have a whole team, working together and staying healthy for the entire season. It's not on one man to make that happen."

"Oh, it's on you," Dayton snapped. "With that fifty-million-dollar contract you're about to sign, you bet it's on you."

Fifty million? Mel thought she might faint. To buy a Fairy Tale Cupcake franchise cost a little less than a million dollars. When Tate had told her the amount, she'd thought it was way too much and no one would ever buy in, but she was wrong. And now they had bakeries all over the country. They'd had people buy in, using every bit of their savings, but for these guys she realized one million was pocket change. It boggled.

"If you don't want to pay me what I'm worth, I can go somewhere else," Keogh said. "Just say the word."

"Oh, no. You're not getting out of signing that contract, Graham," Dayton said. "You're going to play for me until you get me my championship, am I clear?"

Refusing to concede, Keogh crossed his arms over his massive chest and stared down at Dayton. "I guess we'll just see about that."

It was the wrong thing to say. Dayton's head flushed tomato red and he looked like he wanted to slug Keogh. "Yes, we will."

This was about the lamest comeback Dayton could have made and everyone in the bakery knew it. He turned on his cowboy-booted heel and strode to the door, snapping at his wife as he went.

"Let's go, Kendall," he said. "This place is obviously overrated."

Mel sucked in a breath at the insult. She glanced at Tate and Angie and saw that they looked mighty peeved, as well.

Kendall hurried after her husband. She sent an apologetic look to Keogh as she went but he just shook his head. As soon as Dayton left, the bakery erupted into muttered whispers as everyone tried to figure out why there was such bad blood between Keogh and the Scorpions' owner.

Mel felt that she could answer that question quite easily. It was because Dayton was a jerk.

"That was something," Angie said as she and Tate joined Joe and Mel.

"Something is right," Tate agreed. "Do you think he can force the guys to sell the franchise?"

Joe shook his head. "If there was something in their contracts preventing ownership of a small business, it would have come up by now. I get the feeling Dayton's issues with Keogh have more to do with his desire to have his team in the Super Bowl than anything else. He made it pretty clear that he wants a ring."

"Coach Casella appears to be caught in the middle," Mel said. She tipped her head towards Keogh and the coach, who were having an intense conversation at the end of the room.

Coach put his hand on Keogh's shoulder and said something that caused Keogh to shake his head with a small smile. Coach said something else and Keogh actually laughed. The sound of his laughter dispelled the last of the tension in the room and the whispers returned to normal conversation-level chatter.

The counter was quickly mobbed again with customers, and any chance they had to ponder the intricacies of the relationship between the star player and the owner of the team were put aside until the party was over.

When Keogh finally shut and locked the door, they were down to their last two cupcakes. To say the opening had been a success was a flagrant understatement.

Keogh dismissed his newly hired staff, giving them the rest of the day off to recover since they'd have to be back bright and early the next morning to bake enough cupcakes to fill the display case. Tyler had to meet his physical therapist at the gym, so he headed out as did the brothers, Tate and Angie, and Joe.

Mel and Keogh were the last two left in the bakery

and Mel glanced at the remaining two cupcakes and then handed one to Keogh.

"Cheers!" she said, and tapped her cupcake to his.

They were quiet as they made the cupcakes into sandwiches. Mel took a bite and she immediately felt better about her aching feet, sore back, and hurt feelings.

Keogh let out a sigh as the cupcake, which looked ridiculously small in his massive hand, worked its magic on his taste buds.

Once the cupcakes were no more, Mel looked at Keogh and asked, "What's going on with you and Dayton?"

"Going on?" Keogh's eyes widened in innocence.

Mel shook her head. "Yeah, that's the same look my brother got every time he was busted by my parents for something. I'm not buying it. Is it his marriage to Kendall?"

"What?" Keogh looked confused.

"Did she dump you for Dayton and now there's bad blood?" Mel asked.

Keogh shook his head. His expression resembled the sort a person would make when they're annoyed by a buzzing housefly.

"No," Keogh said. "It's mostly that Dayton wants a Super Bowl ring. Straight up, no matter what it takes, that's all he wants and he doesn't want us to have any sort of life outside of the game because he thinks it distracts us from our purpose."

"And what do you think about that?" Mel asked. She picked up a cloth and started wiping down the counter. Keogh took up another one and did the same.

"I think it's a garbage take," he said. His long braids slid over his shoulders as he leaned into the work, his long muscled arm reaching all the way across the counter.

"We're human beings. No one can live for just winning. There's so much more to life. I tell my teammates that all the time. They're never going to be younger than they are now. They're never going to be freer. Now is the time to do the things they want to do because they'll never get this time back."

"You say this to them out loud?" Mel asked.

Keogh smiled. "Yeah."

"Well, I can see why Dayton might take that the wrong way," she said. "Not that he's right. He isn't."

"He thinks just because he has money, he can tell everyone else what to do," Keogh said. "Even in our personal lives. He's a straight-up bully."

Mel doubled back to Dayton's wife. She couldn't shake the feeling that there was more to the story there. "Do you think he resents your former relationship with Kendall?"

Keogh looked at her. "You're really fixated on that."

"Well, yeah," Mel said. "I mean, look at you." She waved her hands at him. "And look at Dayton. And that's just the outside packaging. Add in your charm, personality, and smarts and his incredible lack of all of that and I simply don't get it. Why did she marry him?"

Keogh blew out a breath. Then he said, "Because when she proposed marriage to me, I turned her down."

Six

"Oh." Mel's mouth made a small O and stayed that way while she processed this brand-new information.

"It's not as bad as it sounds," Keogh protested.

"Really? Because it sounds pretty bad." Ray DeLaura stepped through the swinging door that led to the kitchen. They both started at the sight of him.

Mel squinted at him. Ray was always working an angle. "Were you eavesdropping, Ray?"

"Sorry. Didn't mean to interrupt. I left my phone in the kitchen and had to come back."

Yeah, right. Forgot his phone? She wasn't buying that. "I'm sure Keogh had his reasons for saying no."

"I'm sure he did, too," Ray said. "I'm just in a position that if my girl proposed, I'd be saying yes."

"Probably because she's a cop and carries a gun," Mel said.

"It is a motivator," Ray agreed.

Keogh laughed. "If Kendall was packing, I'd probably have said yes, too." He and Ray exchanged a knuckle bump.

Mel rolled her eyes. "If Kendall proposed to you then why did she marry Dayton?"

"Are you kidding?" Ray asked. "The man owns a professional football team. Heck, if he proposed to me, I'd marry him."

Mel imagined Ray in a black leather wedding dress with his gold chain glinting in the sun while he clutched a bouquet. She shook her head. "Thanks for that mental picture."

"What? I think I'd make a pretty bride," he said. He propped his chin on his hands and batted his eyelashes at her. Mel laughed.

"Honestly, I don't know why Kendall married him," Keogh said. "She and I broke up after I said I wasn't ready for marriage and the next thing I knew, about a month later she came back from Vegas as Mrs. Chad Dayton."

"How long ago was that?" Mel asked.

"Midseason last year," he said. "It made for some awkward moments in the run-up to the playoffs."

"I'll say." Ray let out a low whistle.

"Okay, I know I'm overthinking this," Mel said. "But let's flip it, why would Dayton marry Kendall? I mean, he's loaded, he could have anyone he wants. Why rush to marry the woman his QB just dumped?" Keogh winced and she added, "Sorry."

"I have no idea," Keogh said. "When they got back he

called me into his office. They were both there and he
told me they were married. He asked me if this was going
to be a problem for me and I said no. It wasn't. I mean, it
was weird, but not a problem."

"How did Kendall take that?" Mel asked. She couldn't
imagine that Keogh's acceptance of her marriage to Dayton made Kendall happy. Mel suspected that Kendall had
secretly been hoping for Keogh to fight for her. *Gag*.

Keogh glanced away and then back. His voice was
low when he said, "She looked sad."

"Ugh," Ray groaned. "That had to feel lousy."

"Yeah, it did," Keogh said. "But I didn't tell her to
marry the guy."

"Well, it must have worked between them because it's
been almost a year," Mel said. "Maybe they're actually in
love." Both Keogh and Ray looked at her with matching
expressions of doubt. "It could happen."

Keogh shrugged. "Anything's possible, but I suspect
it's more that they found what they were looking for in
each other. She grew up really poor and started working
in cosmetology and then became an aesthetician. She
was working at a spa when I met her and it was clear
from our first date that she was on the hunt for a husband.
That wasn't me. She wanted someone who could provide
for her, and Dayton wanted a hot woman that other men
desired. A mutually beneficial arrangement, if you will."

Mel sighed. "That feels so calculated."

Ray threw an arm around her and said, "Not everyone
can marry for love like you and Joe." She smiled. Ray
kissed her head and then turned to Keogh. "So, hypothet-
ically speaking, if a person happened to have, say, a hundred

of your jerseys, how much would the market value be if you signed them?"

Keogh's eyebrows lifted almost all the way to his hairline.

"Ray." Mel said his name in an almost perfect imitation of his mother, Maria DeLaura.

Ray immediately raised his hands in a surrender gesture. "I'm just asking."

Keogh laughed and shook his head. Mel noted that he looked wiped out. "Come on, let's get out of here. The rest of the cleaning can wait until tomorrow."

"Good call," Keogh said. "I have trained for ten hours a day and not been as tired as I am right now. Who knew owning a bakery could be so exhausting?"

"I knew," Mel said. They shared a smile and Mel switched off the lights. Keogh and Ray checked that the building was secure before the three of them departed out the back door. Keogh locked it and set the alarm.

Ray's Porsche was parked between Mel's Mini Cooper and Keogh's Corvette. Mel frowned. For the first time since she'd bought her car, she thought it might be time to up her game.

She was halfway home when a craving for *pollo fundido* from Someburros, one of her fave Mexican restaurants in the Valley, took over all rational thought. It wasn't suppertime yet, but she simply did not care. The craving was that insistent.

She stopped by the restaurant on her way home and ordered two dinners. She had no idea why she needed to have this right now, but she suspected it was her body's way of regulating all of the sweets she'd eaten today. She noticed that when she was working on a new recipe and taste-testing the cupcakes, sometimes her stomach simply demanded that she eat an entire head of cauliflower. It was all about balance.

When she left the restaurant with her order, she found herself thinking about Dayton's obsession with a Super Bowl win. He'd said he didn't want his players distracted by anything but how could he not realize that marrying his star quarterback's ex was a major distraction? It made his opposition to Keogh and Tyler owning the bakery unreasonable, to say the least.

She didn't like the guy and not just because he'd insulted her, although that would be reason enough. There was something off about Dayton and even Coach Casella seemed to be aware of it. She supposed now that the bakery opening was behind them, she wouldn't have to see Dayton ever again. He had no reason to show up at the bakery and she'd be turning over the managerial work to Cheri Spinelli, so she really didn't have to waste another second thinking about him. Or so she thought.

The sun wasn't even up when the alarm on Mel's phone chimed. Given that the sun rose at five fifteen in the morning in Arizona at peak summer, this was saying something. Mel shut off the alarm and crawled out of bed, leaving Joe sleeping with their dog, Peanut, and their cat, Captain Jack, snoozing at his feet. She took a quick shower and quietly dressed in her jean shorts and her *Bakers Gonna Bake* T-shirt. She finger-combed her short blond hair, knowing the desert heat would dry it in fifteen minutes.

She was driving out to Keogh and Tyler's bakery early today to help train the new staff on the Fairy Tale Cupcake signature techniques. Mel wasn't worried about the quality of Cheri's baking skills—she had an amazing résumé. It was more about teaching Cheri and her staff the signature look of the Fairy Tale Cupcakes, much like their fellow franchise operations, Sprinkles Cupcakes and Gigi's Cupcakes. They each had a trademark and Mel wanted to be sure the team knew how to create theirs. Mel had always been partial to the round-tip swirl, garnished appropriately to match the flavor of cupcake.

There was nothing as cheerful to her as a cupcake with a big old dollop of frosting on it. Of course, maintaining the preferred cake-to-frosting ratio was imperative and that was something she planned to show their new bakers as well.

Mel filled her travel mug with freshly brewed coffee. She slipped on her checkered Vans and headed out the door to her car, which she'd left parked in the driveway. It was already hot outside. Summer in the desert was relentless that way. By midmorning, she'd be able to see the heat rising in ripples from the pavement and it would be absolutely unbearable.

Mel switched on the radio and listened to the news until it became depressing, which took about three minutes, and then she rolled it over to a classic rock station. It took her a moment to realize they were playing music she had listened to as a kid. How could Nirvana be classic rock? How old was she? She shut off the radio.

The highway was empty and the surface streets were quiet. She arrived at the bakery fifteen minutes earlier than expected. This felt like a good omen for the day. Sometimes it was the little things.

There were two other cars in the parking lot. One was Keogh's Corvette and the other she didn't recognize. She wondered if Keogh had decided to pop in before his practice today. It was clear he took the bakery more seriously than Tyler did. While they were equally invested in the enterprise financially, Keogh seemed to actually care about learning how to run the business while Tyler was really a hands-off investor who enjoyed partaking of the merchandise.

Mel climbed out of her car and headed towards the rear entrance. The high-end four-door black sedan parked beside Keogh's Corvette didn't seem like something Cheri would drive, but what did Mel know? Not every person drove a car reflective of their personality.

She grabbed the handle of the back door and found it unlocked. She pulled it open and stepped inside. "Good morning!" she called.

She could feel her coffee's caffeine kicking in, waking her up in preparation for the day ahead. While she loved her kitchen very much, this one was brand-new. It had new-kitchen smell, a lot like new-car smell, and she inhaled deeply, looking forward to breaking it in.

No one answered her greeting. Mel frowned. The kitchen was empty, which was weird since there were cars in the lot. She'd assumed Cheri and Keogh would be prepping to start baking. Maybe they were in front in the customer area, finishing the cleaning from yesterday's party.

Mel pushed through the swinging doors to the front of

the bakery and froze. A man in a suit was sprawled on his back in the center of the room. She glanced around the dining area. No one else was here. Oh, no. Not again. Not now. For a second, a nanosecond really, she thought about turning around and running. But, of course, she didn't.

"Sir, are you all right?" she asked. *Please answer, please sit up and be okay.* He didn't.

Mel dropped to her knees beside the body. His jowly face was slack and his eyes were narrow slits staring vacantly up at the ceiling. She reached forward to check his wrist for a pulse. Before she could touch him a scorpion scuttled out from the cuff of his sleeve. Its little pinchers were raised and its tail curled. Mel yelped and yanked her hand back. It was then that she saw several scorpions swarming over the man. *Gah!*

Mel scuttled backwards away from the body. She felt the room tip sideways and she put her hand on her chest, trying to contain her racing heart. She was not going to faint. She refused to black out and risk having the little critters swarm her body. She felt a scream lodge in her throat at the thought.

Get it together! she chastised herself.

She'd seen scorpions before, many times. She was an Arizona native, after all. There was no reason to feel as if the room had suddenly pitched to the side. She reached out for the service counter and grabbed the edge, trying to steady herself.

She closed her eyes, then snapped them back open as it occurred to her that the scorpions could be all over the bakery. She scanned the area around her even as she felt a creepy-crawly tingle shoot up her spine.

She needed to go back and check to see if the man was

alive, but she didn't want to risk getting stung. She used the counter to pull herself up to her feet. She took a deep breath, trying to steady herself.

"Sir, can you hear me?" she asked. Her voice was faint and she cleared her throat and tried again. "Sir!"

The man didn't move. She had no choice but to get closer to him. Mel dropped into a crouch and began to crawl forward, scanning the ground for any of the terrifying prehistoric arthropods while breathing in through her nose and pushing it out her mouth to keep her dizziness at bay. She'd almost reached the body when an arm scooped her around the middle and hauled her back to the counter.

"Mel, no! Don't go near him. He's covered in scorpions."

She glanced over her shoulder to see Keogh, looking wide-eyed, standing behind her. He set her on her feet and she noticed his hands were shaking. He nodded towards the body and said, "I've already called an ambulance. They're on their way."

Mel slumped against the counter. "Is he . . . ?"

"Dead?" Keogh nodded. "I think so. I couldn't feel a pulse and then a scorpion came at me so I backed away. I thought it was a random one but then two more appeared, so I grabbed my phone and called for help. I didn't know what else to do." He swore under his breath. He was clearly as rattled as she was.

"No, that was a good decision. There's no telling how many scorpions there are or whether they're deadly or not." Mel glanced at the body and saw the little scorpion crawl back up the man's shirtsleeve. A wave of nausea crashed over her and she said, "Let's wait outside."

"Good idea." He took her arm and guided her around the body and out the front door.

They slipped outside, into the early-morning sun. It was already scorching and by mutual unspoken agreement, they moved to stand in the shade of the building. Mel bent over and put her hands on her knees. She concentrated on breathing and keeping her breakfast down. When she thought she was past the worst of it, she rose to her feet.

Sirens sounded in the distance. Good. Help was on the way.

"What happened?" she asked.

Keogh shrugged. "I have no idea. I walked in a few minutes ago and there he was."

"Who is he?" Mel asked. "Why is he in the bakery?"

"You didn't recognize him?" Keogh asked. He looked at her in surprise.

"I only glanced at his face before I saw the scorpion," she said. "After that, I really couldn't see anything but them." She shivered. A trickle of sweat ran down the side of her face. She felt queasy.

Keogh was silent for a beat. When he looked at her, his expression was grave. "It's Chad Dayton. Somehow he ended up in our bakery covered in scorpions, and I think they stung him to death."

Seven

Mel's knees gave out and she landed on the curb with a thump. Keogh reached out and took her arm to steady her. Mel appreciated the gesture.

"I'm okay," she said. He let go and sat down beside her. Mel dug her fingers into her hair. Her brain was swirling with questions. "What was Chad Dayton doing in the bakery? How did he get in there? Why is he covered in scorpions? Do you think someone did this on purpose?"

Keogh shook his head. "I don't know the answer to any of those questions, except the last one."

Mel waited.

Keogh turned to look at her and he said, "A dead man covered in scorpions had to have been done on purpose."

Mel studied his face. Was he telling the truth about not knowing the answers to the other questions? She felt like he was but the fact that Dayton and Keogh had gone two rounds the day before at the opening did not look good for the star quarterback.

"This looks bad for me, doesn't it?" Keogh asked as if reading her thoughts.

"Let's just see what the police think happened," Mel said. "We'll have a better idea then. Maybe it was just a freak accident, like Dayton showed up and somehow disturbed a nest of scorpions?"

"Inside the bakery?" Keogh asked.

Mel shrugged. It sounded improbable but how else was Chad in the middle of the bakery covered in scorpions?

Keogh closed his eyes and muttered, "Wake up! Come on, Graham, wake up!"

He opened his eyes, took in Mel watching him in concern, and ran a hand over his face. His shoulder-length braids were tied back in a thick ponytail at the nape of his neck and he was wearing workout clothes. He'd probably just popped in to check on things and walked into this living nightmare.

"Someone must have let him in. The back door was unlocked when I arrived," Keogh said. "And the alarm system was off."

"That's weird. Only a few of us know the code," Mel said. "Maybe there was a vandal. Perhaps Chad had a change of heart and came here looking for you or Tyler because he wanted to be supportive and buy some cupcakes, and he caught the person that broke in. I bet it was the twerking guy."

"And twerking guy just happened to have a swarm of scorpions, what, in his pocket?" Keogh asked.

Mel shrugged. "I don't know."

Keogh stared at her, letting her know he didn't believe her lame theory any more than she did. Mel would have offered more ideas but an ambulance and two police cars pulled into the parking lot, halting any more conversation between them. She picked up her phone and fired off a quick group text to Joe, Tate, and Angie. She had a feeling they were in for a very long day.

Keogh and Mel were interviewed by the officers who answered the call. They asked basic questions about what had happened, and Mel listened as Keogh explained that he had arrived just minutes before her and was talking to the 9-1-1 dispatcher in the office when she arrived and yelped at the sight of the scorpion. Needless to say, the officers found it all highly suspicious and promptly called for backup.

While they awaited the arrival of the homicide detective and the crime lab, Cheri pulled into the lot. She parked her car in front of the karate studio and looked warily at the two police cars. She rolled down her window and waved Mel and Keogh over to her car. They exchanged a look and then walked over to Cheri in her SUV, which was still idling. She hadn't shut off the engine.

"What's going on?" Cheri asked. She kept her voice low and there was an intensity in her tone that made Mel rush to reassure her.

"It's . . . um . . ." Mel stammered. Unfortunately, there was no way to put it gently. There was a dead body in the bakery on the second day it was open. How was Mel supposed to soft-pedal that?

"There's been an accident," Keogh said. "At least, we hope it was an accident."

"What kind of accident?" Cheri asked. Her hair was up in a messy bun. She was wearing a plain light blue T-shirt and Mel could see her apron folded on the passenger seat.

"A scorpion attack," Keogh said. "I mean, I'm no expert, but that's what it looks like."

"Excuse me?" Cheri asked. "Did you say 'scorpion attack'?"

"Yeah, we found a man in the bakery covered in scorpions," Mel said. She felt her nausea rise up in her throat. She swallowed it down.

"A dead guy covered in scorpions." Cheri stared at the front of the bakery as if trying to grasp what had happened. "That is some crazy mafioso chicanery." Her eyes went wide. "I have to get out of here."

"No, it's okay," Mel said. "There's no one here now. Just us. The police did a thorough sweep."

"Yeah, they're the reason I have to go," Cheri said. "The cops and I have a history."

"What sort of history?" Keogh asked.

"A lot of little misunderstandings," Cheri said. She waved her hand in the direction of the police cars. "I just don't communicate well with the Five-O."

"Do you have a rap sheet?" Mel asked. "Why didn't that come up when we hired you?"

"Didn't it?" Cheri asked. She blinked at them. "Huh. Weird. Okay, so I gotta bounce. If I linger around law enforcement, I start to get hives. It's a medical condition, you get me?"

"Sure," Mel said. Although, she didn't.

"Cool," Cheri said. "Call me when they're gone, although I may not be able to come back for a while. Maybe in a month or two, depending upon how it all plays out. Also, I lost my key during the open house. You might want to keep an eye out for it."

She didn't wait for them to acknowledge her words but shifted her car into reverse and floored it as if the police were after her. As another sedan pulled into the lot, Cheri's car hopped the curb as she sped away from the bakery like she was driving the getaway car in a heist.

"I don't know what to think about that," Mel said.

"Our chief baker has a criminal record," Keogh said. "Do you think she'll actually come back?"

Mel shrugged. "No idea, but I'm guessing no."

"Keogh Graham." A man wearing dark pants and a dress shirt with a blazer approached them. Mel couldn't fathom how he was wearing a blazer in this heat. He was tall, but not as tall as Keogh. He had sandy brown hair, buzzed short, and a square jaw. He took his badge out of his pocket and flashed it at them. Mel read the name *David Rivera, Detective*, before he snapped it shut.

"I'm Detective Rivera," he said. "And I'd like to ask you a few questions."

"Now?" Mel asked. "Shouldn't we have an attorney present?"

"Do you need an attorney present?" Rivera countered.

"Me?" She pointed to herself. "No." She shook her head. "But Ke—Mr. Graham is a celebrity and I don't think he should talk to anyone without representation."

"And you are?"

"Melanie DeLaura. I sold this bakery franchise to Mr. Graham," she said.

"DeLaura?" The detective's eyebrows snapped together, meeting in the middle of his forehead to form one foreboding line. It was the unibrow of a really unhappy man. "Are you the cupcake baker married to Joe De-Laura?"

While prosecutors and police were frequently on the same side, working together to bring criminals to justice, sometimes there were personality clashes. Mel suspected from Rivera's tone that he and Joe might have had one of those clashes.

"Maybe," she answered. He stared at her, the unibrow unmoving. "All right, yes, he's my husband. Is that going to make things awkward?"

Rivera's face was impassive. "Not for me."

Keogh glanced between them as if trying to figure out if they had a problem. Mel would have said that made two of them, but she didn't want to say anything to set Rivera off. Did he like Joe? Did he hate him? Joe was a people person; he navigated the personalities of the court system much like he managed his six brothers and one sister. He was the DeLaura voice of reason, the family mediator, the one who could be counted on to broker a peace treaty between warring factions as needed. Could this detective really dislike him?

"I can answer some questions," Keogh said. "I've got nothing to hide."

Rivera's unibrow split in half and he said, "Very reasonable of you."

Mel made a high-pitched noise. This was not a good idea. She knew it. It was going to go badly for Keogh. He'd say something and the detective would take it the wrong way and the next thing they knew Keogh would be a suspect, which was especially bad given the scene between Dayton and Keogh at the bakery's opening yesterday.

"Keogh, I really th—"

"What time did you get here?" Rivera asked, interrupting her.

"I don't know exactly," Keogh said. He glanced at Mel. "It was just a couple of minutes before you arrived."

"Not even a couple of minutes," Mel said. "More like seconds, don't you think?"

Rivera's eyebrows crept towards each other. Too bad. She was not going to let him place Keogh at the scene of a potential murder with enough time to have committed the murder himself. Nope. Nope. Nope.

"We can probably verify the time," Rivera said. "You know, traffic cameras, what time you placed the 9-1-1 call, that sort of thing."

"Oh." Mel felt thwarted. She didn't like it.

"Did you notice anything peculiar when you arrived?" Rivera asked.

Keogh nodded. "Yeah, there's a car, a sedan, parked in back. I thought it belonged to one of our new staff members and that they'd arrived early."

"But now you think differently?" Rivera asked.

"Well, yeah, I think it has to belong to Dayton." Keogh waved his hand in the direction of the bakery. "How else could he have gotten here?"

"Dayton. The officers said you identified the deceased as Chad Dayton," Rivera said.

"Yes." Keogh nodded.

Rivera looked at Mel. "Can you confirm?"

"Yes . . . well . . . no." She shook her head. "I didn't get a close enough look at his face to recognize him and I've only met him once, but Keogh told me who he was."

"Can you tell me exactly what happened when you arrived, Mr. Graham?" Rivera asked.

"As I mentioned, I parked next to the sedan, thinking it was an employee's. Then I went to the back door and found it unlocked, which I didn't think was too odd, figuring the employee had arrived early. When I went inside, the lights were on and I called out so I didn't startle anyone, but no one answered."

Keogh sucked in a deep breath and puffed out his cheeks as he inhaled as if trying to give himself a second to get it together. "I walked through the kitchen to the bakery and that's where I found him, lying on the floor. When I checked to see if he was breathing—he wasn't—I saw several scorpions crawling on him, so I took my phone into the office because I was freaking out and I called 9-1-1. While I was on the phone, I heard someone come in and found Mel approaching the body, so I grabbed her so she wouldn't get stung."

Rivera turned to look at her and Mel said, "I was trying to check for a pulse when Keogh pulled me away. I saw a scorpion come out of his sleeve, and I was just trying to see if I could help him before I called the police."

Rivera nodded. He asked Mel if she remembered anything else of significance and she shook her head, leaving out the part about Cheri showing up a few minutes ago and taking off, which she noticed Keogh had left out, too.

"All right, if you'll wait here, I want to check on a few things before I take your official statements," Rivera said.

"And then we'll be free to go?" Keogh asked. He sounded nervous about the answer.

"Unless you give me a reason not to release you," Rivera said. "If you'll excuse me, I'm going to have my officers cordon off the area before the press arrives." He turned and walked away. His stride more of a stomp than a glide.

Keogh glanced at Mel. "I feel like this isn't going to be that simple."

"In my experience, it usually isn't," she said.

"Your experience?" he asked.

"I may have stumbled across a dead body or two in my time."

"But you're a cupcake baker," he said. He looked at her as if he couldn't make sense of what she was saying.

"Yeah," she agreed. "But any job working with people is fraught with the potential for . . ." Her voice trailed off. She wanted to find the right word and not cause him to doubt the wisdom of opening his franchise.

"Murder?" Keogh asked. "Is that what you're trying to say? Mel, are you a murder magnet?"

"I'll say she is." A man in a shiny dark gray suit and pointy-toed black dress shoes approached them. Mel squinted.

"Steve? Steve Wolfmeier?" She gaped. She hadn't seen the notorious defense attorney in ages.

Steve put his hand on his chest and said, "You remember me."

"Of course," she said. "You've helped with some rather sticky situations. What are you doing here?"

"I was just cruising by, and I heard the hullabaloo on the police scanner, so I thought I'd join the festivities." He gestured to the Mercedes he'd parked beside the police cars.

"Is that how you get work these days, listening to the scanner?" Mel asked.

He shrugged. "If nothing else, it's never boring." He glanced from her to Keogh, clearly wanting an introduction.

"Oh, sorry, where are my manners?" she asked. "Keogh Graham, this is Steve Wolfmeier, defense attorney." She turned to Steve, and said, "Keogh is—"

"I know who Keogh is," Steve interrupted. He held out his hand to the quarterback and said, "I'm a huge fan."

"Thanks, man." Keogh shook his hand. He waited a beat and asked, "Defense attorney, huh?"

"One of the best," Mel confirmed.

"I prefer to think of myself as *the* best," Steve said.

"And modest, too," Mel added. Steve grinned and Mel was almost blinded by the whiteness of his teeth. His hair was as neatly trimmed as ever but Mel thought she saw a bit more silver than brown in it.

"Modesty is for amateurs," he countered.

Mel shook her head in exasperation but was also comforted by the fact that Steve had changed so little over time.

"So, here's a hypothetical," Keogh said. "If a man found himself in a situation where his boss was discovered dead on the premises of his new business the day after he and the boss had a fight in public, how bad would it look for the man?"

"Hypothetical, huh?" Steve asked.

"Yeah."

"Not bad at all with the right representation," Steve said. He glanced at the two of them. "You haven't spoken to the police yet, have you?"

Keogh and Mel exchanged a look.

"Aw, Mel, you're married to an attorney, you know better," Steve chided her.

"Sorry." She shrugged. "We only told Detective Rivera what occurred once we arrived here. I mean, all we did was find the body and call 9-1-1."

Steve took out his phone. "Let me clear my schedule for the morning. Neither of you are to talk to anyone without me being present. Understood?"

They nodded.

Steve put his phone to his ear. "Sarah, move all of my appointments this morning. Something has come up." He ended the call and said, "I'm going to talk to Detective Rivera and make sure we're all on the same page." He glanced at Keogh. "Call your agent and any of your other people and make sure that no one speaks to the police or the press without my say-so."

Keogh's eyes went wide. He gestured between himself and Mel and asked, "Do you think we're in trouble?"

"Not yet," Steve said. "And my plan is to keep it that way."

They watched him walk away and Keogh turned to Mel and said, "He's really that good?"

"Don't tell him I said so, but he really is the best," she said.

"I heard that," Steve called. He glanced at them over his shoulder and flashed his toothy shark grin that weirdly always soothed Mel in times of high anxiety.

She took out her phone to call her uncle Stan when two cars pulled into the lot, parking just outside the newly strung crime scene tape. Angie and Tate hopped out of one car, while Joe and Uncle Stan got out of the other. Mel put her phone away. She should have known Joe would bring his own detective to the potential crime scene.

"Tell me this isn't happening," Tate said. He glanced at the two police cars and looked as if he'd swallowed a bug.

"This isn't happening," Mel said. Joe pulled her into a quick hug, checking her over as if to reassure himself that she was fine.

"Not funny," Tate said. "This could ruin the franchise before it even opens."

"Tate," Angie said. "A man is dead inside there. Adjust your priorities."

"Sorry," Tate said. He looped his arm around his wife and pulled her into his side and kissed her head. "You're right. That was incredibly insensitive of me."

"Insensitive or not, it's strange that Dayton was in the bakery, and did we all read your text right that he appears to have been swarmed by scorpions?" Joe asked.

"You read it right," Mel said.

"So, we're talking murder?" Angie asked. Her voice was soft as if she didn't even want to say the words. "Murder by scorpion?"

"Possibly," Mel said. She raised her hands in the air. "We have no idea."

"But who would murder him?" Tate asked. "I mean, yeah, he's a je—" Angie cut him off with a swift elbow to his side. "Sorry. But you know what I mean. He certainly did his best to turn the opening of the bakery into a fiasco."

"He had a lot of enemies," Keogh confirmed. "Not just some players and staff but other football owners and even the commissioner all hate . . . hated him."

"Given the method of his demise and the location, I have to wonder if the reason he was murdered inside the bakery was to shut it down," Joe said.

"Do you think so?" Keogh asked. "That makes me feel as if Dayton wasn't the only target, but maybe Tyler and I were as well."

"Everything is a possibility at this point," Uncle Stan said. "Just like everyone is a suspect. Who's the detective in charge?"

"Detective David Rivera," Mel said.

"Unibrow?" Uncle Stan asked. His eyes went wide and he immediately started fishing in his pocket for an antacid tablet.

"Is that a problem?" Mel asked.

"No," Uncle Stan said. He glanced at Joe, who looked equally ill at ease. "No problem at all."

Mel didn't believe him, not even a little.

Eight

"Talk to me," Mel said to Joe. "What's the deal with Rivera?"

"It's nothing, really, he and I just—" Joe said but was interrupted.

"DeLaura."

Mel and Joe turned their heads and saw Detective Rivera walking towards them. His unibrow was fully engaged and Mel could tell that he and Joe were not on good terms, which was astounding to her. Everyone loved Joe. Walking beside Rivera was Steve Wolfmeier. Joe groaned audibly.

"What's he doing here?" Joe asked.

"I'm looking out for my new client, Mr. Graham," Steve said.

Uncle Stan muttered a curse. Tate and Angie both

looked at Mel for an explanation. She shrugged. "He arrived while we were waiting for all of you."

Tate looked at Keogh and asked, "Have you officially hired him?"

"No." Keogh shook his head. "I'm still hoping that I don't need an attorney."

"Everyone needs an attorney," Steve said.

"Rivera, can we talk?" Uncle Stan asked.

"I've got nothing to say to you, Cooper." He turned to Keogh and Mel. "You're both needed at the station to give formal statements."

"What's going to happen to Dayton?" Keogh asked. "I mean, has anyone informed his wife, Kendall?"

"I'm going over to their house as soon as I finish up here. I'd appreciate it if no one spoke to her or the press in the meantime," he said.

Keogh nodded. "And Dayton's body?"

"Will be taken to the medical examiner's office for an autopsy," Rivera said.

"When will we be able to reopen the bakery?" Tate asked. Angie gave him a reproving look and he added, "Not to be insensitive, but there is food in there that will spoil and we have employees to inform, things like that."

"You're going to need to keep the bakery closed until a pest control company can make certain the place is clear of scorpions," Rivera said. "When the crime scene unit is done, you can call someone to sweep the place."

"When will that be?" Tate persisted.

"I'll let you know," Rivera said. "Leave your contact information with one of the officers. I'd say someone will be in touch in a week or two."

Tate gaped.

"Aw, don't be like this, Rivera," Uncle Stan said. "Think of the brotherhood."

Rivera stepped forward, a menacing scowl on his face. "There is no brotherhood between me and you. You took that away when you stole the basketball championship by putting in this ringer."

"I'm not a ringer," Joe said. Mel glanced at him and noted that despite his denial, he looked pleased.

"Aw, come on," Rivera snapped. "You played point guard at university. If you were a few inches taller, your scoring record could have taken you pro."

Joe puffed his chest a little with pride, but he sounded contrite when he said, "It was just a friendly game, Rivera, you need to get over it."

"It was the championship!" Rivera snapped. He turned to Keogh. "We have a basketball league for employees in the criminal justice system. Anyone working in law enforcement can play. The season runs three months and we go to a championship. This one"—he pointed to Uncle Stan—"brings this guy in"—he pointed to Joe—"halfway through the season. I ask you: Is that right? Is that fair?"

Keogh glanced at the faces all staring at him as if he were the referee in a pickup game. "Have we lost sight of the fact that there is a dead man in there?" He pointed to the bakery behind him, and the energy level immediately shifted.

"He's right," Uncle Stan said. "We need to focus on the situation at hand."

"I need to focus," Rivera said. "You're out of your jurisdiction, Cooper." He glanced at Mel and Keogh. "Meet me at the station in fifteen minutes. I'll get there when I can. The rest of you, clear out. I'll let you know when you can enter the bakery again."

"I need to call my agent," Keogh said.

"Already did it," Steve said. "He's going to meet us at the station."

"You know my agent?" Keogh asked.

Steve just looked at him, slipping on a pair of sunglasses that he took out of an inside pocket in his suit jacket. Like Rivera, how was he wearing a suit and not sweating? Mel marveled.

"I told you I'm the best." Steve smiled at Mel. It was a slash of brilliant white. "Would you like me to represent you as well?"

Mel gave him a reproving look and looped her hand through Joe's arm. "Thanks, but I'm good."

A crime scene tech, dressed from head to toe in her white Tyvek suit, walked over and muttered something in Detective Rivera's ear. He stared at her. "Are you sure there was no other indication of foul play?"

"Nothing is for sure until the medical examiner weighs in, but if this is an Arizona bark scorpion, which seems likely, its poison is deadly. And we found eleven of them on the deceased." She held up a plastic vial with a lid. Inside was a dead scorpion just like the one Mel had seen climb out of Dayton's sleeve.

The group collectively recoiled.

"This could be your killer," the crime scene tech said.

Rivera took the vial and studied the little arthropod. "But it's so small."

"Bark scorpions max out at two inches," she said. "Never judge a scorpion by its size. The victim was stung at least a dozen times that we can see on his exposed skin. It appears someone set a nest loose on this guy."

"Did the venom kill him?" Keogh asked.

"Likely, yes," the crime scene tech said. "In a fatal scorpion sting, the cause of death is usually heart or respiratory failure, but again we won't know for sure until after the autopsy and tox screens."

Nausea punched Mel right in the throat. Surprising her with its force, she dropped Joe's arm and spun away from the group. She hurried to the side of the building. She was covered in sweat and gulping in air, while she braced herself against the solid brick wall.

"Hey, cupcake." Joe put his hand on her back. "You okay?"

"Yeah, I just can't imagine what that must have been like," she said. She took a long steadying breath. "My only interaction with Dayton was unpleasant but I just can't believe he's dead and in such a gruesome fashion. Maybe it's just the heat on top of the horrible circumstances of his death, but I don't feel so well."

"Let's get out of here," Joe said. "I'll take you to the station. Tate said he'll stay here until they're done and then he'll arrange for a pest control company to come out."

"Okay," Mel agreed. While they were still away from the group, she asked, "Between you and me, as a prosecutor, how bad does this look for Keogh?"

Joe's expression became grim. He glanced past her at the road that had been blocked off with yellow crime scene tape, and there was a wall of news vans with reporters and cameramen ready and waiting.

"Honestly? After their dustup yesterday, it's pretty bad."

Mel felt her nausea spike again, but she shook her

head. She was not going to give in to this. They had a franchise to save, and she was not about to let Keogh be accused of a crime she was sure he didn't commit.

Their time at the police station was mercifully brief. Partly, it was because Steve really was the best defense attorney money—a lot of money—could buy, but also because Mel requested a barf bag and the police seemed to want her out of there before she actually vomited.

Unsurprisingly, it was the local media that slowed their departure. It seemed they'd been tipped off about Keogh's appearance at the station, as the place was quickly overrun with reporters chasing down the story of Chad Dayton's grisly death in the bakery owned by Keogh Graham and Tyler Matthews. Mel and Keogh were sequestered in an interview room while they awaited the okay to leave.

Mel wondered if Rivera was drawing it out just to torture Joe. He and Steve were both standing outside the interview room working their contacts in the justice system to protect Keogh and Mel. It was one of the many times Mel was grateful she had married an attorney.

Keogh stood up and started to pace. Mel stayed seated, still recovering from the heat and her queasy stomach. The industrial wall clock ticked relentlessly, but for Mel, time had ceased to have meaning and she was sure they were going to be in this room forever when Tyler appeared in the doorway, looking frazzled.

"Bro, what's happening?" he asked.

"I have no idea, except I'm sure it's not good," Keogh said.

"I'm sorry I wasn't here sooner," Tyler said. "I was with the doc, getting my knee aspirated. Then I went to the gym to do arms with Quinn and Trevor and we were all wondering where you were."

"Here." Keogh held his arms wide.

"Yeah, Coach came into the gym and told everyone what happened to Dayton. He also said you were at the police station. I came right away to see if I could help. What can I do?"

"Thanks, brother." Keogh took Tyler's extended hand and then pulled him into a chest bump hug sort of thing that Mel had seen the DeLaura brothers do upon greeting each other. "I appreciate you."

"We're partners," Tyler said. "I'm here for you just like you'd be there for me."

Keogh patted his friend's shoulder and nodded. It was obvious he appreciated the loyalty.

"Is it true what the media is saying?" Tyler asked.

"That depends, what are they saying?" Keogh asked.

"The mainstream news outlets or the gossip ones?" Tyler asked.

"Oh, let's start with the gossip," Steve suggested as he entered the room. "I love those."

"Of course you do," Joe said, following Steve.

"What? I get loads of business from them," Steve said. Joe rolled his eyes.

"This is potentially my attorney, Steve Wolfmeier." Keogh gestured to Steve and then to Tyler. "My teammate and business partner, Tyler Matthews."

The two men exchanged a handshake. "Big fan," Steve said.

"Thanks," Tyler said. He took a deep breath and said, "All right, you know the rumors about you retiring early have been swirling for a while?"

Keogh nodded.

"The gossip channels are now all abuzz speculating that Dayton wouldn't let you out of your contract, so you—"

"Killed him off with a nest of scorpions?" Keogh asked. He sounded outraged.

"Yeah. Other outlets are saying it was revenge because Dayton stole your girl," Tyler said. He cringed as if he hated that he had to repeat the story.

"But *I* broke up with *her*!" Keogh protested.

"Yeah, no one cares about facts," Tyler said. "And there's one other story circulating . . . but . . . it's not worth repeating."

Mel noticed he wouldn't look at either of them. She frowned. "What's the story?"

"It's dumb," Tyler said. He looked at Joe when he said this, and Mel knew immediately that it was about her.

"Tell us, Tyler," she demanded. Her tone was no-nonsense and he looked pained.

He ran a hand through his sandy brown hair and said, "All right, but don't kill the messenger."

They all stared at him, waiting.

"Okay, a local news station is speculating that you and Keogh are having an affair and that the scorpions were really meant for your husband and Dayton was killed by mistake."

Mel glanced at Keogh and then Joe. They both looked perplexed and she was right there with them. She burst out laughing. Joe grinned and then he started to laugh, too. Keogh's lips twitched and then he let out a hearty chuckle.

Tyler looked relieved while Steve just shook his head. He glanced at Mel and said, "It's like they don't know you at all. You'd never give up Joe, and I should know since I tried to change your mind."

Mel smiled and hugged Joe to her side. It was true. She'd never give him up.

"And what are the legit news outlets saying?" Steve asked.

They all sobered up and glanced at Tyler. He put a hand behind his neck, looking uncomfortable. "They're more careful, but they are saying it was a suspicious way to die and that no one has an answer as to what Dayton was doing in the bakery. They have reported that Keogh called 9-1-1, and I heard they're trying to get a copy of the tape."

"So, they're accusing me without accusing me," Keogh said.

"Yeah." Tyler nodded. "I'm really sorry, man."

Nine

"How do we know the bakery is free of scorpions?" Marty asked.

"Because our pest control company said so," Mel answered. They were driving out to Keogh's bakery. Cheri had yet to reappear, and it had been three days since the discovery of Dayton's body in the middle of the bakery.

"Those little psychopaths are like four hundred million years old," Marty said. "They're older than dinosaurs and they can survive radiation. Did you know they found some alive in the desert in the 1960s after nuclear testing? Do you really think 'pest control' can eradicate them?"

"Relax, old man," Ray said from the backseat. "I've got reflexes like a bird of prey. We see any scorpions and I'll stomp on them before they know what's coming."

Marty rolled his eyes. "Reflexes like a chicken with its head cut off, you mean. And who are you calling 'old,' Mr. Receding Hairline?"

"My hair is not receding." Ray scowled. "I simply have a very high forehead, which signifies a lot of brains. Unlike you, Chrome Dome."

"Ha!" Marty barked a laugh. "Any brains you've got, you're sitting on."

"Listen, you—" Ray began but Mel cut him off.

"Enough you two, do not make me pull this van over," she said. "You will not enjoy walking to the bakery in this heat."

"But he said—"

"He started it—"

Mel slowed the car as if she was going to pull over.

"All right, all right," they said together.

"I'm sure the exterminator went over the bakery with a black light, which would illuminate the scorpions' exoskeletons, making them easy to find. Besides, we still don't know if it was the scorpions that killed Dayton. Joe told me the only species in Arizona that's deadly is the bark scorpion, and no adults have died from a sting in over fifty years."

"Were the ones found on Dayton bark scorpions?" Marty asked.

"The crime scene investigator thought they might be," Mel said.

"Then it seems to me it's a safe assumption they're what killed him," Ray said.

"Possibly," Mel conceded. "But we won't know for sure until the medical examiner confirms it in the autopsy. Why don't you both have a cupcake and relax? We'll be there in ten minutes and we can see what we're dealing with."

"I thought you'd never ask," Ray said. He turned in his seat to access the cupcakes Mel had packed. He opened a lid and took out two. He handed one over the seat to Marty.

Mel had packed enough stock to open the bakery today, and she planned to bake more cupcakes to carry them through until Cheri came back or they hired someone new. She really hoped Cheri came back. Despite her unfortunate relationship with the police, she was a stellar baker.

"Thank you, Brainless," Marty said.

"Hey!" Ray protested. "Was that nice?"

"Marty." Mel used her sternest warning tone.

"Sorry, couldn't resist," he said.

"You're forgiven, Baldy," Ray said.

"Yo!" Marty cried. "No lecture for him?"

Mel could feel his indignant gaze on her while she drove. She felt her right eye twitch. She stuck her finger on the lid, trying to make it stop. "Eat. Your. Cupcakes."

Her feral growl must have gotten through because they tucked into their cupcakes at the same time. Mel glanced at Marty's as he unwrapped the cake. He had their signature vanilla and vanilla. It was a very pretty cupcake and she loved decorating its swirl of icing with confectionary pearls of matte white.

The scent of the cupcake hit her then, but instead of the usual dopamine rush she felt when she smelled a baked good of any kind, she immediately became sick to her stomach. She tried to swallow the bile down, but her mouth pooled with saliva and she started to feel her throat convulse.

She flicked on her signal and jerked the van to the side of the road. Unprepared, both Ray and Marty got a face full of cupcake, frosting-side first. Mel had no time to appreciate their looks of surprise as they blinked at her through face masks of icing. She was out of the driver's seat and hustling to the side of the road to retch before either of them knew what was happening.

When her stomach was emptied of its contents, she turned to find Ray holding a bottle of water and Marty a fistful of napkins.

"You okay, boss?" Marty asked.

"Yeah," Mel said. She reached for the water. She swished some in her mouth and then spit. She dabbed her lips with the napkins. "I think I must have eaten something that didn't agree with me."

"Nah," Ray said. "I've seen this before. You've got PTSD."

"Huh? I have what?" Mel asked. She was still woozy and the sun beating down on her head wasn't helping.

"Yeah, you know, post-traumatic stress disorder," he said. "Going back to the scene of the trauma is triggering you and making you sick."

Marty looked at Ray and nodded. "I think he might be onto something there."

Ray looked surprised and said, "Thank you."

"You also have a gob of frosting in your right nostril," Marty said.

Ray scowled and took a napkin from Mel and blew his nose.

"If it's not PTSD," Marty said, "it could be just straight up terror. Those little buggers are deadly and we're walking right into the place where they killed a man. You saw it up close and personal. It has to be freaking you out on a subconscious level."

In truth, Mel thought he was right. She felt a creepy-crawly tingle go right up her spine at the thought of the scorpion she'd seen, but she wasn't about to admit it to Marty when they were on a mission to reopen Keogh and Tyler's bakery. The press had hounded Keogh incessantly about Dayton's death during the past twenty-four hours. Because of that, they had agreed that he and Tyler couldn't go anywhere near the place.

With Cheri gone, it was up to Mel to do the baking. She figured she'd hide from any reporters in the kitchen while turning out product. Marty and Ray would man the front counter with the staff they'd hired, who were hopefully still willing to show up.

Joe didn't love the idea but relented when Ray volunteered to keep an eye on Mel and Marty. To cover all their bases, Angie would do the baking at their bakery in Old Town while Tate worked the counter in Marty's stead. It felt as if they were spread as thin as a layer of caramelized sugar on a crème brûlée, but they'd manage until the media found something else to fixate on. At least, Mel hoped so.

She took a deep breath and waved everyone back into the van. They arrived at the bakery moments later to find one lone reporter staked out. He glanced at the three of them and began to walk towards them until Ray stepped out of the car and took a menacing step in his direction.

The reporter, a young man in his twenties, stopped short, rethinking his approach. Smart guy.

Mel, Marty, and Ray entered the bakery through the back door, locking it behind them. They stood just inside, pressed up against each other as if no one wanted to walk any farther into the kitchen.

"After you, reflexes of a bird of prey," Marty said.

Ray huffed a breath and stepped forward right as the swinging doors opened. He let out a yelp and jumped back, throwing up his arms in front of Mel and Marty as if to protect them from a giant scorpion that could open doors and attack them.

"Sorry! Didn't mean to startle you." A man in a bright yellow pest control uniform stepped into the kitchen. He had on a matching yellow ball cap and was carrying a flashlight. "I was just doing a last sweep of the place." He waved the flashlight in the direction of the bakery and Mel realized it was actually a black light. She recognized him as the pest control specialist they used to maintain their main bakery in Old Town.

"Hi, Nick," she said. "How are you?"

"Hey, Mel. I'm good. You?"

"You know this guy?" Ray asked before Mel could answer.

"Tate hired him as our exterminator a few years ago," Mel said.

Ray dropped his arms and crossed them over his chest. "Where's your work truck? I didn't see it in the back."

"I parked out front," Nick said. "There was some creepy guy lurking around out back, so I didn't want to park there in case he jumped me or something."

"Yes, we saw him, too. He's actually a reporter so you made a good call there. Thank you for coming out, Nick," Mel said. She moved to stand in front of Ray. "We're hoping to reopen tomorrow. Do you think that will be all right?"

"Sure," he said. "It's been a few days since the dead dude was found and the place has been gone over multiple times. I came this morning just to do one more safety check. I feel confident that I can declare this establishment scorpion-free."

Marty sagged in relief. He rubbed his hands together and said, "Good. DeLaura, let's get the van unloaded so Mel can start baking."

"I'll help," Mel said.

"Nah, you're too recognizable. That reporter out there needs to be chased off first," Marty said.

"I have a spray for that," Nick said. They all glanced at him with their eyebrows raised. He widened his eyes and added, "It was a joke."

"Pity," Ray said. Nick looked alarmed but Mel chuckled as she knew Ray did not love the media.

"He's also joking," she explained.

"Ah." Nick nodded. "Ha-ha. Good one."

Ray rolled his eyes and he and Marty left the kitchen to go unload Mel's supplies.

"Pretty crazy that a nest of bark scorpions got in here, right?" Mel asked. She was very curious to hear Nick's hypothesis on how that happened, mostly because she didn't want to worry about it happening again.

"Oh, those weren't bark scorpions," he said.

"They weren't?" she asked.

"No."

"But I thought Dayton died from the multiple stings of the bark scorpions," she said. "I mean, I saw one crawl out of his sleeve."

"Yeah, no. The ones we caught in here were Arizona stripe-tailed scorpions, also called devil scorpions. They're much less venomous than most varieties. Their tails are thicker than the bark scorpion, that's how you tell them apart," he said. "We clear nests of them out of residential areas all the time."

"So if the scorpions didn't kill Dayton, what did?" Mel asked.

"No idea." Nick shrugged. "Pretty weird though. Scorpions are generally solitary dudes. They don't travel in packs, except for the bark scorpion, which moves in a pack in the winter. I mean, if you find one, you'll likely find more because one scorpion indicates that they've discovered an ideal habitat, but they don't pal around."

Mel stared at him, trying to wrap her brain around this new information.

The back door opened and Ray and Marty entered, carrying tubs of supplies.

"Call me if you have any more issues, but unless you let that reporter in, you are pest-free," Nick said. He left the kitchen through the swinging door that led to the front of the bakery. Mel followed just to make certain no one was lurking outside to bother him.

It was all clear. Nick climbed into his bright yellow pickup truck and drove away with a cheerful wave.

Mel watched him go, considering what he had said. If Dayton hadn't been killed by the scorpions found crawling all over him then how had he died? Heart attack from fright? A dozen scorpions would do that to her. But how did they get into the bakery? She refused to believe that the bakery offered the arthropods an ideal habitat and that the designers and construction workers who'd re-modeled the place had missed rogue scorpions on the premises.

If it wasn't fright that had killed him, what had? And what was Dayton doing in the bakery after hours? Why was he here? Did he meet someone, and if so, who? What did they want? These were the questions that had been plaguing Mel since Dayton's body was found.

There was no way his death was a coincidence. There was a reason it happened here in the bakery and the only thing she could think was that whoever murdered Dayton wanted Keogh and Tyler to take the fall for it. In her opinion there was only one person who fit those criteria.

Kendall Dayton, Chad's wife. She had to regret marrying him so impulsively in the aftermath of her breakup with Keogh. And she was likely harboring some bitterness at being dumped, so why not set up her ex-boyfriend and ruin his life?

Mel wanted to share her theory with Joe and Uncle Stan, but she knew they would both tell her to leave it to the police. As Marty and Ray went out to the front of the bakery to start setting it up for tomorrow's customers, Mel set to work baking her first few batches of cupcakes. She chose the time-honored classic chocolate cake with vanilla frosting as well as one of the bakery's signature almond flavor, the Blonde Bombshell.

She'd called Cheri and the two assistants they'd hired, but all of their phones had gone to voice mail and no one had returned her calls. She assumed they were going to have to hire more help, which would keep them short-staffed at both bakeries. She tried not to feel overwhelmed. Owning a small business was always unpredictable, and when a franchise opened with a dead body found in it, the situation spiraled into chaos.

She baked an industrial-sized tray of cupcakes and while they cooled, she started on her vanilla buttercream after putting a batch of almond cupcakes in the oven. Working in a bakery with product like this had a rhythm of its own, and working alone reminded Mel of the early days when they had just the one shop and life felt simpler, even though she spent every waking hour worried about whether they would be successful or not.

Using the bakery's smaller standing mixer, she began adding the ingredients for the frosting. She inhaled deeply, knowing the scent would calm her down. It was her own sort of self-soothing. Except, it didn't.

Instead, Mel's stomach immediately turned, and she felt the nausea from earlier return. She recoiled from the mixer and dashed to the staff restroom, where she dry-heaved since there was nothing left in her stomach after being ill earlier.

"Boss!" She heard Marty call her name.

"In here," she cried. She staggered to her feet and splashed some cold water on her face. She stepped back into the kitchen to find Marty standing there, looking concerned.

"You all right?"

"I really think I ate something bad," she said. "My stomach is not right."

"I'll call Oz and see if he can come out to help with the baking," Marty said. "The crime scene folks made a mess of the shop with fingerprint kit residue and whatnot.

Ray and I are going to have a heck of a job cleaning it up."

"That's a good idea," Mel said. "If I don't hear from Cheri and the other bakers, we're going to have to hire the second string, assuming any of them are available. I have all of their applications in the office. I can do that while my stomach settles."

"What did you eat last night?"

"I'll only tell you if you don't judge me," Mel said.

"Never," Marty said.

"I woke up starving in the middle of the night and microwaved a frozen bean burrito," Mel said.

Marty said nothing but his eyebrows lifted.

"See? Right there, you're judging," she said.

"I'm not judging so much as I'm surprised," Marty said. "This is my surprised face."

"Sure, it is," Mel said. She went over to the mixer and shut it off. She took the bowl off the stand but when the smell of vanilla hit her, she flinched, feeling her stomach rebel all over again. She shoved the bowl at Marty and backed away.

"Cover that and put it in the cooler, please," she said. She covered her nose and shuffled away. "I can't believe I'm reacting badly to the smell of frosting. Frosting!"

Before she got sick, she shut the door to the office behind her. She could hear Marty calling Oz and she hoped their former employee was available because the mere thought of frosting a cupcake made her gag. This was a nightmare.

Ten

Oz arrived forty minutes later, giving Mel time to recover from her nausea and hire bakers to replace the ones who hadn't shown up. Marcella Gibbons and Cecily Donovan were culinary students planning to work part-time at the bakery around their course loads. As for a chief baker, Mel hadn't had any luck. She was still holding out hope that Cheri would appear and take on the new hires who would start in the next few days.

"Hey, chef." Oz appeared in the office door. "Ray and Marty wiped down the front of the bakery and loaded the merchandise I brought into the display case, but we're going to need a lot more. I have no idea when the gawkers will show up, but they will."

Mel nodded. "I'm feeling better. I'll help."

Oz gave her a dubious look but said nothing. Together

they donned their aprons and set to work. Mel decided to whip up a batch of their Death by Chocolate while Oz finished her earlier efforts with the vanilla buttercream.

Mel felt her strength returning and she smiled at Oz as she passed him. "Thanks so much for coming here on your day off. I really appreciate—"

Oz had taken the lid off the tub of vanilla buttercream and Mel stopped in her tracks. She immediately felt physically ill at the whiff of vanilla.

She hurried to the other side of the kitchen and cried, "Cover that!"

Oz looked at her in alarm and slapped the lid onto the tub. "What's wrong?"

"It's the smell of vanilla that's making my stomach turn," Mel said. She turned her head and took a deep breath through her mouth.

"Do you think there's something wrong with the vanilla?" Oz asked.

"No, it's me," she said. She gestured to the ganache she was making. "The chocolate isn't bothering me."

"That's weird."

"Totally."

"We can manage this," Oz said. "You work over there and I'll take this stuff to the front and finish these cupcakes out there."

Mel nodded, relieved when Oz left the kitchen, taking the bucket of vanilla buttercream with him. Vanilla. She loved vanilla. Why was it hitting her so wrong today? Maybe she was coming down with something. She tried to think if she'd been in contact with anyone who was sick lately, but no incidents came to mind. She was spooning the ganache onto the chocolate cupcakes when

Kendall swept into the kitchen from the front of the bakery with Marty and Ray following her like two puppies.

"Hi . . . um . . ." Kendall paused as she glanced at Mel. It was clear she didn't remember her name.

Mel waited a beat but when Kendall said nothing, she decided to help her out. "I'm Mel."

"Of course, the chef woman with the man's name and haircut." Kendall shook her long waterfall of dark silky hair and it shimmered under the fluorescent lights of the kitchen. "Keogh mentioned you. I'm sorry I forgot your name. Things have been . . . hectic."

Man's name and haircut? Mel dropped the spoon of ganache into the bowl, lest she give in to the temptation to flick her wrist and accidentally splat Kendall with some ganache. Also, "hectic" was not the word she would have used had her husband just been found murdered.

"Can I get you a cupcake, Mrs. Dayton?" Marty asked.

"Or a cup of coffee?" Ray offered.

"How about a seat?" Marty suggested.

"No, no, I'm fine, thank you." Kendall smiled at them and they both looked dazzled under her regard. Mel rolled her eyes.

"Don't you have things to do out front?" Mel asked them.

Kendall lowered her gaze and it was as if they were released from a spell.

"Right. Out front," Marty muttered. He turned to leave. When Ray didn't follow, Marty hooked Ray's elbow with his hand and tugged him forcibly from the kitchen.

Mel stared at the woman before her. There was no question she was stunningly beautiful. Kendall ticked all the boxes of what was popular at the moment, heart-shaped face, large doe eyes, narrow nose, full lips, and a curvy figure with a tiny waist. She was the sort of woman whom people noticed when she entered the room. The type who was always escorted to the front of the line, given the best table at the restaurant, and never got ticketed no matter how fast she drove or where she parked.

Mel knew that the pretty people lived in an entirely different world than the plain ones and she'd never really resented it as much as she did right now. Because the truth was that the person with the most to gain from Chad Dayton's death was his widow. Wasn't it always the spouse? Unless the Daytons had an unusual arrangement, at the very least Kendall would get a nice chunk of Chad's wealth upon his death.

Mel didn't think Kendall should get away with murder just because she had a tiny waist and a nice head of hair. She might be able to employ her wiles on others, but Mel was not about to be manipulated by this beautiful black widow into feeling sorry for her.

"Was there something I can help you with?" Mel asked.

"I was in the area, so I thought I'd stop by and see if Keogh was here," Kendall said. She looked at Mel expectantly. Mel noticed that her face, which was flawless, also lacked expression. Keogh had said she was an aesthetician. Mel wondered if she'd overdone her own Botox treatments and now had the facial expression range of a potato. She decided to test out the theory by seeing if she could provoke some emotion.

"He's not." Mel picked up her spoon and continued pouring the ganache. She glanced at Kendall to see if her short answer annoyed the woman, but it was impossible to say as her expression didn't alter a bit.

"Do you know where he is?" Kendall persisted.

Mel moved on to the next cupcake. When she finished she glanced up and said, "No."

Kendall met her stare and tipped her chin up. "You don't like me."

"I don't know you," Mel countered. She watched Kendall's face. Absolutely no emotion was visible. It was like conversing with a plastic doll. Creepy.

"I've met your type before," Kendall said. She leaned forward and stared into the pot of ganache like a fortune teller glancing into her crystal ball.

"My type?" Mel asked.

"You think I manipulate people into doing what I want by using my looks," Kendall said as she glanced from the pot to Mel.

Mel raised her eyebrows. It was exactly what she thought, and she didn't appreciate being called out for it.

"You think when Keogh broke up with me that I turned to Chad to punch back and hurt Keogh," Kendall continued. "But that's not true. I loved Chad."

Mel pressed her lips together. She didn't trust herself to say a word. She'd met Chad. She considered Keogh a friend. Even putting her loyalties aside, there was no way Chad was more lovable than Keogh.

"You don't believe me," Kendall said. She tossed her long hair over her shoulder in what Mel realized was a practiced move. It was also the only way Kendall could express any emotion. "That's to be expected since you didn't know Chad. He loved me. He called me his little 'Fire Starter.'" She glanced past Mel as if she was remembering something special about Chad, before she continued, "He could be very kind, and thoughtful, and—"

"That's not the Chad I met," Mel said. She was finished with this conversation. "Keogh's not here but if he should stop by, I'll tell him you were looking for him."

Kendall's lips tried to form a small pout but they moved only a millimeter or two. Realizing that her effort would be wasted on Mel, she immediately stopped. "Thank you," she said. "I appreciate that."

Mel watched as Kendall sashayed from the kitchen through the swinging doors into the front of the bakery. She almost followed her to see if Marty and Ray made fools of themselves again but to what purpose? As far as Mel was concerned Kendall was not to be trusted. Not even a little.

It wasn't Kendall's fault she was pretty, but it was Kendall's decision to use her looks to her advantage, and there was simply no way that Mel believed that she and Chad had been a love match. The guy had been horrible, and while Mel didn't think he deserved to die, it wasn't a big surprise, given the level of hostile energy Dayton emitted, that someone felt the need to remove him from the equation.

Mel finished her batch of Death by Chocolate cupcakes, setting the large trays onto the rolling carts to be wheeled into the cooler. Nervous about her reaction to vanilla, she decided her next batch of cupcakes would be lemon. Thankfully, her stomach seemed okay with the citrus smell, and when Oz came back into the kitchen with the vanilla cupcakes he went straight into the walk-in cooler, keeping the vanilla scent away from Mel as he went.

"How are you feeling?" he asked.

"Better," she said. "And lesson learned. No more midnight frozen bean burritos for me."

"TMI, chef," Oz said. He wrinkled up his nose at the mere idea of frozen food and Mel laughed. She handed him a pastry bag and together they started working on the lemon confections that she had nicknamed Pucker Up cupcakes.

They were almost finished when Keogh and Tyler came in through the back door.

Tyler's eyes lit up at the sight of the cupcakes and he immediately helped himself, barely greeting Mel before he stuffed one into his mouth and reached for another.

Keogh caught his wrist, blocking the move, and said, "Those might be a special order. You should ask first."

"Sorry," Tyler said through a mouthful. He swallowed and asked, "Are they?"

"No." Mel shook her head. Keogh let go of Tyler, who then grabbed two cupcakes.

"Dude!" Keogh snapped. "You're literally eating our profits."

Tyler shrugged. "So what? We're paying for the ingredients. Doesn't that mean we can eat as much as we want?"

"No, it doesn't."

"Aw, come on, man, this is just a side hustle," Tyler protested. "It's not like it matters if we succeed."

"We've sunk a lot of money into this place," Keogh argued. "Of course it matters."

"You're getting awfully intense about a bunch of cupcakes," Tyler said. "Maybe you have taken a few too many shots to the head lately."

"That's not it." Keogh rolled his eyes. "Let me break this down for you. The average profit for a bakery is three hundred and twenty-five thousand to four hundred and fifty thousand dollars."

"Sweet!" Tyler said.

"No, not 'sweet.'" Keogh shook his head. "Most of that profit is going right back into the business for the first three years. We have to pay for the cost of food, which is estimated to be thirty percent, and labor at forty percent. That leaves us with thirty percent—"

"One hundred grand?" Tyler's eyes lit up.

"Which will be wiped out by our lease, insurance, utilities, marketing, and . . ." Keogh looked at Mel. "What did I miss?"

"General operating costs," she said. "You know, for when you have to replace your oven or if you want to invest in point-of-sale technology, which I highly recommend."

"See?" Keogh asked Tyler. "Now do you see why you can't just plow a dozen cupcakes?"

"Yeah, and it sucks the joy out of owning a bakery," Tyler said. He glanced at Oz, who had not moved since the two football players had entered the shop.

Mel studied Oz's unblinking face. It was the same look that Ray and Marty had worn when they'd been talking to Kendall. Oz was starstruck.

"Oz, this is Keogh Graham and Tyler Matthews."

"Hi." Oz barely got the word out.

"Nice to meet you," Keogh and Tyler said together. Oz nodded and Mel suspected he needed something to do to get him over his celebrity awe.

"Oz, why don't you take Tyler out front and see if there are some extra cupcakes out there?" Mel asked.

"Now you're talking," Tyler said. He rubbed his hands together.

"Yeah, sure, happy to," Oz said. He gently put down his pastry bag and led Tyler through the doors to the front.

"I've seen that guy before," Keogh said.

"He does cooking segments for the local morning show," Mel said. "He used to work for us, but he's just helping out today." She didn't mention it was because the other bakers were no-shows and she suddenly inexplicably couldn't abide the smell of vanilla.

"That's nice of him," Keogh said.

"Yeah, he's a great guy. That got a little intense between you and Tyler," Mel said. "Are you two good? Opening a business with friends can be stressful."

"He's an idiot," Keogh said. The words were harsh but his voice was affectionate. "He thinks he can play ball forever. It's like he doesn't get that football players have an expiration date. His knee is already giving him trouble but he won't even think about retiring."

"Speaking of which, and not that it's any of my business, but are the rumors true? Are you planning on retiring?"

"Now you sound like the press," Keogh said.

She stared at him, waiting for him to continue.

"This doesn't leave this room," he said. He gestured between them. "You can't tell anyone, not Joe, not Tate or Angie, no one."

"Okay."

"The docs say if I get another severe concussion, I'm at high risk for chronic traumatic encephalopathy, or CTE."

"Oh, no," Mel said. "I'm so sorry, Keogh." She lowered her voice. "You have to retire then, don't you?"

"It feels like the smart thing to do," he said.

"What would happen to Tyler if you retired?" she asked. "Would the team keep him?"

"Yeah," Keogh said. "He'd be fine even though he should retire, too."

Mel noticed he sounded unsure about his friend's career. She was about to call him on it when Tyler came back into the kitchen, carrying a plateful of cupcakes, with a sharply dressed man who looked as if he belonged in a boardroom, following him.

"Hey, Key, look who I found," Tyler said. "Your agent, the one and only Blaise Benson."

"Hey, Blaise," Keogh said. He didn't sound overly happy to see him. "This is Mel." She waved and the forbidding-looking man nodded at her, clearly impatient to get to his business.

"Keogh, we need to talk about your potential incarceration," he said.

Eleven

"Whoa, whoa, not those cupcakes," Oz cried as he dashed into the kitchen. "Tyler, not the ones with the vani—"

"Why not vanilla?" Tyler interrupted. He sounded as happy as a little kid. He picked up the vanilla-topped one and handed it to Blaise. "You said these are the most popular flavor. You gotta try these, Blaise. They're amazing."

The scent of vanilla hit Mel and she reared back. Not again, she thought. She barely managed to excuse herself before bolting to the bathroom. She immediately started to gag but she tried to keep it quiet, putting her hand over her mouth and pretending to cough. There was silence on the other side of the door and then a soft knock.

"You all right, chef?" It was Oz.

"Yeah, I'm good," she answered. She was mouth-breathing, trying not to throw up the chocolate cupcake she'd eaten earlier.

"Hey, guess what this is from?" Oz said, and then he started to chant, "'Show me the money.'" He was obviously trying to distract her with a movie quote, and it actually worked a little bit.

"*Jerry Maguire*," Mel answered.

"All right, now I know you'll live," Oz said. "Call me if you need me. In the meantime, I'll put away anything with vanilla."

"Thank you," she said. "I'll be out in a minute."

She heard Oz walking away and sank to the floor. The nausea felt relentless. She leaned forward, putting her head between her knees. Why was she reacting this way? Ugh.

"What's up with Mel?" Tyler asked. "Is she okay?"

The door to the bathroom was thin, and Mel could hear the men talking as clearly as if they were standing in the bathroom with her. She thought about the retching noise she'd just made and felt her face get warm.

"No idea," Keogh said. "It seems like the smell of the cupcake in your hand hit her wrong. Maybe take those cupcakes back out front?"

"Oh, sorry, that's a bummer," Tyler said. "I'll be sitting in a booth eating my body weight in yummy goodness if you need me."

"Ty." Keogh's voice held a warning note.

"I'm joking, sheesh," Tyler said.

It was quiet for a beat and then Keogh said, "What's going on, Blaise? You only show up when there is something major happening, so let's have it."

"I'm not going to sugarcoat it. There's a distinct

possibility that you are going to be arrested for the murder of Chad Dayton," Blaise said.

Mel gasped. She wondered if they could hear her and she quickly put her hand over her mouth. She waited a beat, afraid to breathe too loudly.

"Why would I get arrested?" Keogh asked. Either they hadn't heard her or didn't care. "What reason could I possibly have to murder Dayton?"

"For starters, he married your ex."

"I broke up with Kendall first," Keogh protested. "I couldn't care less that she married Dayton."

"The police are not interested in that little detail," Blaise said. "They suspect you got jealous when they showed up at the opening of your bakery and you murdered Dayton in a fit of jealousy."

"With a swarm of scorpions?" Keogh asked. "Did I just happen to have them on hand? How do they think I got a bunch of scorpions? I'm a football player not an entomologist."

There was no answer and Mel thought Blaise had likely shrugged. All thought of her nausea was pushed aside as she listened in on their conversation, which she knew was rude but it wasn't as though she had a choice to be in the restroom while they talked.

Being the chief suspect in a murder investigation would doom Keogh's bakery dreams for good. Who was going to buy cupcakes from a guy who was suspected of murder? She felt sick but it wasn't her stomach this time, it was her heart.

"I can't believe this," Keogh said. He sounded upset. "It's such a load of garbage. Even if I was jealous, which I'm not, I wouldn't murder a guy over a woman. That's insane."

"I'm just keeping you in the loop about what's being said," Blaise said. "The agency is vetting some public relations people for damage control and they should have a plan for how to go forward soon."

"What if I retire from the team?" Keogh asked. "You know I've been thinking about it. Would that end the speculation?"

Blaise muttered something Mel couldn't hear.

"What do you mean, I can't retire?" Keogh asked.

"Let me put this as clearly as I can," Blaise said. "A quarterback on a team bound for the Super Bowl is much more likely to get a pass on a murder rap than a retired old has-been. You feel me?"

"What you're saying is if I'm playing, I'm protected," Keogh said.

"Yeah."

"That's crazy," Keogh said. "That just proves what everyone always accuses sports figures of—that fame means the rules don't apply to us."

"It's not fame," Blaise said. "It's skill. That fifty-million-dollar arm of yours and your killer instincts—"

The kitchen went abruptly silent.

"Sorry, that was a poor choice of words," Blaise said. "I'm just pointing out that you have what it will take to make the Scorpions Super Bowl champions, which is the one thing Dayton wanted more than anything."

"I know, believe me, I know," Keogh said.

"Dayton had heard the retirement rumors swirling about you. That's why he freaked out about the bakery. He took it as one more sign that you were breaking away," Blaise said. "He was so worried you were going to retire before the season began, he was calling me several times a week to discuss how to keep you happy."

"I remember," Keogh said. "He was relentless."

"A quality he was known for," Blaise agreed. "It's been noted by more than one media outlet that he was single-minded and had a well-deserved reputation for heaping retribution on those who went against him."

"What are you trying to say?" Keogh asked.

"That there have been grumblings that you murdered Dayton to get away from him," Blaise said. "Despite your medical records being private, the media knows how many concussions you've had. They know you're at risk for CTE. There's been some buzz that you were escaping Dayton to save your life."

"Wait, I thought everyone believed I murdered him over Kendall?" Keogh asked. "Can't they make up their minds about a motive?"

"I think the point is that there are multiple reasons for you to have wanted to end Dayton," Blaise said. "And if they do arrest you, you could find yourself riding the bench in a courtroom instead of on the sidelines if you don't make your next move very wisely."

"Meaning stay in the game," Keogh said. "Whether I want to or not."

"I'm just saying there's a lot at stake," Blaise said.

"Including your career as a sports agent. If I retire and you no longer represent me, your biggest client, who are you?" Keogh said.

There was another very heavy silence.

"Um . . . ouch," Blaise said. "I don't think I deserved that."

"Just speaking the truth," Keogh said. "I know there's a lot more riding on me than a Super Bowl win. There are many, many careers at stake. Believe me, I get it."

"Well, you'd better," Blaise said. It was the first time Mel had detected some heat in his voice. "Before you do anything rash like handing in your jersey, you might want to think over all of the ramifications to yourself, your team, your best friend, Tyler, and yes, even me. Call me if you want to talk or if you have any questions."

There was silence and Mel rose to her feet. Poor Keogh. The season hadn't even started yet, and now he was going to have to play, not only with the risk of a possible CTE hanging over his head but also a potential arrest for murder, which was absolutely crazy. There was no way he was a murderer. Mel felt sure of it.

She took a minute to breathe even though she wanted to run right out and find out if he was okay. Instead, she splashed water on her face, making certain she wasn't going to be sick. She washed and dried her hands, checking that she was steady before she went back into the kitchen.

Keogh was standing by the stove. There was a pot on one of the burners and steam was rising from it. Mel hesitated in the doorway. She didn't know what he was cooking but she didn't want to risk getting sick from it.

"It's all right," Keogh said. "This is a recipe my grandmother taught me to soothe the stomach."

Mel crossed the kitchen, cautiously. She slipped onto one of the stools at the worktable.

Keogh stirred whatever was in the pot. He was staring into it as if it could give him the answers he sought.

"I didn't mean to eavesdrop," Mel said. "But I heard what Blaise said, at least most of it."

"About my potential arrest for Dayton's murder?" Keogh asked.

"Yes."

"Hmm."

"Do you have an alibi?" Mel asked.

"Given that they suspect it was the middle of the night when he died, no," Keogh said. "I was asleep in my bed alone. Not a great alibi."

"Are there cameras on your house, proving you were there?" Mel asked.

"There is one that shows me, or more accurately my car, pulling into my garage," he said. "But I don't have cameras in my house because I'm leery about security breaches and my privacy going viral, if you know what I mean."

Mel nodded. She could see where that would be a concern for a man as famous as Keogh.

"Nothing concrete then," she said.

"No." He took the pot off the stove and grabbed one of the coffee mugs from a cupboard over the sink. He carefully poured the steaming liquid into the cup and put it in front of Mel. "Sip that slowly. It should make you feel better."

She cupped the mug, letting the warmth fill her hands before she lifted the mug to her lips. The scent of ginger hit her nose and she paused. She took a cautious sip. The spice lingered on her tongue but it didn't cause her stomach to rebel.

"Thank you," she said. "Who else would have wanted Dayton dead?"

"You met the man," Keogh said. "The easier question to answer would be, Who wouldn't want him dead?"

"How about Coach?" Mel asked. "What was his relationship with Dayton like?"

"Complicated," Keogh said.

"Meaning?" Mel sipped her tea. She could feel her stomach settle and she sighed in relief.

"Coach's job is to win, he crushed it last year, but we still didn't win the big game," Keogh said. "Dayton's been on him all during the off-season to be sure to win this year. The pressure has to be insane."

"Was it bad enough that Coach might feel like his position was in jeopardy?" Mel asked.

"This is professional sports," Keogh said. "The entire industry is built on an attitude of 'What have you done for me lately?' There is no job security. Everyone is in jeopardy all the time."

"Who is going to own the team now that Dayton is gone?" Mel asked.

"Good question," Keogh said. "He has some grown sons from his first marriage, but I would think it would be Kendall."

"But they weren't even married that long," Mel said.

Keogh shrugged. "His sons rarely come to any of the games. They've shown no interest in the team. I don't think they're close at all, but by all accounts, Dayton loved Kendall . . . you know, as much as he was capable of loving anything or anyone."

"Do you think she knew she would inherit the team?" Mel asked.

Keogh studied her. "I think I know where you're going with that, and I have to disagree. Kendall is not a murderer."

"You sure about that?" Mel asked.

"Yes," he said. Mel couldn't help but notice the slight hesitation before he said it.

"If Kendall is the owner, do you think she will keep the team or sell it?" Mel asked.

"No idea." Keogh shrugged. "I haven't really spoken to her one-on-one since she married Dayton. It seemed best for all that I keep my distance."

Mel sipped her tea and thought about the rarity of a woman owning a major sports team. She liked the idea even though she wasn't terribly fond of the woman herself.

"How are you feeling now?" Keogh asked.

Mel took another sip and paused to consider. She drew in a deep breath. The ginger was definitely helping. She was feeling much more settled.

"I think your ginger tea worked," she said.

"I'm glad," Keogh said. "My grandmother swore by it."

"Well, I for one am grateful," Mel said. "I can't believe how sick I've been all day. I couldn't seem to shake it."

"When are you due?" Keogh asked. His smile was warm and full of understanding.

"Excuse me?" Mel said. "Due for what?"

"You know, when is the baby due?"

Mel blinked at him and then she laughed. "Baby?"

"Yeah," Keogh said. "Isn't that what's making you sick? I mean, why do you think you suddenly can't stand the smell of vanilla? It's a classic symptom of morning sickness."

"No!" Mel scoffed. "I'm not . . . I can't be . . ."

"Mel, do we need to have a talk about the birds and the bees?" Keogh asked. His tone was gentle and there was a glint of humor in his eyes.

"No," Mel said. She felt her face get warm in embarrassment. "How . . . why . . ."

"That tea you're drinking is what my grandmother made for my mom every time she got pregnant. With me, Mama June couldn't stand the smell of lemon but with my younger brother, it was barbeque sauce. I'm the oldest of four. I remember when Nana came and made the tea and by the time my youngest sister was born, I was able to make the tea, too."

"But I . . ." Mel tried to think if pregnancy was possible. It hit her then that it definitely was. She and Joe hadn't been trying, but they hadn't exactly been *not* trying, either. She could be carrying her husband's baby right now! The wooziness hit her full force and she slumped against the back of her chair.

Twelve

"Drink your tea," Keogh said. "It'll help."

Mel did as he suggested, feeling as if she couldn't quite get a grip on what was happening. A baby? She needed confirmation.

"I have to take a test," she said. "I mean, it could be just a stomach flu in which case if I've given it to you, I'm sorry."

"Could be, but I've never known a stomach flu to be triggered by the smell of vanilla," Keogh said. His logic was sound.

"I have to go," Mel said. She glanced up at him. "Don't say anything to the others, please."

"Of course not," he said. "But are you sure you're up for driving? You might want to wait until later."

"No, now that it's out there, I have to know or it will

drive me crazy," she said. She rose from her seat to go and grab her purse from the office. When she returned she said, "Will you ask Oz to take Ray and Marty back to Old Town with him?"

"Sure," Keogh said. "And if he can't, I'll make sure they get home. Don't worry about it."

"Thanks," Mel said. She impetuously hugged him. It was very similar to hugging a brick wall.

Keogh patted her back with one large hand. "Happy to help."

She hurried out the back door, rushing to her car before the reporter, who was still outside, could do more than yell a few questions at her. They were ridiculous.

"Did Keogh murder the owner of the Scorpions?

"Will the bakery close its doors?

"Is Keogh going to be arrested?"

Mel ignored him completely. She started her vehicle and zipped out of the parking lot, heading for the first pharmacy she could find. There was one halfway to home and she parked and dashed inside. The summer sun was heating up and she texted Angie to find out if she was still at the bakery.

Angie responded that she was home, putting Emari down for her nap while Tate managed the bakery. Mel texted her that she would be over in a little while for a project. She stood confronting the wall of pregnancy tests and decided to buy several just in case. The cashier said nothing to her, for which Mel was grateful, and she hurried back to her car.

Mel parked in Angie's driveway and just as she stepped out of her car, Angie opened the front door. She looked at Mel's face and asked, "What's wrong? What's the project? We don't have to fire someone, do we? I hate having to do that."

"No, nothing's wrong. Not exactly," Mel said.

"Are we sleuthing then?" Angie asked. She lowered her voice to a whisper as they stepped inside. The house was very mid-century modern, and Angie had decorated it sparsely, mostly with photographs of her family and friends.

"Sort of," Mel said.

"I knew it," Angie cried. "Someone murdered Dayton and we're going to figure out who. I've been thinking about this all night and I think—"

"I already know who did it," Mel said.

"What? Who?" Angie led the way into her kitchen. Mel glanced around for any sign of anything flavored with vanilla. The coast was clear.

"It has to be Kendall Dayton," Mel continued. "She's the only one with a real motive."

"I'll bite," Angie said. "What's her motive?"

"Keogh told me she's the one who will inherit the team," Mel said. "That's a powerful motive."

"True," Angie said. "But it's well known that Chad Dayton was not well liked. There must be loads of people who wanted him gone."

"It's Kendall," Mel said. She made a face. "She coasts through life on her looks and I'm sure she thinks she can avoid a conviction if she bats her eyelashes and tosses her hair enough."

"Mel, I have to be honest. I feel like you're choosing her just because she's pretty, and it annoys you," Angie said.

"No!" Mel cried. It came out loud and defensive even

to her own ears. She sat on a stool at the kitchen island and Angie slid onto the one beside her. "Sorry, I didn't mean to raise the volume like that."

"It's okay," Angie said. "Emari has been a champion napper, lately. I think a parade could march up and down the hallway and she'd sleep through it."

"Thank goodness for that," Mel said. She took a breath and said, "I can see where you might think I'm choosing Kendall because she's so obnoxiously gorgeous, but that's not it. She has the most reason to murder Dayton. Period."

"Is there any evidence?" Angie asked. "Like where was she when he was murdered?"

"No evidence yet," Mel admitted, "and I don't know her alibi, either. Shoot, I should have asked her that when she came to the bakery today."

"She came to the bakery?"

"Yes, first she couldn't remember my name and when I introduced myself she said, 'the chef woman with the man's name and haircut.'"

"You're right, she totally did it," Angie said. She looked peeved, which was just the solace Mel needed.

"She was looking for Keogh, which I also find very suspish," Mel said.

"So is that what we're doing today?" Angie asked. "Looking for evidence that Kendall murdered her husband?"

"Not exactly," Mel said.

"Good," Angie said. "Even though you're probably right, I think we need to go wide. We can't just play into your bias."

"My whatis?" Mel asked.

"Bias," Angie said. "Mel, ever since we were in middle

school, you've had a bias against excessively pretty women."

Mel leaned back in her seat and studied her friend. She was shocked. "I. Have. Not."

"Yeah, you have," Angie said. "And I get it, they can be horrible." She shuddered. "But even though Kendall was nasty to you, I don't think we can accuse her of murder just because she's a mean girl. We need evidence."

"That's not what I was doing," Mel protested. "I really do think she has the most motive."

"Are you sure that's it?" Angie asked.

"Yes," Mel said. "I'm not even here about that."

"I thought you said we were sleuthing."

"We are, but not about Dayton or his murder."

Angie looked confused. "Then what are we doing?"

"This." Mel handed her the bag from the pharmacy.

Angie looked bewildered. She opened the bag and peered inside. She stared for a beat and then looked up at Mel.

Her eyes were wide but she also looked wary. "Are you pranking me?"

Mel shook her head.

"Ah!" Angie leapt out of her chair and threw her arms around Mel's neck, hugging her so tight it almost strangled.

"What happened? Are you late? Have you been trying? Why didn't you tell me?" She fired questions at Mel not giving her a chance to answer.

When Angie let her go, Mel said, "Let's not get crazy. I have to take the test. I might not be, but today all of a sudden the scent of vanilla made me violently ill. And not just once but several times."

"My old friend morning sickness," Angie said. "Can I get you anything? Plain crackers seem to help."

"No, I'm feeling better," Mel said. "Keogh actually made me some ginger tea when he suspected that I was pregnant."

Angie frowned. "Keogh?"

"Yes, I was so sick at his bakery this morning—"

"Do you mean to tell me that Keogh knew you were pregnant before I did?" Angie looked offended.

"Um, we're not sure that I am yet," Mel said. "And technically, he knew before I did. He was the one who suggested my upset stomach was because I might be pregnant."

"Oh." Angie thought about it. "That's different then."

"Exactly," Mel said. "As of now, he has an unconfirmed suspicion."

"You did swear him to secrecy, yes?"

"Of course."

"Are you ready to find out?" Angie asked. With a look of excitement she held up one of the kits.

"I think so," Mel said. Her stomach whooshed for an entirely different reason. Was she ready? She honestly wasn't sure.

\ ' \ ' / \

"How long do we wait?" Mel asked.

They were sitting on the floor in the hallway, leaning against the closed bathroom door as if they'd trapped a wild creature in there. Angie was holding the test box and reading the pages and pages of instructions that came with it.

"It says to wait for at least ten minutes," Angie said.

"How long has it been?" Mel asked. She was certain it had to have been an hour.

"Three minutes," Angie said.

"Ugh." Mel flopped over on the floor, lying in a fetal position.

"Let's think about something else," Angie suggested.

"Not cupcakes," Mel said. "I'm afraid I'll be sick."

"Okay, then, what about Dayton's murder?"

"Not if you're going to lecture me on my pretty-woman bias," Mel said. "I still say Kendall is the most likely suspect."

"Except how did she murder him with scorpions in Keogh's bakery?" Angie asked. "It makes no sense."

"She was going for the ultimate revenge," Mel countered. "Murder her dud of a husband and frame her ex, using scorpions, which just so happens to be the name of the team she'll inherit. It's like a calling card."

"Deadly scorpions?" Angie asked. "That seems a tad dramatic."

"Oh, I have some information on that from our exterminator," Mel said. "The scorpions weren't deadly bark scorpions. They were devil scorpions and they're not nearly as poisonous."

"So, Dayton wasn't killed by scorpion stings?"

"Not according to Nick," Mel said.

"That changes everything," Angie said. "Did Nick tell the police?"

"Detective Rivera?" Mel asked. "I don't know. I imagine the medical examiner will figure it out, but maybe I can call the detective and share the information, you know, as a concerned citizen."

"It's the right thing to do," Angie said.

They were quiet for a moment. Mel glanced at her friend. Angie's transformation into motherhood had been an amazing journey to watch. She used to be a feisty hot-head whose first response to insults and threats had been to punch back, but now she was infused with a patience for life and people that made every moment something to be mindful of and to be shared through Emari's eyes. Sure, she had her moments when she needed to tap out of motherhood for a spell and turn it over to Tate but over-all, she'd had a true metamorphosis.

Mel pushed herself up to a seated position. "What if I'm not good at it?"

"What? Solving the murder?" Angie asked. "I think your résumé speaks for itself."

"No," Mel said. Her voice was low when she added, "The whole mom thing. What if I mess it up? What if I'm too impatient or critical? What if I give the baby my own insecurities? What if it hates me? What if I'm a terrible mother?"

"That right there is why you're going to be just fine," Angie said. "Look at how much you care about doing a good job. That means you're going to be an amazing mom."

She looped her arm around Mel's shoulders and gave her a half hug. Mel relaxed against her friend. Angie was right. She did care. So much. And Mel had Joe. Dear Joe. She couldn't ask for a better man to father her children.

She wondered if she should call him. But then, what if she wasn't pregnant? She didn't want him to be disap-pointed. He hadn't said anything, but when they talked about having a family, his face lit up with excitement like all he'd ever wanted in life was to have a family with her.

Mel glanced at her phone. There were mere seconds

left on the timer. There was no way she could wait for Joe to get here to find out the results, besides this way she could find a really special way to tell him, instead of being hunkered in a hallway waiting for her phone to ding.

Ding!

"It's time!" Angie let her go and sprang to her feet.

Mel sat, afraid to get up and see what the stick said. She couldn't decide if she'd be relieved or disappointed. She didn't particularly want to feel either one of those emotions right now.

"Come on, Mel," Angie cried. "Moment of truth."

"I can't go in," Mel said. "You go look."

"Are you sure?" Angie asked.

"Yes." Mel nodded.

Angie met her gaze and held it for a moment and then turned and went inside the bathroom.

Mel sat there waiting. She had assumed Angie would dash in and then scream if it was positive. The lack of noise made her concerned. Angie, who had wanted Mel to have a baby so they could be moms together, was likely disheartened by the results.

Had Keogh been wrong? He had seemed so sure. Was she not pregnant? She'd really thought she was. The disappointment that washed over her was surprising in its intensity. She felt her throat get tight and tears flooded her eyes. She blinked them away, trying to get it together.

Well, she supposed the upside was that she didn't have to even mention this test to Joe. The disappointment would be hers alone to carry.

Angie appeared in the doorway, holding the test in her hand. Tears were streaming down her face and Mel rose to her feet to hug her friend.

"It's okay, Ange," Mel said. "I'm fine with not having a baby yet. Joe and I haven't given it our best efforts." She forced a laugh, trying to lighten the moment. "I'm confident we'll have a better outcome next time."

Angie shook her head. She held out the test to Mel and said, "No, you . . . it . . . Mel, it's positive. You're pregnant."

Thirteen

Mel spent the rest of the day in a daze. When she left Angie's house, after a long session of laughs and tears, she sat in her car. She pondered the steering wheel. She put her hand on her abdomen. She tried to wrap her head around the fact that she was now the very thing she had spent most of her adult life actively avoiding being—pregnant.

When Angie came out with Emari in her arms, she rapped on Mel's window and asked if she needed a ride home. Angie was laughing and Mel took a moment to take in the picture of her friend with her toddler on her hip. That was going to be her. It boggled.

Mel shook her head and laughed. Then she drove home. She wandered around her house, played with her pets, and decided to make a special dinner for her and

Joe. She put candles on the table, set it with the good china, and snipped some magenta bougainvillea blossoms from the bush in front of the house to put in a vase, finishing it off.

She set up her tablet in the kitchen, watching the news while she cooked. She was only half listening while trying to figure out what she would say to Joe. How should she tell him? She didn't know if she wanted to be serious or joyful or teasing. She was imagining his response to each variation when the newscaster's voice broke in.

"The police have taken Keogh Graham in for questioning in connection with the murder of Chad Dayton, owner of the Arizona Scorpions."

Mel dropped the spoon she was using to stir her homemade sauce and focused on the small screen. The display showed a video of Keogh being led into the police station. He was flanked by his attorney, Steve Wolfmeier, Coach Casella, and his agent, Blaise Benson. He wasn't handcuffed and Keogh held his head high. He wore sunglasses and a sharp suit and didn't acknowledge any of the shouts or jeers directed his way by the gathering crowd.

The story rolled to the next news segment and Mel switched it off. She shut off the stove, putting the lid on the sauce pot and removing it from the heat. She grabbed her phone and called Tate.

"Did you see the news?" she asked.

"No, what happened?"

"Keogh's been taken in for questioning," Mel said. "We have to get over there."

"Taken in as in arrested?" Tate cried.

"I don't know," Mel said. "They just said questioning, but his attorney, his agent, and his coach were with him."

"That's crazy!" Tate cried. "What can we do?"

"I don't know," Mel said. "Show support?"

"I think we have to," Tate said. "I mean, this could se-riously damage his business—not to mention ours, since we're partners and all."

"Tate." Mel said his name exactly like Angie did when she was correcting him.

"Sorry, sorry," he said. "You can take the guy out of the investment office but you can't take the investment office out of the guy. Clearly, this is more than a business situation. We should go because we're his friends."

"Exactly." Mel heard the sound of the garage door. She scooped her handbag off its spot on the side table and patted Peanut and Captain Jack on their heads. "Joe just pulled in. I'll grab him and we'll pick you up in less than five."

"I'll be ready," Tate promised.

Mel stepped into the garage from the house. She hur-ried to the passenger side of the car and opened the door.

Joe opened his mouth to speak but she said, "Keogh's been brought in. We have to go. Tate can take me if you can't, otherwise we're picking him up."

"Tell him to be waiting outside," Joe said.

"Already did."

Tate was outside the house with Angie, who was hold-ing Emari. He turned and kissed his baby on her head and then his wife on the lips and said he'd call as soon as he knew something. Angie waved at them. Her gaze met Mel's for a moment and Mel shook her head. She'd sworn Angie to secrecy, aside from Tate, and she knew Angie was asking if she'd told Joe. Angie nodded, indicating message received.

As Tate climbed into the car, he said, "Congratulations."

"For what?" Joe asked.

Mel whipped her head around and stared at Tate with wide eyes.

He frowned in confusion, but Mel ignored him and said, "I developed a new cupcake flavor." It sounded ridiculously lame even to her.

"Oh? Need a taste tester?" Joe asked.

Tate slowly nodded and Mel knew he understood that she hadn't told Joe the news yet.

"Why do you think they brought Keogh in?" Mel asked. "What could have happened?"

"We'll only know if they choose to tell us," Joe said. "But I suspect he's a person of interest for a variety of reasons, but primarily because Dayton was found dead in his bakery."

"That doesn't seem fair," Tate said.

"But the medical examiner hasn't even said what the cause of death was," Mel said. "And from what Nick the exterminator told me, it wasn't the scorpions that killed Dayton."

"What?" Joe asked. "When did you find that out?"

"This morning at the bakery," Mel said.

"And you didn't call me?" Joe asked.

"I would have, truly, but it was a crazy busy day," Mel said. Oh, he had no idea how busy.

"I understand," Joe said. He reached across the car's console and squeezed her hand in his. "I imagine trying to run two bakeries and crafting a brand-new flavor kept you busy."

"Hmm." Mel hummed noncommittally. This was one of the many reasons she loved her husband. He was always impressed with her even if it wasn't warranted. "According to Nick, the scorpions found on Dayton were devil scorpions, not bark scorpions, and much less lethal, although their sting is pretty nasty."

"So, if it wasn't the scorpions that killed Dayton, what did?" Tate asked.

Mel shrugged. She glanced at Joe, who was frowning at the road in front of them. She would have told him the news about the baby right then and there but with Tate sitting in the backseat like a golden retriever, his head swiveling back and forth while they talked, she just couldn't. She wanted it to be special.

"What's going to happen to Keogh?" Mel asked.

"Depends upon what happens during questioning," Joe said. "He's got solid representation with Wolfmeier, who should keep him from being arrested, for the moment."

"That's not as reassuring as you'd think," Mel said.

Joe parked in the lot of the police station. It was a small squat building built of stone in the center of town. She realized every time she'd ever had to go into the station in Old Town, it was with the knowledge that her uncle was there, somewhere, and even if he wasn't happy to see her, the rest of the department was because she usually brought cupcakes. She felt oddly barehanded not bringing cupcakes into the station.

Joe went and spoke to the officer at the front desk. They were shown to a line of hard metal chairs on the far side of the room. Mel and Tate sat down while Joe took out his phone.

"I'm going to make some calls and see what I can find out," he said.

He wandered away and Mel sat with Tate. As soon as Joe was out of earshot, Tate whispered, "You haven't told him yet? How could you not have told him?"

"Um." Mel gestured to the building around them. "Kind of busy."

"Mel." Tate looked at her and she knew her friend wasn't falling for her distraction technique.

"I was going to tell him," she said. "I was. I cooked a nice dinner, I even put a vase of flowers on the table. I wanted it to be special, not something I yelled at him while we picked you up on the way to the police station."

"I get that, but you need to tell him as soon as possible," Tate said. He gestured to where Joe was pacing, while chatting. He was still in his suit and tie from work and Mel felt her heart flip-flop. He was the father of her child. Oh, how she hoped the baby turned out just like him. Kind, compassionate, funny, and smart.

"I know," Mel agreed. "He deserves to know."

"It's not even that," Tate said. "I don't think Angie and I are up to the challenge of keeping a secret of this magnitude."

"You have to," Mel said. "If you blab to him, I will never forgive you."

"Then tell him soon," Tate said.

"I will," Mel said. "I promise."

Joe took his phone away from his ear, sliding it into his pants pocket as he walked towards them. His face was grim.

"What's wrong?" Mel asked. "What happened?"

"Nothing yet," he said. "But apparently, Keogh was sent to the hospital a month ago for a scorpion sting."

Mel's eyes went wide at the implication. "And?"

"And Detective Rivera seems to think it's tied to Dayton's murder," he said.

"How?" Mel asked.

"I'm just guessing, because I suspect Rivera is thinking that Keogh, having just been stung by a scorpion, thought it would be a grand way to get rid of the man who married his ex," Joe said.

"But that's totally circumstantial and coincidental," Tate protested. "He can't base his case on that."

"Agreed," Joe said. "But it was enough for them to bring Keogh in for questioning."

"Are they going to release him?" Mel asked.

"Most likely," Joe said. "Because if I know Wolfme—"

"Hey, hey, hey. If it isn't my favorite assistant district attorney," Steve Wolfmeier greeted them as he came around the corner with Keogh. There was no sign of Coach Casella or Blaise Benson. "Isn't this a conflict of interest for you, DeLaura?"

"It is," Joe said. "Which is why I would recuse myself from the case."

"Always the straight shooter," Wolfmeier said. It didn't sound like a compliment.

Keogh had taken his sunglasses off and he looked scared. Mel hopped up from her seat and hugged him. "Are you okay? Is there anything we can do to help?"

"You're here?" Keogh glanced at Mel and Tate. "You came here for me?"

"Of course," Tate said. "We're partners."

Keogh blinked. Mel wasn't certain but she thought he appeared a little choked up. "Thank you. I appreciate the support. Honestly, I'll be better when I'm out of here."

"Mr. Graham?" A uniformed officer approached them. "There is a swarm of reporters out there, you may want to take the lesser-known side exit."

Keogh looked at Wolfmeier, who nodded and said, "That's a good idea. Nice of you to show up, kids, but I'm taking my client home and we have a lot of planning to do. You can catch up tomorrow."

"All right," Mel said. "Keogh, we'll keep the bakery going for you. Don't you worry."

He smiled at her and it was one of pure happiness, which given the circumstances was surprising.

"Oh, I'm not worried," Keogh said. "I talked to my mama earlier and she is flying in from Savannah tonight. Everything will be fine now that Mama June is en route."

His joy was infectious and Mel grinned at him. "I can't wait to meet her."

٠٠٠٠٠

Mel was working in the kitchen of Keogh and Tyler's bakery when Mama June Graham arrived. She was a burst of bright colors and flashed a big smile when she saw Mel working at the large steel table in the middle of the kitchen. Mel had opted to make her Cinnamon Sinner cupcakes, hoping that her stomach wouldn't rebel if there was no vanilla involved.

"Hello there, you must be Mel," Mama June said. Her hair was combed out in a stylish Afro and she wore a sundress with a pattern of brightly colored lime and lemon wedges and big dangling lemon earrings to match.

Mama June's warm wide smile was positively contagious, and Mel found herself returning it when she said, "And you must be Keogh's mom, Mrs. Graham."

"Call me Mama June," she said with a wave of her hand. Her nails were short and polished in bright yellows and greens and a big diamond sparkled on her finger. "Everyone does."

"It's wonderful to meet you, Mama June," Mel said. "I know Keogh was very excited for your arrival."

"Me, too," Mama June said. "I wanted to be here for the bakery opening, but I was wrapping up the semester with my students."

"Mama is a professor at the Savannah College of Art and Design," Keogh said.

"What do you teach?" Mel asked.

"Ceramics," Mama June said. "I've always enjoyed working with my hands. Honestly, creating was the only thing that got me through losing Keogh's father twenty years ago."

"I'm so sorry," Mel said to both of them. "I lost my dad over ten years ago and I still miss him every day."

Mama June nodded and Mel could tell by the look in her eyes that she understood completely.

"Let me show you around the bakery, Mama," Keogh said. "You're going to love it."

"I already do," she said. "Anything that gets you safely off the field is A-okay with me."

Keogh shook his head and toured her around the kitchen and then took her out front, where Mel could hear him introducing her to Marty. Mel wasn't sure what to expect after Keogh was brought in for questioning last night, but they had still opened today. They'd had a steady stream of customers, and much to Mel's surprise, it wasn't just gawkers wanting to know what had happened to the Valley's favorite player. In fact, Mel had felt as if it was almost a show of support. She took it as a good sign.

She filled her pastry bag and was frosting the cinnamon cupcakes when the kitchen door opened and Mama June returned. She glanced at the wall and saw the rack of aprons and asked, "Keogh is out there signing autographs and it looks like he'll be there awhile. Is there anything I can do to help you?"

"I never say no to help." Mel hadn't slept well and was feeling exhausted. She would have accepted assistance even from all seven DeLaura brothers, which normally she'd never consider, given the chaos that would ensue.

"I was hoping you'd say that." Mama June smiled and lifted the bright pink apron over her head, tying it around her waist as she joined Mel at the table. "What can I do?"

"Dust each cupcake with a light coating of cinnamon after I put the frosting on?" Mel asked.

Mama June nodded. She picked up the jar of ground cinnamon and sprinkled it on the top of the cupcakes as Mel went.

"Forgive me if I'm being impolite," Mama June said. "But how far along are you?"

"How did you know? Did Keogh tell you?" Mel asked. She paused between cupcakes to look at the woman beside her.

"Oh, no." Mama June shook her head. "He didn't have

to tell me. You have that glow. Personally, I never felt as if I glowed during my four pregnancies, but my mama assured me that I did."

"I don't feel very glowy, either," Mel said. "More like nauseated and exhausted."

"What smell is triggering you?"

"Vanilla," Mel said. She resumed frosting. "Keogh made me the tea that your mother made for you, the ginger one, and it helped."

"Oh, I'm glad. That poor kid had to make it for me when I carried his sister. Oh, honey, I was so sick. I'm surprised he remembered, but then again his happy place always was the kitchen," Mama June said. "I suppose it's a natural fit that he wanted to open a bakery. He was always a sweet-over-savory person."

"Me, too," Mel said. "I don't see why we can't have cake for every meal."

Mama June laughed. "Would you like me to bake and frost any of the cupcakes that have vanilla in them, so you don't have to smell it?"

"My sous chef is working his other job today and the two part-timers we hired are students in culinary school, so if you're willing, that would be amazing. I will be forever in your debt."

Mama June clapped her hands. "No, it's me who owes you. I love baking and I have a recipe for a peach cobbler cupcake that is to die for . . . oh, sorry, that's probably not the best turn of phrase given the circumstances."

"It's okay," Mel said. "Things are a bit wonky around here since Dayton's death. I feel for Keogh and Tyler. Opening their bakery and then having the owner of the team found dead inside, it's the stuff of nightmares."

"It is," Mama June said. "When Keogh called to tell me, I couldn't believe it. And the idea that it was murder is just . . ."

"Mama June!" Tyler swept in through the back door with his arms held wide.

"Tyler!" Mama June stepped into his hug, squeezing him around the middle. "How is it you get handsomer every time I see you?"

Tyler beamed and said, "It's because your eyesight is failing."

"Oh, you." Mama June swatted his arm. She laughed and rejoined Mel at the table. "Keogh is out front if you're looking for him."

"Thanks," Tyler said. "Hey, Mel." He scooped two cupcakes on his way and she shook her head.

"Hi, Tyler." She glanced at Mama June and said, "Keogh is afraid Tyler is going to eat all their profits and he might not be wrong."

"I hear that," Mama June said. "I used to feed Keogh's high school football team once a week after practice. I'd make an enormous Crock-Pot full of baked beans and pulled pork and then trays and trays of corn bread. There was never anything left. Not even a crumb."

Mel didn't want to dim Mama June's light, but she had to ask, "Are you worried about Keogh? Do you think he might be falsely arrested?"

Mama June stopped sprinkling the cinnamon. She met Mel's gaze and her warm brown eyes were as certain as her mother's love for her child. "No. I know my boy, and I know he could never do such a thing. My faith is strong that the killer will be caught and my son will be vindicated."

Mel stood up straighter. "I think so, too, and I'm willing to do whatever it takes to prove Keogh is innocent."

Mama June gave her a half hug. "I knew buying a bakery was a good move for him."

Mel hoped she was right. At the moment, she couldn't help but fear that the bakery had given the person who really murdered Dayton a place to plant the body, setting Keogh up for a murder rap that could ruin his life.

Fourteen

"I'm staying with Mel," Mama June said when Keogh and Tyler returned to the kitchen.

"Are you sure?" Keogh asked. "You used to love watching us practice."

Mama June didn't say anything and Tyler's eyebrows rose. "Is this because Kendall is probably the owner of the team now?"

Mama June brushed an invisible bit of lint off her sleeve. "Maybe."

"Ma—" Keogh said, but Mama June interrupted.

"Also, I'm going to make my peach cobbler cupcakes for your bakery, since Mel could use a hand."

"Oh, yes!" Tyler pumped his fist. "Are those the ones with the peach-flavored cake and the vanilla buttercream with the brown sugar–cinnamon peaches on top?"

"Yes."

"Come on, bro, let's not stand in her way," Tyler said. He nudged Keogh towards the door.

"I didn't have you come here to make you work," Keogh said.

"Look at this kitchen," Mama June said. "This is a dream come true. Now shoo. I'll bring some cupcakes to your practice so you and your teammates don't miss out."

Keogh opened his mouth to protest and Mel said, "I'll deliver her safe and sound to you with cupcakes. I promise."

"All right, but be careful," Keogh said. "Both of you."

"We will," Mama June said. She kissed Keogh's cheek and waved him away.

The players exited out the back door and Mel noted that Keogh locked it behind him.

"This is going to work out very well," Mama June said.

"Oh?" Mel asked.

"Yes, because now we get to bring cupcakes and snoop around their practice," Mama June said. "We can get into all sorts of places if we show up with cupcakes."

Mel laughed. Mama June was a woman after her own heart. "Absolutely, we can."

⌣⸜⸝⸜⸝

Mel left Marty to oversee the bakery when she and Mama June departed. Two of the DeLaura brothers, Tony and Al, had arrived to help him and Mel tried not to think of what shenanigans the three of them would get into while unsupervised.

Having carefully covered the peach cobbler cupcakes because the vanilla frosting still made Mel queasy, she and Mama June drove over to the stadium, which was only a few miles away, where the players were practicing for the upcoming season.

The vast parking lot was surprisingly empty compared to game days. They were able to get a spot near the door and the security guard recognized Mama June and greeted her with a big smile.

"Good afternoon, Mrs. Graham," the man said. His badge read *Hector*.

"Hector, you know better than to get formal with me," Mama June said. "Here. Have a cupcake." She handed him one out of the tub in her arms and he beamed.

Mel made certain to stay upwind of the scent. She didn't want to embarrass herself any more than she already had. She'd never had access to the enormous stadium before unless she'd had a ticket in hand, so it was thrilling to be escorted in by Hector.

"The guys are on the field," he said. "They're just finishing up and I'm sure Coach Casella won't mind you being here."

They walked through a series of doors and long hallways, through the locker room, and out onto the field. There was a man sitting on a bench, wearing a bright orange, multi-legged costume beside an enormous scorpion head. His posture was forlorn. He had a shock of dark hair that fell over his forehead and he was wearing glasses.

"Hi, Jamie," Mama June greeted him. "What's the matter?"

Jamie glanced up and caught sight of Mel standing beside Mama June and tried to cover his face with his elbow. "Ah! No one is supposed to see me. I am not a person. I'm Scotty the Scorpion!"

He hopped off the bench and grabbed the head part of his costume and yanked it on. He looked like Barney the purple dinosaur except he was vivid orange. The rest of his costume was a body made up of the same orange but had two pincher arms and a long forked tail that curled up. Not exactly the sort of mascot you wanted to give a hug.

"Relax, Jamie, have a cupcake," Mama June said. "Mel is our friend and she won't tell anyone she saw you."

Jamie lifted the mask off. He took the cupcake and sighed. "I don't suppose it really matters. I heard Dayton was planning to fire me before he died, so it's probably just a matter of time before I have to hang up my costume."

"Dayton was going to fire you?" Mama June asked. "Why?"

"Something about how I didn't move fast enough for him," Jamie said. He jerked a thumb at his costume. "He should have tried sprinting in that thing. The tail alone is fifteen pounds."

"That does seem unfair," Mel said. "You have a new owner now. Maybe Kendall won't be so harsh."

"Doesn't matter." Jamie picked at the wrapper around his cupcake. "I heard they're going to change the team name and the mascot because it now has a bad association for the players and the fans."

He slumped back onto the bench. Mama June patted him on the shoulder. "Don't worry. I'll bet they pick a great new mascot and you'll be first in line to bring it to life."

Jamie looked at her over the top of his glasses. "You think?"

"Absolutely," she said. "Look at how well you sell that scorpion. Why, I think you can be and do anything you put your mind to, Jamie."

"Thanks, Mama June." He took a huge bite out of his cupcake, looking infinitely better than when they'd arrived. They left him to ponder his future and made their way down the sideline.

"I used to think cupcakes worked mood magic," Mel said. "But I think that was all you."

"After four kids, you gain some skills," Mama June said. "But the cupcake was a perfect closer." They exchanged a smile.

The men were out on the field, so they carried their tubs of cupcakes over to the table where the water station was set up. A few yards away, Coach Casella was having an intense conversation with Kendall Dayton and even though she knew it was none of her business, Mel was desperate to hear what was being said.

She glanced at Mama June and noted the other woman was watching the coach and Kendall as well, her eyes narrowed with speculation.

"What are you thinking?" Mel asked.

"I was just wondering what sort of relationship those two have," Mama June said. "Close? And if so, how close?"

Mel turned back to Kendall and the coach in time to see her reach out and squeeze the coach's biceps, accompanied by her patent-worthy hair toss and gleaming smile. Mel felt her stomach rebel and this time it had nothing to do with the scent of vanilla.

"From here, it looks as if she has him wrapped around her finger," Mel said.

"Enough to kill for her?" Mama June asked.

Mel glanced back at the couple. Could it be? She watched the coach jog back out to the field to run practice. Mel supposed anything was possible, but Coach hadn't struck her as the sort of guy who'd plot a murder that didn't include touchdowns. She felt like any killing he did was strictly on the field.

"Kendall, we demand to talk to you, right now!" A man stormed out of the same door Mel and Mama June had used. He was thirtysomething, had a receding hairline, and was wearing a bespoke sports coat over a dress shirt and expensive jeans. There was another man walking beside him, and judging by the similar sports coat and hairline, they were brothers.

Kendall turned away from the field, tipped her chin up, and planted her hands on her hips. Just then the breeze picked up and blew the hem of her long dress and the tendrils of her dark hair in a very Wonder Woman pose. Mel half expected Kendall's personal soundtrack to start playing over the loudspeaker. It was too much.

To Kendall's credit, she was clearly not intimidated by the men charging forward. In fact, she looked bored. Although, maybe that was just because she couldn't make any facial expressions. She lifted her hand to lower her sunglasses and glanced over them as she said, "Now is not a great time, C.J. and Thad."

"Oh." Mama June's eyebrows lifted.

"What?" Mel whispered. "What did I miss?"

"Those men are Dayton's two sons," she said. "Chad junior, aka C.J., and his younger brother, Thad."

"The ones from his previous marriage." Mel remembered Keogh telling her Dayton had sons.

"Uh-huh, and from what I understand it was a very

bitter divorce, since Dayton threw over his wife of forty years for Ms. Kendall," Mama June said. She gave Mel a side-eye. "This might get interesting."

They watched the men stop just short of crowding Kendall. The one who appeared to be the older of the two, presumably C.J., said, "We know what you did, Daddy's Little Midlife Crisis, and you're going to pay."

Kendall rolled her eyes and blew out a breath. "What exactly do you two brain surgeons think I did?"

"You murdered our father," Thad said. "And we can prove it."

"Ooh-wee." Mama June reached for a cupcake and started peeling off the wrapper. "Here we go."

Mel wished she could eat a cupcake, too, but she didn't want to risk it. Instead, she focused on Kendall to see how she was going to handle the situation.

"If this is because your 'Daddy' left the Scorpions to me, I'm sorry, but accusing me of something I didn't do is not going to reverse his decision," she said.

"If you are found guilty of his murder, then the team ownership will automatically revert to us," the younger brother, Thad, said. "We checked with our attorney."

"I didn't murder Chad," Kendall said. "I would never. I loved him." Her voice broke and she spun away from them, putting the back of her hand to her face. It was a very dramatic posture that worked on the brothers as well as it worked on Mel, which was to say, not at all.

"More accurately, you loved his money," C.J. spat. "You can't prove your alibi of being home alone, but even if you could it doesn't matter. We know how you murdered our father. And you got your old boyfriend to do the dirty deed for you."

"Excuse me?" Kendall and Mama June said at the same time.

"Uh-oh." Mel had a feeling the Dayton brothers had just invited more trouble than they'd ever imagined. She tried to distract Mama June. "We should probably hand out the cupcakes, don't you think?"

Mama June ignored her, carefully putting the lid on her tub. One eyebrow shot up high on her forehead and her mouth was pressed into a firm line as she strode towards Kendall and her accusers. Mel glanced at the field. Keogh was throwing the ball to Tyler, seemingly unaware of the drama unfolding on the sidelines.

Mel raised her arm and waved at him. "Keogh!"

He didn't hear her as someone out on the field was blasting rap music through a Bluetooth speaker. Mel cupped her hands to her mouth and yelled, "Keogh!" Still nothing.

She glanced up and down the sidelines trying to figure out how she could get his attention.

There was nothing at hand but a tub full of cupcakes. Peach cobbler cupcakes with vanilla buttercream. Mel took a huge breath and held it while she popped the lid off the tub and grabbed a cupcake. As if she were trying out for the team, she drew her arm back and threw the cupcake with all her might.

The cupcake sailed through the air, making a perfect spiral right before it went splat onto the ground at Keogh's feet. She'd been aiming for his shoulder, but she figured this was probably for the best. His head turned from the cupcake to the sidelines where he squinted. When he saw her, he raised his arm to wave but stopped as he took in the sight of his mother, striding forward to take on the Dayton brothers.

"What did you say about my son?" Mama June asked. Her voice did not invite anything less than the absolute truth.

"Mrs. Graham . . . uh . . . we didn't see you over there," C.J. said.

"Good to see you again, Mrs. G," Thad said.

Mama June pulled up to stand next to Kendall and said, "I'll ask you one more time, what did you say about my son?"

Mel noticed that she did not invite them to call her Mama June. Keogh was jogging in from the field with Tyler beside him. When they joined the group, they towered over the Dayton brothers.

"Is there a problem here?" Keogh asked.

"No, no pro—" Thad began but C.J. interrupted him.

"Yeah, there's a problem," he said. He stepped forward, which Mel thought was a pretty bold maneuver given that Keogh and Tyler were big enough to pick him up and twist him into a little balloon animal if they wanted to. Tyler took a step forward and C.J. stopped, clearly realizing that he was poking the bear.

"Yes? What problem would that be?" Mama June asked.

"It seems to us that our stepmonster here likely had her ex kill our father so that she could inherit the team," C.J. said. Mel was impressed that his voice cracked only once while spouting this nonsense.

"You did not just accuse my son of murder," Mama June said. "I know you wouldn't be that foolish."

Both Keogh and Tyler crossed their arms over their chests, which managed to make them appear larger than ever. C.J. and Thad exchanged a nervous look and Thad was about to speak when Coach Casella joined them.

"Hey, fellas, what's going on?" he asked.

"It could have been him," Thad whispered as an aside to C.J.

"Could have been me what?" Coach asked.

"Could have been you that's in league with this home-wrecker to steal the team from us," C.J. said.

"Excuse me?" Coach Casella said. He pushed his hat back on his head and scratched his hairline as if that would make what C.J. said make sense.

"The brothers here think that I had someone murder their father for me so I could inherit the football team," Kendall said.

"Oh." Coach pondered that for a beat. "Wait, did they just accuse *me* of murdering my boss?"

"Yes, they did," Mama June said. "They tried to blame Keogh first, but when they had to do it to his face, they had second thoughts."

Coach glanced from the wall that Keogh and Tyler had formed and nodded. "So, they aren't entirely stupid."

"Hey!" Thad protested.

"Here's the problem with your theory, guys," he said. "Both Keogh and I have alibis. I was at home, watching reels of our opposing teams, while he was also at home recovering from a grueling practice, which the security cameras at both of our residences show."

"Well, that's . . . it doesn't . . ." Thad stammered.

"Then why did the police bring you in for questioning yesterday?" C.J. asked Keogh.

"They wanted me to tell them who I thought Dayton's

killer was," Keogh said. He stared at the brothers. "Guess who I told them it was?"

C.J.'s jaw dropped while Thad looked confused.

"You better not have said it was us," C.J. cried.

"Why not?" Keogh said. "You seem to have the most to gain, especially as you're throwing around wild accusations. How pissed were you when you found out Dayton left most of his property, money, and his beloved team to his new wife?"

"She's not keeping one damn dime of it!" C.J. yelled.

"Yeah, we'll see you in court, you basic Barbie," Thad added. C.J. frowned at him and Thad shrugged.

"By all means, have your attorney call mine," Kendall said. "I'm sure he'd love to discuss the many ways you've been cut out of the will."

"I hate you," C.J. spat. "Do you even care that you broke up a family? A family. We were supposed to inherit everything. We're his sons, his pride and joy, his legacy—"

"That's interesting," Kendall interrupted him. "When your father talked about you, he called you his two greatest disappointments."

"You lie," Thad said.

"You both failed out of college, you still live at home with your mom, you've never had jobs that lasted more than a month or two at the most, and you blew through your dad's money like it bubbled up from an endless well," Kendall said. "Why would he have left any of it to you? You're a couple of spoiled children who want what they want when they want it. In fact, if anyone murdered Chad for his money, it seems pretty clear to me that it was you two."

Fifteen

Mel was surprised that neither of the brothers physically attacked Kendall for what she said. Of course, the hulking figures of Keogh and Tyler were a solid deterrent, still her accusation was brutal. C.J. was so furious he was shaking and Thad had lost his powers of speech. All he could manage were inarticulate grunts of protest.

Security, alerted by the yelling, arrived and escorted the brothers out. C.J. kicked up a fuss, demanding names as he planned to fire everyone as soon as he and his brother took over ownership of the team. The rest of the players slowly joined them on the sideline.

"Don't listen to them, bro," Quinn said. The enormous defensive lineman improbably made Keogh look average-sized as he towered over him and patted his shoulder.

Mel glanced at the ground half expecting Keogh to have been planted like a tree. "There's no way you had anything to do with Dayton's death. We all know that."

There were several cries in support of Keogh and his mouth tipped up in the corner. "Thank you, brothers. I appreciate you."

Mama June left the group to go and grab the tub of cupcakes. She held them out to the players, and said, "Have a cupcake or two. You boys need to keep up your strength."

Keogh caught Mel's eye and smiled. He'd been right. His mama had a way of making everything better. Mel watched the players consume their cupcakes. There was good-natured teasing about how many cupcakes Quinn could eat and Tyler was in the thick of it. Mel realized that while Keogh was the natural-born leader of the team, he kept himself a bit removed. Tyler was the approachable one who was friends with everyone, making himself the liaison to Keogh.

Mel had no idea there was such a hierarchy on a sports team. Having never been much of an athlete, she had no clue how team dynamics worked. It was clear from the players' words and actions that they respected Keogh, and Mel knew that if the Dayton brothers did get possession of the team, it would be useless to them. These guys were loyal, and she doubted they'd be eager to play for the Daytons, especially if they believed the brothers wrongly accused Keogh of murdering Chad Dayton.

"I hope you won't listen to what those two idiots were saying," Kendall said to Keogh. "The team stands by you, as do I, since you and I both know you had nothing to do with Chad's death." Her voice broke a little before she said "death," and Mel studied her face. Her expression was stuck in neutral but her eyes glistened with tears. Kendall was either a very good actress or she was genuinely upset by her husband's murder.

"No, they can't bother me. I know I'm innocent," Keogh said. "They can try and stir up trouble but I know that the murderer will get caught."

Mel wondered if Keogh was saying this for the team's benefit. Given the sudden lift in everyone's spirits, she assumed he was. Then again, maybe it was just a matter of fake it till you make it.

"He's a natural-born leader." Mel turned to find Coach Casella at her side. "I think these guys would run through fire for him."

"I was just thinking the same thing," Mel said. She hesitated and then added, "You won't be able to replace him if he retires, will you?"

The coach shook his head dismissively. "He's not going to retire."

"You sound very certain of that," Mel said. "With the potential of another concussion causing him a CTE, don't you think he should retire?"

"It's a very very slight possibility," Coach said. He looked as if he'd had this discussion a time or two. "Keogh and I have talked about it and I'm positive he'll make the right decision for the team, regardless of what his mother thinks."

"Mama June wants him to retire?" Mel asked.

Coach shrugged. "Who do you think gave him the idea to buy a bakery franchise? I swear, she would be happier to have him anywhere but on the football field where he belongs."

He raised his voice as if wanting to be heard by Keogh and his mother. It appeared to work as both of them turned to look at him. The formerly laid-back coach crossed his arms over his chest and stared Keogh down.

Keogh shook his head and said, "This is not the time or the place."

"Why not?" Coach Casella spread his arms wide. "You've been dragging your feet about making a decision on the upcoming season. We've humored you, letting you practice, even though you haven't formally signed your contract. How long do you think you can stall, Keogh?"

The entire stadium went quiet. Mel felt her heart hammer in her chest. She really didn't like conflict of any kind, not even conflict that had nothing to do with her. She glanced over her shoulder, wondering if she could slip back into the locker room and out that maze of tunnels to the parking lot.

"I told you I need to wait," Keogh said.

"For what?" Coach snapped. "To see if your bakery is successful so you can leave us high and dry without a quarterback?"

"You have a second string," Keogh argued. "And he's great."

Mel saw one of the players duck his head, so she assumed that was him.

"He's not you," Coach said. "You have a god-given gift—"

"That doesn't mean he should put himself at risk to become a potato just so you can win a championship!" Mama June snapped.

"You stay out of—" Coach said, but Keogh interrupted.

"Hey now," Keogh said. "I know we're all on edge

after Dayton's death, and I know it's been difficult to plan for the season when I am still trying to decide what to do." He turned to the other players. "I am sorry about that, but you all know that this game comes with risks and I'm just trying to make the best decision that I can for the long haul."

"Absolutely," Quinn said. "I said it before and I'll say it again. We've got you."

Mel saw the other players nodding. More than anyone else they knew the potential harm that could happen to their bodies every time they took the field. Despite Coach's impatience, the team seemed okay with Keogh's need to make the right choice.

"You don't get it," Coach snapped. "The one thing Dayton was right about was that by refusing to sign your new contract and by doing this wait-and-see dance, you're showing that you're not one hundred percent committed to the team. You can't be a leader if you're not one hundred percent committed."

"You're wrong," Keogh said. "I'm waiting specifically to make certain that if and when I do sign my contract it's because I am one hundred percent committed. That's what my teammates deserve and I won't give them anything less."

The rumbling of the players sounded as if they approved and Coach looked furious, as if Keogh had outmaneuvered him and he didn't like it one bit. "You're running out of time, Keogh. If you don't sign and soon, there won't be a place for you here. I'm putting you on notice, right now, that I'm looking to trade you."

"Do what you have to do, Coach. Then the decision will be made for me, won't it?" Keogh asked.

Coach shook his head as if he just couldn't understand that sort of thinking and stormed off the field, leaving his assistant coach to follow him. Mel squinted after him, wondering what that had been about. At the opening of the cupcake bakery, Coach Casella had seemed so supportive. Had something changed? If so, what?

She glanced back to where Mama June was standing by her son and reflexively put a hand over her stomach. How would a mother feel if her son made a decision that could put him at risk for brain damage and ruin the rest of his life? How far would she go to protect him? Mel blinked. She did not just think that. Mama June wasn't even in town when Dayton was murdered. There was no way she was a part of it.

Mel knew she must be getting wacky. Maybe it was the pregnancy hormones. She glanced around the group. There were so many people who had more of a reason to murder Dayton than Keogh or Mama June. Dayton's sons being cut out of his will were solid suspects, or his young new wife wanting to be rid of him so she could inherit it all, even Coach Casella, who had to be sick of defusing every volatile situation Dayton created, had more of a reason.

"Tyler!" A man in dark blue scrubs approached the wide receiver. "It's time to aspirate that knee." The doctor held up a syringe and Tyler blanched.

"Now, Doc, really?" he asked.

"Yes, now. We have to keep draining it to relieve the pressure and the discomfort," the doctor said. "We can discuss the next steps in your treatment after an updated MRI."

"But I hate needles," Tyler said. He looked miserable

and Mel couldn't help but smile. Tyler glanced at her and asked, "What?"

"You get crushed by grown men on a regular basis but a needle bothers you?"

Tyler pondered this and said, "At least I can try to outrun someone trying to tackle me."

"Well, you won't be outrunning anyone if you don't treat that knee," the doctor countered.

Tyler snagged another cupcake from the bin Mama June held and followed the doctor to the locker room.

"If you're a good boy maybe Doc will give you a sticker, Ty," Keogh called after him. Ty's response was a one-fingered salute, which made Keogh laugh.

The last remaining coach on the field called practice, and the players headed to the locker room. Mel asked Mama June if she wanted a ride home on her way back to the bakery, but she declined, saying she'd go with Keogh. Mel nodded.

As she walked back through the maze of corridors, Mel tried not to think about how these hallways were the perfect place for a murderer to hide out. She picked up her pace, relieved when she stepped back out into the hot Arizona sun.

Joe was due home in a matter of minutes. Instead of cooking, Mel had ordered their favorite Italian takeout from Uncle Sal's Italian Restaurant and Bar to make up for not being able to get home the evening before in time to tell him. She hoped for a do-over tonight and wanted to set the mood for the happy news she had to share.

After her time at the stadium with the team yesterday afternoon, she'd gotten back to Keogh's bakery to discover that there'd been a run on cupcakes. Apparently some Scorpions fans had found the bakery and wiped them out of every last cupcake. Mel had stayed to work until late that night trying to restock.

It was particularly annoying to her that because of her reaction to the smell of vanilla, Marty had called in his girlfriend, Olivia Puckett, Mel's bakery rival, to help her with the late-night baking.

"What's wrong with you, princess?" Olivia had asked as she entered the kitchen in her blue chef smock.

"Stomach bug of some sort," Mel fibbed. She'd be darned if she'd tell Olivia about the baby before she told Joe.

"Either that or it's your own baking making you gack," Olivia suggested. She nudged Mel with her elbow. "I know your cooking does that to me."

Mel glared at her and Marty gave his girlfriend a stern look and said, "Now, Liv, is that nice?"

"Aw, come on, I'm just joshing you," Olivia said. Her topknot of gray corkscrew curls bounced as she set to work, making the cupcakes Mel couldn't tolerate the smell of. It was very humbling.

By the time Mel arrived home, she was tired and grumpy and Joe was asleep. She didn't want to wake him to tell him the news. She wanted it to be an epic moment between them, not one where he had drool crusting one side of his mouth and she was feeling stabby. She'd decided to wait until today, hoping things would be calmer.

To facilitate her opportunity to talk to Joe, Tate and Angie had gone to work at Keogh's bakery today while Mel and Marty stayed in Old Town. Mel had enjoyed the feeling of normalcy and had spent all day thinking about how she would break the news to Joe.

She'd just put their take-out chicken Parmesan in the oven when there was a preemptive knock on her front door and then the sound of a key unlocking it.

Peanut went into a frenzy of barking while Captain Jack bolted for the back bedroom. Mel left the kitchen, wondering which one of their family members had arrived. It was either one of their parents or siblings. When they'd bought the house, they'd given out so many keys, Mel wondered why they bothered to lock it at all.

She was halfway through the living room when her mother, Joyce, appeared in the doorway. Peanut loved Joyce and she threw her portly Boston terrier body at her until Joyce squatted down and gave her all the love her doggy heart required before Joyce was allowed to enter. This took a moment.

"Who is Gammy's good girl? Who's her pretty girl?" Joyce asked the dog as Peanut wiggled herself into a frenzy. Sometimes Mel wondered why the dog didn't dislocate a hip, she was shaking her booty so hard. "That's right, you are. You are Gammy's best doggy. Yes, you are." Then she reached into her pocket and handed Peanut a little doggy biscuit.

"Mom, she's on a diet," Mel protested.

"One little biscuit won't hurt her," Joyce argued. She glanced around the room. "And where's my handsome grandkitty?"

"Hiding."

"Well, I'm sure he'll come out for some kisses and cuddles when he's ready," Joyce said. "He's such a good kitty."

Mel's mind suddenly flashed forward, imagining a time when she was trying to discipline her toddler and ~~Joyce swooped in to undermine her authority with toys~~ and candy and other Gammy bribes. She'd seen Joyce do it to her nephews and while they'd turned out okay, she suspected it was because her brother Charlie and his family lived in Flagstaff and had a few hours of buffer to deprogram the kids on the ride home. Mel lived minutes away. Mere minutes!

"What's wrong?" Joyce asked. "Why do you have that weird look on your face?"

"Me?" Mel asked. "What do you mean? I don't have a weird look."

"Yes, you do," Joyce insisted. She rose to her feet and fluffed her blond bob. She was wearing long shorts, sandals, and a cute pink top, looking like the quintessential gammy that she was.

Why this reality punched Mel in the face so hard she had no idea. Joyce had been Gammy to her nephews for more than a decade. This wasn't a new role for her, but in relationship to Mel, as a mom, it was huge. Huge.

"You're not fighting with dear Joe, are you?" Joyce asked.

Mel did not roll her eyes, although it took monumental effort. Joyce had been calling her husband "dear Joe" since they'd started dating. Joe loved it, Mel not so much.

"No, Joe and I are fine," Mel said. "In fact, I was just fixing dinner as he should be home soon."

"Oh, that's nice," Joyce said. "How good of you to have a home-cooked meal waiting for him after he's worked so hard all day."

"It's takeout," Mel said.

"Oh, honey." Joyce's voice carried a forkful of disappointment.

Mel frowned. "It's as good as it gets, because I work all day, too."

"I know, dear." Joyce patted her arm. Mel was certain her mother didn't mean to be so old-fashioned and condescending and yet, it still felt that way.

"Was there something you needed?" Mel asked.

"Yes, my large blue salad bowl," Joyce said. "Stan and I are hosting dinner tomorrow night for some of his work friends, and I need a bigger bowl."

"No problem, it's in the cupboard." Mel led the way into the kitchen and Joyce followed.

Mel opened the cabinet and stretched up onto her tiptoes to grab the bowl off the top shelf. When she turned around with the bowl in her hand, Joyce was staring at her with her mouth slightly open. Mel looked at her shirt to see if she'd spilled something on it. Nope.

"You okay, Mom?" she asked.

"How far along are you?" Joyce asked. She clapped her hand over her mouth as tears filled her eyes. "And why didn't you tell me?"

"Wait, what?" Mel asked. "How did you know?"

"Your butt is bigger." Joyce dropped her hand.

Mel stared at her. "Excuse me?"

"Your butt is bigger," Joyce repeated. She held her hands out wide to demonstrate as she spoke as if it was the most reasonable observation in the world. "When I was pregnant with both you and Charlie, I went all pear-shaped until my belly caught up to my rear end then I just looked like a big apple."

"How have I never heard of this before?" Mel asked.

"You've never been pregnant before," Joyce said.

"Huh." Mel grunted. "Still, you might have mentioned it. How big is my butt?"

"It's just a little extra padding, don't worry about it. And you could have told me the good news and not leave me to figure it out by myself," Joyce said. There was a note of hurt in her voice.

"Don't take it personally. I haven't even told Joe yet," Mel said. "I've been trying to find the right time. I want it to be special, you know?"

"In that case, I forgive you," Joyce said. Her voice cracked and she looked like she was about to cry. "My baby is going to have a baby."

Mel felt her throat get tight and her eyes watered up. "Oh, Mom."

Joyce opened her arms and Mel stepped in for a hug. The familiar scent of Joyce's perfume, a faint floral scent, engulfed her and suddenly Mel felt as if she were a kid again. Joyce rocked her gently back and forth.

"I'm so happy for you," Joyce said. "Dear Joe is going to make such a wonderful father."

Sixteen

Mel laughed. Of course there was no mention about her being a good mother. Maybe it was just assumed. She figured she'd go with that.

Mel heard the sound of a car in the driveway and knew Joe was home.

"Ack! You have to go!" Mel said.

"But—" Joyce began to protest but Mel cut her off.

"No, I want to tell Joe all by myself," Mel said.

"I know, dear, but that's not Joe. It's Tate." Joyce pointed to the window.

Mel hurried to the front door. What was Tate doing here? It was late. The bakery was closed. She felt a beat of panic that something might be wrong with Emari or Angie, but then why wouldn't he call?

Tate was halfway up the walkway and his expression

was grim when Mel and Joyce stepped outside. Mel closed the door on Peanut's barking so she could hear Tate speak.

"Why are you here? What's wrong?" she asked.

"I don't know how to say this gently, so I'm just going to say it."

"Say what? Tate, what's happened?"

"Coach Casella was shot and killed," he said.

"What?" Mel cried. "How? When?"

"I don't know the details, but it gets worse," Tate said.

"Worse?" Mel cried. "How can it be worse?"

"Keogh is considered the primary person of interest," Tate said.

Mel stumbled back and Joyce steadied her with an arm around her waist.

"It'll be okay, Melanie," Joyce said. "Breathe and try to stay calm. You have to manage your emotions since it's not just you now."

"But I just saw Coach and Keogh and all of the team yesterday," Mel said. "Sure, they exchanged a few words about Keogh and his contract but that doesn't mean Keogh shot him."

"I'm headed over to Keogh's house now in a show of support," Tate said. "Do you want to come?"

Mel thought about telling Joe their good news while all of this was happening. She couldn't picture it. She couldn't imagine being happy with Coach murdered and Keogh potentially arrested for a crime he didn't commit.

"Yeah, I'll come with you," she said. "Let me grab my bag." She turned to Joyce and said, "Not a word to anyone about you know what. Promise me."

Joyce made a gesture like she was zipping her lips. "I

promise. You two go. I'll take care of your dinner and the pets until dear Joe gets home."

Mel studied her mother. Was Joyce capable of keeping a secret?

"Do you remember when you were nine and you asked me not to tell your father that you won the spelling bee for your grade because you wanted to tell him?" Joyce asked.

"Yes."

"Well, it about killed me not to say anything, but I kept my promise," Joyce said.

"This is kind of a bigger deal than a spelling bee," Mel said.

"At the time it did not feel that way."

"I can imagine." Mel stepped forward and kissed her mom's cheek. "Tell Joe I'll be home soon."

"I will. Be careful," Joyce said. She glanced past Mel at Tate and said, "Keep her safe."

"Always, Joyce." Tate put his hand over his heart and Joyce seemed satisfied.

Mel got into Tate's car after moving the container of baby wipes off the seat so she could sit down. "Tell me everything you know."

"Apparently, Coach Casella was found shot to death in his office early this morning," Tate said.

"And this is the first we're hearing of it?" Mel asked.

"In light of it being the second murder in regards to the Scorpions, the team kept it quiet as long as they could," Tate said. He was silent for a minute. "It gets worse, Mel. There's a reason Keogh is the chief suspect."

She took a deep breath and leaned back in her seat. "Hit me."

"The gun found on the office floor beside the body was registered to Keogh Graham."

"No!" Mel gasped.

"Yes."

"That can't be," she said. She thought about how Keogh had made her tea when he realized before anyone, even her, that she was pregnant. "He'd never shoot anyone. I'm sure of it."

"Unsurprisingly, the police do not feel the same way. He hasn't been formally charged but it may just be a matter of time."

"Why hasn't he been charged?" Mel asked. "Not that I want him to be, but it seems odd."

"I don't want to sound like a jerk, but I suspect it's because he's Keogh Graham and he's the Scorpions' best shot at a Super Bowl title."

"So what his agent Benson said was true." Mel shook her head. "A quarterback with a future title was going to get a pass on murder, whereas a cupcake baker wouldn't."

"So it would seem."

"How is he?" she asked. "Have you spoken to him?"

"He's at home, meeting with his attorney and public relations people," Tate said. "I wouldn't go over there right now, but Tyler reached out and asked that we come."

"No, it's a good idea," Mel said. "We have to be ready to deal with the press tomorrow. You know they're going to show up at the bakery and we'd better be prepared with whatever talking points they want us to use."

"That's what I thought, too," Tate said.

They drove in silence to Keogh's house, which wasn't far from their neighborhood, except in value. Keogh's neighborhood was easily ten times more expensive than Mel's, which given his pending fifty-million-dollar contract was not a huge surprise. On Lincoln Drive in the heart of Paradise Valley, Keogh lived in a gated mansion in the shadow of Camelback Mountain.

Even if the GPS didn't guide them right to his gate, the gathering of news vans parked on the street and outside his home was a hot clue. The vans with their mini satellite dishes congested the entire area and Mel knew his neighbors were likely peeved that the superstar athlete had brought this scourge upon them.

Tate rolled right up to the gate. A security officer checked his ID while another kept the reporters at bay. The media shouted questions and pointed their cameras at them and Mel felt a nervous flutter that she was exposing her baby to such intensity. It couldn't be healthy for either of them.

The guard waved them through and the gates slowly opened. Tate drove carefully inside what looked like a well-fortified compound and Mel breathed a sigh of relief.

There were several police cars and sports cars and assorted other vehicles. She wondered what was happening inside the low-slung white brick building with the black trim. The shape of the house was very angular with lots of floor-to-ceiling glass and very precisely landscaped grounds. Each tuft of ornamental grass was trimmed into exactly the same shape and spaced perfectly along the walkway to the front door.

Tate parked and they climbed out of the car. Mel felt as if they were intruding but no one chased them away. They approached the large double doors that had been painted an accent color of apple green. Before Tate could ring the bell or knock, the door was pulled open and Keogh stood there.

"Thank you for coming," he said. "I know what the news is saying and I just want you to know that I didn't do it. I'm innocent."

His voice shook and Tate reached out and squeezed his shoulder. "We know that. We know you're innocent, Keogh, and we'll stand by you."

"Mel?" Keogh asked her.

"Of course," she said. "I know you didn't do this."

Keogh bobbed his head and let out a breath as if he'd been holding it for hours. "Thank you. I didn't really know what was important to me until all of this happened, but now I'm beginning to see. I don't want this." He gestured for them to follow him inside. "For the first time, I am really grasping what a fishbowl my life is. I want to run my own business and be my own boss. I want to live my life without all of this constant scrutiny." He paused to gesture at the street with the news vans. "I just want to run the bakery and settle down, maybe start a family." He looked at them with eyes full of fear. "That isn't going to happen if I'm in prison."

"You're not going to prison," Tate said. "We won't let that happen."

Mel took in the open floor plan of the home. The lighting was perfect and the furniture looked custom-made for this particular building. There was art on the walls that appeared to be an original Rothko and a Pollock. Keogh's home was understated and refined and positively reeked of money. This was not the sort of abode a person lived in when they owned a bakery. Could Keogh really walk away from all of this?

"What's happening, Keogh?" Mel asked. "Where's Mama June?"

"After she cussed out Detective Rivera—" he began but Mel interrupted.

"She didn't."

"Oh, yes, she did." He shook his head. "Then she went to her room to lie down. She's feeling a bit overwhelmed and if Mama June is tapping out, you know it's bad."

"Mr. Graham, I think we have all we need for now." Detective Rivera appeared in the vast foyer. "Thank you for your cooperation."

Mel noticed Steve Wolfmeier was standing behind him. He was clearly shadowing the detective, not letting him have one second of unsupervised time with his client or in his house.

"Sure, no problem," Keogh said. He looked nervous as if he expected Rivera to cuff him and drag him out of there. "And I'm sorry about my mom."

"No need," Rivera said. "I have kids. I get it."

Keogh's shoulders dropped in relief.

"Mrs. DeLaura. Mr. Harper," Detective Rivera greeted them. "I'm surprised to see you here."

"Keogh is our business partner," Tate said. "Where else would we be?" His voice held a note of challenge.

Detective Rivera raised his hands, indicating he meant no insult and yet Mel still felt on edge. Potentially, it was because she knew of the bad blood between Joe and Rivera, but then again it could be the predatory light in Rivera's eyes when he looked at Keogh. Despite his affable manner, it was easy to see that Rivera had made up his mind that Keogh was guilty and it was just a matter of time before he was caught.

They watched the detective leave, taking his fellow officers with him. They were silent until the door shut behind them and then Keogh said, "This is bad, so bad."

"You're not under arrest," Steve said. "Let's take that as a win."

"They'll probably be back tomorrow with a warrant," Keogh said glumly.

"If they had the proof to arrest you now, they would have," Steve said. "Try not to worry. I'm heading out. I have calls to make and I want to tap some of my sources at the police department."

"Thanks for coming," Keogh said.

"It's why I'm here," Steve said. "Tate, Mel, try to cheer him up. It's going to be okay."

Keogh looked dubious but Mel knew that if anyone could help him, it was Steve. With a wave, he left, closing the door behind him.

"Keogh, *SportsCenter* is asking for an exclusive interview," Blaise Benson called from across the great room. His tone made it clear he didn't think Keogh should do it, but he let the quarterback make his own decision.

"No, no interviews," Keogh said. "Not until we absolutely have to."

"Understood," Blaise said. He disappeared back into the room that appeared to be an office.

"Keogh, what can we do for you?" Tate asked.

"I don't know." Keogh walked through the house, leaving them to follow. They passed a kitchen Mel could only imagine in her dreams, a living room that was massive with a television big enough to host the entire football team for a watch party.

Keogh strode across the terrazzo floor to the sliding glass doors on the far side of the house. They were already open and he stepped out onto a patio that was almost the same size as his house, which boasted a misting system and free-standing air conditioners to keep it cool, an outdoor kitchen, a dining area, and plenty of lounge chairs arranged in clusters all around the pool, which glowed a brilliant blue. The dark form of the mountain loomed beyond the yard and small lamps lit up the line of palm trees that delineated the edge of his property.

Keogh sank onto one of the many rattan chairs, decorated with fat, teal-colored cushions. Mel and Tate took the other two. The backyard was quiet, with only the sound of the trickling water from the waterfall built into the end of the pool, which seemed to relax Keogh as he sighed and leaned back in his seat.

"What happened?" Mel asked. "I mean, and I'm not trying to sound like I'm judging you, but . . . a gun, really?"

"I know." Keogh put his head in his hands. "I'm such an idiot, but I kept it in a safe and, honestly, I'd forgotten that I even owned it."

"Statistically, most people get shot with their own weapons," Tate said. Both Mel and Keogh looked at him. "Sorry. That's probably not helpful at the moment."

"Why did you have a gun, Keogh?" Mel asked.

"I bought it a few years ago for protection."

"Protection from who?" Mel asked.

"Oh, I don't want to go there," Keogh said.

"Did you already tell the police?" Tate asked.

"Yeah," Keogh said.

"Then you might as well tell us," Mel said.

"It's so embarrassing," Keogh said.

"We're your friends," Tate said. He waved for Keogh to continue. "Out with it."

"All right, but you'd better not laugh." He stared at them and Mel made her face expressionless and glanced at Tate to make certain he did the same. "A few years ago, I had this obsessive fan who started showing up at all the games. I was new and green and thought it was so nice of her to be there to cheer me on. Then she started replying to every social media post my public relations team put up."

"Boundary issues," Tate said.

"You don't know the half of it," Keogh said. "She escalated to replying to all the posts as my wife."

"Eek!" Mel cried.

"It was awful," Keogh said. "She stalked me every single day at the field, at home . . . Anywhere I went, she appeared. She parked outside the gate, tried to break into my house, and generally dogged my every move."

"I'm sorry," Mel said. "That's a lot."

"When I refused to acknowledge her, she became angry and the threats started," Keogh said. "When I was dating Kendall, she was absolutely vicious in her social media posts and we had to block her, which did nothing. She just made up new identities and popped up again and again. She was furious and, frankly, really scary. Apparently, she believed I was her fated mate—"

"Her fated what?" Tate interrupted.

"Fated mate," Mel said. "It's a term used in paranormal romances."

"There was nothing romantic about it. She actually broke into my house one night and got one of my arms tied to the bedpost before I woke up and was able to fight back," Keogh said. "I didn't want to hit her, so I ran out of my house in the middle of the night in nothing but my boxer shorts with my phone clutched in my hand. It was humiliating."

"And terrifying," Tate said. "Why would she do that?"

"Because we live in a world where athletes and artists are now so accessible thanks to social media that people believe they have a relationship with us that doesn't actually exist. There is an expectation that we owe it to them to share every detail of our lives and then they forget that they don't really know us. We're not family. We're not friends. They see the highlight reel of our lives. They witness the image of us carefully curated by our publicists and it gives them a distorted sense of who we are and their relationship to us."

"I can see why owning a bakery seems like a nice respite from all of that," Tate said. "It must be exhausting being your level of famous."

"I certainly didn't sign up for that when I fell in love with the game as a kid," Keogh said.

"From my view in the cheap seats, it seems like the world has changed," Mel said. "These days people seem to think you owe them a relationship of some sort whether they're reviewing your cupcake bakery on social media or you're a star on a football team. Honestly, it feels as if our two most precious commodities have become our privacy and our time."

"Exactly." Keogh leaned back in his chair and stared up at the dark sky. There were only a few stars visible, given the light pollution of the city, but he pondered them and said, "Also, I think someone is trying very hard to frame me for murder."

Seventeen

"I wish I could say you're wrong, but I don't think you are," Tate said.

"But who would do this?" Mel asked. "And why?"

Keogh shrugged. "I wish I knew but I haven't got a clue. First, Dayton is murdered and covered in the same type of scorpions that bit me right over there by my pool and his body was found in our bakery. Why?"

"It has to be over his ownership of the team," Tate said. "It's clear that his sons thought they were going to inherit. Maybe they got tired of waiting, knew about you being stung by the scorpion, and used a nest to terrorize their dad and he had a heart attack and died."

"Is that what officially killed him?" Mel asked. "Our exterminator didn't think it was the scorpions."

"No, that's just a theory," Tate said. "I mean, if a

swarm of scorpions crawled all over me, I'd have a heart attack."

"Same," Mel said.

"It's a good theory," Keogh said. "There's also Kendall. She had to know she was going to inherit the team. Maybe she killed him so she could inherit that much faster."

"I'm not the biggest Kendall fan," Mel admitted. "And for a while, I did consider her a black widow sort, but she seemed genuinely upset at Chad's death. Besides, she's so much younger than her husband, all she really needed to do was bide her time and wait it out."

"Unless something happened and she was forced to move more quickly," Tate said.

"What could have happened?" Mel asked.

Tate shrugged. "No idea, but I'm guessing it would have to do with Coach being shot."

"Good point," Mel said. "That can't be coincidence. The two murders have to be connected. We just have to figure out who wanted both of them dead and why."

No one spoke. There was no reason for Kendall or the brothers to have wanted to kill Coach Casella. He had nothing to do with them inheriting the team.

"The only thing the two murders have in common is that both men fought with me right before they were murdered," Keogh said. He looked physically ill. He glanced up at the sky and said, "I'm trying really hard not to freak out right now."

"I think you just solved the murders," Mel said.

Keogh dropped his hands and stared at her, a look of deep hurt in his eyes. "You think I did it?"

Mel shook her head. "No, I think you're right. Someone

is framing you for the murders and they're killing their victims right when it will make you look guiltiest."

Tate nodded. "You're right. That makes the most sense. Both murders happened after a public falling-out with you. The first public argument was in your bakery, where the first body was found, and the second one was in the football stadium, which is practically your second home and also where the second body was discovered."

"Who knew that you were stung by a scorpion?" Mel asked. "Because the fact that the killer used scorpions seems significant to me."

"Everyone knew," Keogh said. "My leg swelled up and I couldn't walk for two days. Pretty hard to try and hide."

"And who knew you had a gun in a safe in your house?" Tate asked.

Keogh made a face. "Again. Everyone."

Mel raised her eyebrows. "You told people?"

"I told most of the team," Keogh said. "A lot of them crash here and when my stalker kept trying to break in, I felt it was important for anyone on the premises to know that I had a gun and to know the code to the safe if they needed it. Again, so stupid."

"Do any of the players have a grudge with Dayton and Coach Casella?" Mel asked.

"I don't think so," Keogh said. "But I can ask Tyler if he knows anything. He's more of an extrovert than I am and is closer to our teammates."

Mel glanced around the patio, making certain they were alone. "I'm going to ask a sensitive question."

Keogh tipped his head to the side. "Okay."

"Is there anyone in your life, your agent, a family

member, a friend, who might go too far when trying to protect you?" Mel asked.

Tate pursed his lips but said nothing while Keogh frowned, a deep crease appearing between his brows.

"Are you accusing Mama June—" he began but Mel interrupted.

"No!" She shook her head. "I'm merely asking if there is someone in your life who might be overly protective. You don't have to answer right now. You can think about it."

"Other than my mom, I can't think of anyone," Keogh said. "My dad died when I was young and for as long as I can remember, it was just Mama June, my siblings, and me. But it can't be any of them. They all live in Savannah and were in Georgia at the time of Dayton's murder."

Mel nodded. "Good. I hated to even mention it, but family can be very protective."

"Which is not necessarily a bad thing," Tate said.

Mel and Tate exchanged a smile, thinking of the family they'd both married into, which made them officially family as well.

"I know what you mean," Keogh said. "My team is like that—what do they call it?—a found family. I'd take a bullet for any of those guys, and I know they'd do the same for me."

"Are you sure?" Tate asked. "Even the second-string quarterback who's waiting for his shot?"

"Titus?" Keogh shook his head. "He's like a little brother to me."

"If you're sure," Tate said. "Sometimes ambitious people can hide their true natures."

"No, not Titus," Keogh said. "He's from Kansas."

"Oh, well, then," Tate said, letting it go because it was

obvious that Keogh had made up his mind about his replacement.

"What about Kendall?" Mel asked. "Did she have any issues with Coach?"

"Not that I know of," Keogh said. "But we haven't exactly been confiding in each other over the past year, either."

"Oh, I know!" Tate said. "What about that crazy fan who was mooning the bakery? The one Ray almost ran over with the cupcake van. Could it be someone like that? Someone who wants the Scorpions to lose their shot at the Super Bowl this season?"

"It's quite the preemptive strike to hit before the season even starts," Keogh said. "But we could ask the public relations people if they've seen anything suspicious or threatening on our social media feeds."

Mel nodded. "What happens next?"

"Steve said I'm to stay home and not go anywhere except practice unless he's with me," Keogh said. He glanced at the dark shape of the mountain. "Making this feel even more like a cage."

"I'm sorry," Mel said. "I know it's unpleasant, but I think it's wise for you to stay away from the bakery and out of the public eye until things settle down."

"Is that a euphemism for 'until the police find Dayton's and Coach's killer or killers'?" Keogh asked.

"It has to be the same person, doesn't it?" Tate asked. "I mean, what are the odds that both of them would have a murderer after them?"

"Ah," Mel gasped. Keogh and Tate turned to look at her. "What if the murderer has more victims in mind?

What if they are murdering people associated with the Scorpions one at a time until there is no one left?"

Keogh frowned and Tate said, "That's a terrifying thought. As much as I hate to admit it, Keogh, you have to be very careful, like seriously, trust no one."

Keogh nodded. "I think that's why Steve said not to leave my house at all if possible."

Mel and Tate exchanged a look and Mel knew what he was thinking. If there was a murderer taking aim at anyone associated with the Scorpions, then the bakery and anyone working there was a potential target, too. Mel felt her gut twist, but this time she was certain it had nothing to do with morning sickness and everything to do with fear.

/\

Mel was at Keogh and Tyler's bakery the next morning with Marty and Ray, per usual, as well as an off-duty police officer because Joe and Tate had insisted.

The officer was a tall, muscular, redheaded woman named Eve Danner, who looked like she feared nothing and no one. She sat at a booth out in the main room and scrolled through her tablet while keeping an eye on the bakery.

Marty had offered her a cupcake and she'd helped herself to three. Mel was impressed. Officer Danner had a sweet tooth to rival Joe's. Still, Mel didn't want to answer any questions Officer Danner might ask of her, so she hid in the kitchen.

Mel was whipping up her half-pistachio, half-chocolate cupcakes with the chocolate ganache frosting when Tyler walked through the back door. Mel hadn't seen him since before the coach was found and she noted that he looked highly stressed.

"Hi, Tyler," she said. "Want to try my newest flavor? I think it's pretty good."

"No, thanks." He shook his head with a sigh. He sank onto a stool at the table and watched her pour the ganache on the top. "Wait. What's the flavor?"

"Chocolate-pistachio," Mel said. She paused spreading the ganache to sprinkle some crushed pistachios on the top of the chocolate.

"Well, maybe just one," he said. "You need a taste tester, after all."

"Exactly," Mel said.

Tyler bit the cupcake in half, chewing thoughtfully. Then his eyes went wide and he said, "That is so good. The chocolate and pistachio complement each other perfectly. It's so rich, it's like there's a whole stick of butter in there."

"I take it you approve?" Mel asked.

"Double thumbs-up," he said. He reached for another and Mel let him. She knew comfort eating when she saw it.

"Do you want to talk?" she asked. "I'm a good listener."

"No . . . yes . . . maybe. I just don't understand why all of this is happening," Tyler said. "We're going into potentially the greatest season of our careers and someone shot our coach, using Keogh's gun. Why? Not to mention that the owner is dead, too, murdered by scorpions, of all things. I mean, what is happening?"

Mel didn't mention what Nick the exterminator had told her about the scorpions not being deadly. She suspected the medical examiner had figured that out and it was information for the police to share or not as they saw fit.

"It does feel as if the intent is to stop the team," Mel said. "Tate and I talked to Keogh last night and asked if any of the players might have a grudge. Can you think of anyone?"

"I'd be interested in hearing this, too."

Mel turned as Blaise Benson entered the kitchen through the swinging doors that led to the bakery.

"Blaise," Tyler said. His greeting was less than warm but Blaise didn't seem to notice or care. Mel wondered about that. "I can't think of anyone on the team with an ax to grind. We're like a well-oiled machine. Keogh and I have a mind meld like Rice and Montana or Brady and Gronk and all of the players around us are support."

"You're putting yourself in some rarefied air," Blaise said. "You really think you're worthy of such a comparison?"

Tyler glared and opened his mouth to argue but Mel interrupted, holding out a cupcake to Blaise. "Cupcake?"

He shuddered. "No." As if his manners were on a time delay, he added, "Thank you."

"Keogh and I are unbeatable and you know it," Tyler said.

"Keogh is unbeatable, but with that bum knee of yours, how much longer do you really think you can keep up?" Blaise asked.

"We're a team on the field just like we're partners in this bakery," Tyler said.

"Until you get cut, which is seeming more and more likely," Blaise said. "Enjoy your time as a starter while it lasts."

Now Mel was annoyed. Keogh's agent or not, she didn't like the way Blaise was goading Tyler.

"Was there a reason you stopped by other than to insult us?" she snapped.

"I was looking for Keogh," he said.

"He's either at his house or on the field," Mel said. "Weird that you don't know that."

"I've been busy managing the news outlets." A hot splash of color suffused Blaise's face and his tone was defensive. He nodded stiffly, turned, and left. He didn't exactly flounce but Mel felt that it was implied.

"Hoo hoo," Tyler crowed. "That was an awesome takedown, Mel. That guy is such a jerk."

"Yeah, he is. I mean, unless you're allergic, what sort of person doesn't eat cupcakes?" Mel asked. "Not one you can trust."

"Right?" Tyler asked. "I've never liked that guy. He's been riding the coaches to bench me because of my knee, but Keogh refuses to let that happen."

"You and Keogh really are brothers," Mel said. She thought about Angie and Tate. "Some friendships are like that."

"The best ones," Tyler agreed. Mel packed up a big box of cupcakes for Tyler to take to the team. She supposed she shouldn't cut into the bakery's profits, but she also thought the team could use the morale boost. Tyler was happy to deliver them on his way to practice.

She spent the rest of the day baking and planning how she would tell Joe about the baby. It had been three days since she'd found out and she was desperate to tell him. Nervous, too. While they had talked about having kids, they hadn't set a date and she didn't know if he was ready right now.

She thought about how he was with all of his nieces and nephews and knew that even if he wasn't completely prepared, he would manage it by the time the baby arrived. She supposed that meant they would have to turn the spare bedroom into a nursery. The mere thought of a nursery made her woozy.

She sank onto a stool at the metal table and that's where Marty and Ray found her, staring into space.

"You okay, boss?" Marty asked.

"Yeah, not for nothing, but you've been acting a little off lately," Ray said. "And I'm not just talking about the vomiting."

"Huh?" Mel glanced up and realized she was sitting there with a bag of cream cheese frosting in her hands while three dozen naked carrot cake cupcakes sat in need of their icing. "Oh, yeah, I'm fine. I was just thinking."

"About the murders?" Marty said. "Yeah, it's so weird. Just so you know, I have maintained constant vigilance and there have been no scorpion sightings."

"It wasn't the scorpions that killed Dayton," Ray said. They both looked at him and Ray looked startled and added, "You know, that's what the bug killer guy said."

Mel studied his face. He wasn't making eye contact. He reached for an unfrosted cupcake, probably so he could shove it in his mouth and avoid answering questions, but Mel knew his sweet tooth and there was no way he wanted an unfrosted cupcake. He might as well eat a muffin if that was the case. She smacked his hand away.

"Tell us what you know," she said.

"Hey, is that nice?" he asked. "I'm working myself to death out there—"

Marty scoffed.

"I am!" Ray protested. "And I can't even have a cupcake?"

"Do not try to change the subject," Mel said. "What do you know?"

"You can't say anything," Ray said. "Tara will kill me."

"Tara?" Mel asked. "Isn't the west side out of her jurisdiction?"

"It is, but she's friends with one of the medical examiners for the county," Ray said. "Her friend told her that the scorpion stings on Dayton's body were done posthumously."

"He was stung after he was dead?" Mel asked. She was glad she was sitting down because that was just plain grisly.

"Yeah," Ray said. "Whoever murdered him used the scorpions to distract from what they did."

"What did they do?" Mel asked. Ray's information confirmed what the exterminator had told her, so what had the medical examiner discovered? "How did Dayton die?"

"I don't know. The only gossip was that the scorpions didn't do it." Ray watched as Mel frosted a cupcake. When she waved him in, he took it and chomped it in two bites. "You saw the body, Mel. How do you think he died?"

Mel shook her head. "I don't know. I didn't see any obvious wounds on his body. No strangulation marks, no stab wounds or blood. Who killed Dayton and why do it in the bakery?"

"No idea. You know why? Because it's not our job to

solve the murder," Marty said. "Especially not in your condition."

He clapped a hand over his mouth.

"You know?" Mel asked.

"Know what?" Ray was chewing and glanced between them with a confused look on his face.

"That I'm suffering from severe allergies," Mel said. It wasn't a complete fib. She'd been having terrible allergies because clearly the vomiting, heartburn, and insomnia weren't enough suffering.

"Oh, I thought you were pregnant," Ray said. Then he grinned at her.

Mel gasped. "You, too?"

He nodded, looking quite pleased with himself.

"How did you guys know?" Mel asked. "And why didn't you say anything?"

"I have two daughters," Marty said. "This isn't my first pregnant rodeo."

"You've seen my family. Heck, you are my family," Ray said. "Someone is always pregnant. Looks like 'tag, you're it.'" He tapped Mel on the shoulder and surprised a laugh out of her.

"Okay, fine, yes, I'm pregnant. But you can't tell anyone else, because I haven't had a chance to tell Joe yet," she said. "And I don't want him finding out from anyone but me. Understood?"

"Roger that," Marty said.

"Noted," Ray agreed. "But you'd better tell him soon. My mom can spot a pregnancy from half a mile away and she will not be able to contain herself if she sees you."

"No problem," Mel said. "I have decided that tonight is the night. One way or another, I am telling Joe the news."

Eighteen

Mel didn't tell Joe the news. Instead, she woke up on her couch, with Captain Jack and Peanut sprawled all over her, to see her phone vibrating across the coffee table.

She glanced at the clock on the living room wall. It was after eleven o'clock at night and she realized she must have fallen asleep while waiting for Joe to come home. She grabbed her phone, assuming it was him calling to tell her he was on his way. It wasn't Joe.

"Tate, what's wrong?" she answered.

"The bakery was vandalized," Tate said.

"Our bakery?" Mel felt her body go cold and she sat up. Captain Jack sprang away from her and Peanut hopped onto the floor. She wondered if they could tell from her tone that something was wrong.

"Not ours, Keogh and Tyler's," Tate said. "I just got the call from Keogh. He stopped by on the way home from a late practice and found the place had been destroyed."

"Oh, no," Mel said. "He must be devastated."

"He sounded pretty upset," Tate said. "I'm headed over there. I'm going to call their insurance company and see what can be done to expedite the repairs."

"Even expedited, it could take a while," Mel said. She put her hand on her forehead. "Come by and pick me up. I'll go with you."

"Don't you think you should rest?" he asked. "You know, given your . . . you know."

"It's okay. You can say pregnancy. Joe's not on the phone." Mel smiled. "In fact, I fell asleep on the couch waiting for him to get home from work. I had a really good nap, so I'm good to go. Besides, I won't be able to sleep until I see how bad it is."

"All right, I'll be there in five," Tate said.

Mel checked her messages. Sure enough, Joe had texted. He was working late on a case that was going to trial next week. He didn't expect to be home until after midnight. Mel knew that there was no way she and Tate could get out to the bakery and back by then, so she texted him that she was working late, too, and would see him when she got home. She didn't tell him about the vandalism as she didn't want to worry him.

She wondered if she'd ever get the chance to tell Joe that he was going to be a father. At this rate, she hoped she got to mention it before the baby started kindergarten.

\\ '/'\ '\

Tate and Mel arrived at the bakery forty minutes later. Keogh and Tyler were seated on a bench on the sidewalk in front of the bakery. At a glance, Mel saw that the curb was covered in broken glass. She glanced through the gaping holes that used to be windows to assess the damage inside and flinched. The tables and chairs had been overturned. The large display case was smashed. The chalkboard listing their flavors and daily specials was cracked as if someone had thrown something heavy at it.

Taking it all in, Mel staggered on her feet. Keogh immediately hopped up and helped her to his seat.

"I know how you feel," he said. "I thought I was going to pass out when I saw it."

"Same," Tyler agreed. He leaned forward and rested his elbows on his knees, hanging his head down.

Mel reached over and patted his shoulder. "I'm so sorry, Tyler."

He shrugged. "It's whatever. I mean, it's just a side hustle. It's not like it's how we make our living."

"I'm beginning to think this endeavor is cursed," Keogh said.

"Agreed," Tyler said. "Nothing has gone right for us since we opened the bakery. Maybe we should close up shop, take the trade that's been offered, and bail."

"Trade?" Tate asked.

"Yeah," Keogh said. "There's been some talk about trading us to a different team."

"Is this Kendall's idea?" Mel asked.

"No, apparently Coach put it out there before he . . . died." Keogh cleared his throat.

"I think we should do it," Tyler said.

Keogh frowned. "So, we just walk away from this?"

"It's a bakery, Key," Tyler said. "We're football players."

"I don't know, bro," Keogh said. "I've played for the Scorpions for ten years. I have a home here. I've put down roots, and I really like the community."

"The same community that thinks you're a murderer?" Tyler said.

"Would the trade be for both of you?" Mel asked. "I mean, if Tyler wants to go, he could, and you could stay here and run the bakery."

"We're a package deal," Tyler said. "Wherever Key goes, I go."

Mel exchanged a knowing glance with Tate. "I know that feeling."

"I just don't think Phoenix is the place for us anymore," Tyler said. "Look at everything that's happened. It's a sign to take the trade."

Keogh looked back at the bakery. His eyes were sad and it made Mel's heart hurt. She felt terrible. She knew it was ridiculous because it wasn't as if she had anything to do with the bad things that were happening. Still, out of all the franchises they'd opened, they'd had only one other bakery, their very first, be so fraught with danger.

She glanced back at the shop. The lights were on and the police were inside. She wondered with a small pang in her chest what had happened to the cupcakes she'd spent all day baking. She tried not to take it personally. The destruction was likely from a disgruntled fan, or perhaps a random bit of violence that got out of hand. Or maybe it was the same person intent on murdering everyone connected to the team. She hushed that thought. She didn't want to believe it.

Tate took out his phone and asked Keogh, "Did you use the insurance company I recommended?"

"Yeah." He nodded.

"Okay, I'm going to call them and see what we can expect," he said. "At the very least, we have to board up the windows tonight so you don't get robbed. The kitchen appliances alone are worth a fortune."

Tate wandered down the sidewalk away from them. Mel glanced at Keogh. He looked shell-shocked. She wondered if he would decide to take the loss and quit on his dream. She hoped not but at this point she couldn't blame him if he did.

"Have the police said anything?" Mel asked.

"No," Keogh said. "They asked some questions but then went inside to assess the damage and see if there was any evidence of who did it."

They waited in silence. Mel was eager to get inside but she knew better than to push. The police would be done when they were done and not a second before. Instead, she called Joe to let him know what had happened.

"Is everything okay, cupcake?" Joe asked. "I got your text about working late, but I thought you'd baked all day to get the franchise fully stocked?"

"I did," Mel said. Her voice wobbled and she felt her throat get tight. Without any warning, she sobbed.

"Cupcake? *Ack!* What's wrong?" Joe cried.

Mel wanted to answer him but she was in a crying

spin cycle that she couldn't get out of. With a hiccup, she handed her phone to Keogh.

"Hey, Joe, it's Keogh," he said. "Mel's . . . uh . . . well, the truth is our bakery got vandalized."

There was silence while Joe peppered him with questions. Mel couldn't hear their conversation over her sobs. Tyler hopped up and entered the building. An officer yelled at him, but he waved the guy off. In seconds, he returned and handed Mel some napkins that he'd snatched from a napkin holder.

Mel took the wad and dabbed her face. "Th . . . thank . . . y . . . you. That was so nice of you." Inexplicably, Tyler's act of kindness made her sob even harder. "I don't know what's wrong with me."

Tyler looked very uncomfortable as if he wasn't sure what to do about the moisture exploding out of her eyeballs. Mel tried to get it together, but her emotions were on a stampede and she was just along for the ride. She bunched up the napkins and held them to her face while she sobbed it out.

Keogh sat down beside her, handed her phone back, and put his arm around her shoulders. "It's okay," he said. "Everything is going to be okay."

"No, it isn't." Mel sobbed. She leaned her head on his shoulder and said, "Someone is trying to destroy your dream and you're probably going to quit and then all of this will be for nothing."

"Not nothing." Keogh pulled back so he could meet her gaze. His smile was wide and warm and he said, "Look at the friendships Tyler and I have made with all of you. That's not nothing."

"Aw, that's so niiiiice," Mel wailed.

"Is she broken?" Tyler asked. "Because this level of crying over cupcakes is . . ."

"Pregnancy," Tate said as he joined them.

"Oh . . . Ohhhh," Tyler said. His eyes went wide as he grasped the situation.

"Hey, Mel." Tate crouched down in front of her. He pulled her hands away from her face and said, "'Remember to eat a green thing every day, and have lots of calcium.'"

Mel blinked and sniffed before she identified the movie quote. "*Dazed and Confused*, which is very on point right now."

"That's my girl," Tate said. "Better now?"

Mel nodded. "Yeah, I'm good."

"Good, because Joe is on his way," Keogh said. "I told him you were just upset about your cupcakes being smashed."

Mel nodded. "Well, that was incredibly rude of them."

"Keogh, Tyler, I think it's time for you to leave." Blaise Benson approached them. "The press is on the way and I don't think it will do you any good—"

A pickup truck roared into the parking lot and honked. They all jumped. The tinted window slid down and Quinn Lancaster stuck his head out and said, "Anyone need some plywood?"

Mama June was in the passenger seat. She leaned around Quinn and said, "Mel, what are you doing here? You know you need to be resting."

Mel grinned. "Oh, you know, just having a good cry— as you do."

Mama June climbed out of the truck and hurried over to Mel, giving her a big hug. "It's perfectly normal."

"Yeah, just surprising," Mel said. "Ambushed by all of these emotions. I'm just not prepared."

"It'll pass," Mama June said. "In the meantime, you just have to ride it out. Cry when you need to, laugh when you can."

The officer in charge of the incident, whose badge read *Bishop*, came out of the bakery. "We've dusted for fingerprints and taken photographs, Mr. Graham. Mr. Matthews, I'm afraid unless you have some security camera footage, that's all we can do."

Keogh shook his head. "Sorry, Officer Bishop. That's been on my list ever since . . . well, shoot. I just didn't get to it."

"Me, either," Tyler said. "The past week has been a lot."

"We did find one item that I'd appreciate your help in identifying," Officer Bishop said. He held up a plastic bag. Inside was a Scorpions football jersey. With a gloved hand, he lifted it out and held it up so that it was fully visible. He glanced at Tyler. "Do you recognize this?"

"That's my jersey," Tyler said. "My name and number are on the back. What was it doing here?"

"Judging by the glass shards in it and the rips, whoever broke into your bakery, wrapped their fist in this shirt and punched their way in."

Tyler stared at the shirt. He looked as if someone had punched him in the chest. Keogh glanced at his friend and for the briefest second, Mel thought she saw suspicion in his gaze, but then it was gone.

"I own a lot of jerseys," Tyler said. "This could have come from anywhere."

"Yeah, I figured as much," Officer Bishop said. He was young and when he looked at the two football players, he seemed in awe, and not just because they were both a head taller than him. "We'll come back tomorrow morning and check with the neighboring shops. Maybe we'll get lucky and one of them has security footage of the parking lot or exterior of the building."

"Is it okay if we go ahead and board up the windows?" Keogh asked. "We want to keep the place secure."

"Sure," Bishop said. "We're done. You can go ahead and clean up inside, too."

It was then that Mel noticed the parade of vehicles entering the small parking lot. These were not average-people cars. These were high-end sports cars, trucks, and sedans that most people would never own in their lifetime. It took her a second to realize that it wasn't just Quinn, the entire team had turned out to help.

The lift in Keogh's spirits was immediate. He clapped Tyler on the shoulder and said, "See, look at this. We can't leave these guys. We're fam."

When Joe picked up Mel from the bakery, the players were still hard at work setting the bakery to rights. Mel and Tate agreed that the best thing they could do would be to open the bakery just like normal tomorrow. Whoever had smashed in the windows would not win.

Mel thought about telling Joe their happy news on the ride home, but she fell asleep. The cool air from the car's vents washed over her and the next thing she knew he was gently jostling her arm to wake her up. She barely had the stamina to brush her teeth and put on her pajamas before she was asleep.

Up before the sun, Mel was out the door and at their bakery in Old Town, raiding their supply of cupcakes to stock Keogh and Tyler's. Tate was there and Oz arrived to help with the baking to replace all that Mel was taking. She wanted a cupcake for breakfast but chose a banana instead, grumbling all the way to her car. Eating intentionally for two was definitely going to require some discipline.

She walked in through the back door of the bakery to find Keogh, Mama June, Tyler, Steve, and Blaise sitting in the kitchen watching the news. Ray and Marty had followed her in a separate car as they were planning to stay later than she was. This worked for her as it gave her a chance to practice telling Joe the news on the drive over. She felt a flutter of excitement. Today was definitely the day.

The first thing Mel noticed was that Mama June and Keogh were wearing aprons. Judging by the ingredients on the worktable and the smell of freshly baked cupcakes, they had clearly been doing some baking. Mel was impressed.

"I didn't want you to have to smell the vanilla," Keogh said. "So we decided to bake those early and get them out of the way."

"Aw, thanks," Mel said. "I really appreciate that."

"Uh-oh, here it is, the lead news story," Tyler said.

They all glanced at the television that was mounted on the wall. Mel had one like it in her kitchen and she mostly watched old movies when she stayed late baking specialty orders. This one, she noticed, was mostly tuned to the sports networks. This morning, however, it was the local news.

"Late last night, a vandal targeted the local bakery owned by two stars of the Arizona Scorpions football team," the newsperson read the story off the teleprompter. "Video taken from a security camera installed by the shopping center's property owner shows the suspect punching their way into the bakery."

They all watched speechless as the grainy video played, showing a person, dressed in dark clothes, white sneakers, and a dark ball cap, approach the front door and then punch the glass until it shattered. Swiftly, the person reached inside and unlocked the door. The video then cut out.

"That's the vandal!" Tyler cried. "They have them on video. They have to be able to catch them now."

"That video was terrible," Steve said. "As a defense attorney, I'd be able to take that apart frame by frame."

"No suspects were arrested and the bakery is planning to be open today," the news anchor continued. "We go to our live correspondent who is at the bakery this morning."

Mel glanced through the kitchen door to the front of the bakery. With the plywood covering the windows and door, there was no way to tell who was outside.

"What are they doing out there?" Keogh asked, and Mel turned back to the television to see what was happening.

"Hi, I'm Rix Bonano, and I'm standing outside the Fairy Tale Cupcakes bakery owned by quarterback Keogh Graham and wide receiver Tyler Matthews. As you can see, the windows and doors have been boarded up in response to some vandalism that occurred late last night."

Mel watched as the camera panned across the front of the bakery away from the reporter who had slicked-back hair and was wearing a dress shirt that appeared to be too large for him, making him look as if he were a kid dressing up as a reporter rather than the real deal.

"No suspects have been arrested and no motive is apparent, but I have two people with me who have a theory about what might have happened."

The camera came back to the reporter, and Mel finally saw whom Keogh had seen. C.J. and Thad Dayton were standing beside the reporter. A chyron came up with their names, so it was clear that the news team had been prepared for this visit.

"Standing with me are C.J. Dayton and Thad Dayton, sons of the late Chad Dayton, the former owner of the Arizona Scorpions. Can you tell us what you think happened last night here at the bakery?"

"It's a publicity stunt," C.J. said.

"Yeah, totally," Thad repeated.

"What?" Keogh cried. His eyes were huge and he clapped his hands on his head as if to keep the top of his head from blowing off.

"We have hard evidence that Keogh Graham did this 'vandalism' to his own bakery so that the fans would feel sorry for him," C.J. continued. "But you shouldn't because he's a murderer who will stop at nothing to get what he wants."

Rix, the reporter, looked giddy, no doubt imagining this clip going viral and giving him his fifteen minutes of sad manufactured fame. "And what does he want?" Rix asked. He then turned to the camera for a close-up and asked in an overly dramatic voice, "What does Keogh Graham want?"

"To kick your as—" Keogh began but Mama June interrupted.

"Don't stoop to their level, son."

"But—" he protested, but Mama June gave him a look. Keogh nodded.

"Yes, ma'am."

Mel wondered what kind of mother magic this was and how could she get some before the baby came along. She wanted to be able to shut down a tantrum with a look. She glanced back at the television.

"What do you think, Mr. Dayton?"

"I think it's pretty clear that Keogh wants ownership of the Arizona Scorpions," C.J. said. "His refusal to sign his contract proves that the rumors about him retiring are true. What better way to not leave the game he loves than to own a team?"

"Yeah, and we figured out that he and our father's wife Kendall planned the whole thing," Thad said. C.J. turned and gave his brother an annoyed look. It was obvious he'd wanted to be the one to drop the bombshell.

"Are you saying that Keogh Graham is involved with Kendall Dayton?" Rix asked, his voice full of feigned surprise.

"Yeah," C.J. said. "I don't think they ever broke up. She married the old man so that the two of them could off him and take over the team. When Coach Casella caught them, they murdered him, too."

"That's it!" Keogh shouted. He stormed towards the front of the bakery.

Mama June looked at Tyler and said, "Stop him!"

"Stop him? I want to help him!" Tyler said.

"No, Mama June is right. If Keogh's seen as being violent, it's the absolute worst optics he could have right now," Steve said.

"Agreed. If he storms out there, it could destroy his career," Blaise cautioned.

"Argh." Tyler hurried from the kitchen and they all followed him. "Key, wait!"

Keogh was about to shove the door open when there was a commotion from outside. Someone yelped and there was a lot of yelling.

"You guys, get back in here!" Marty called from the kitchen. "You have to see this!"

As one they all turned back to the kitchen. Marty had the remote for the television in his hand and he was laughing so hard he was wheezing. He had paused the television and when they reassembled, he pointed the clicker at the screen and hit play.

Rix and the Dayton brothers filled the screen. C.J. was repeating his theory about Keogh being a murderer and then, out of nowhere, a fat juicy tomato hit C.J. right in the face. He staggered back. Thad shouted at someone off-camera and he, too, got a face full of overripe tomato. And then the pelting began. Tomatoes rained down on the Dayton brothers until they were covered in seeds and pulp. The reporter tried to back away, but he slipped on the tomato droppings and landed on the sidewalk on his rump.

Mel wasn't positive but she thought she heard the cameraman laughing. The image abruptly vanished, switching back to the reporters anchoring the newsroom desk. Both of them stared openmouthed until the woman shook her head and plastered on a fake smile as she sent them to a commercial break.

"Who? What?" Keogh asked.

"Only one way to find out," Mama June said. "Now we can go outside."

She led the way to the front door. Keogh had unlocked it and she pushed it open to find the Dayton brothers and the news van speeding away from an angry mob. A small army of young Scorpions fans were standing in the parking lot. One teen, the self-appointed leader, was at the front of the pack with a grocery bag full of overly ripe tomatoes.

His mouth formed a small O as he took in the sight of Keogh and Mama June. "Mr. Graham!"

Keogh studied the boy, who looked to be about fourteen. "Don't I know you?"

The boy's face lit up. "You remember? You came to see me in the Phoenix Children's Hospital two years ago."

"Miles, right?" Keogh asked.

"Yeah!" The boy looked as if he might pass out.

"Of course, I remember you. How's your arm?"

"All healed, sir," Miles answered. He dropped the bag of veggies and pretended to make a pass. Mel suspected he was the one who had managed to hit the Daytons with such accuracy.

"Clearly," Keogh said. "I know that school is out for the summer, but what are you doing here?"

"My friend Davis—" Miles paused to point at a gangly kid with glasses. The boy waved. Keogh waved back. "Davis was at his dad's coffee shop last night and he heard that reporter talking to those two guys while they planned their news conference. He messaged us all last night and we agreed to come and stop them. You give so much to the community. We know you didn't hurt anyone, Mr. Graham."

Mel glanced at Keogh and saw a sheen of tears fill his

eyes. It was clear that his fans' loyalty meant a lot to him. Mama June opened her arms and hugged the boy. "You know what this calls for, kids?"

The crowd of boys and girls collectively shook their heads. Mama June grinned and shouted, "Cupcakes!"

Nineteen

After a successful day of baking, Mel left Ray and Marty in charge of the new hires while she drove back to Old Town. Feeling inspired, she had made a reservation at Joe's favorite restaurant. Hoping that no one would see them there, she planned to finally tell him the news. She texted Joe to meet her at the restaurant for dinner. He had responded with a very enthusiastic gif.

Mel showered, put on mascara and lip gloss, and wore her favorite pink swing dress with a pair of black low-heeled sandals and her black clutch. It was a go-to outfit for the hot Arizona summer. She fluffed her hair one last time just before she stepped outside to find Steve Wolf-meier striding up the walkway.

"Hey, Mel, sorry to interrupt," he said.

"Is this going to take long?" she asked.

"Not to be overly dramatic, but the future of my client and your friend Keogh depends upon it," he said. "So, yes."

His face was grim. Mel's heart sank. She opened the app on her phone to cancel dinner and sent a quick text to Joe that the plan had changed and to come right home. She knew that whatever brought Steve to her door had to be bad for Keogh.

"Mel, you look . . ." Steve's lips parted in their usual flirty smile but then the corners of his mouth drooped and an expression of alarm came over his face. "Pregnant."

"What?" she cried. "How can you tell?" She put her hands on her belly. She'd never been super skinny but she didn't think she was showing yet, either.

"You have a look," he said. He studied her for a beat. "There is a softness to you and a glow. Frankly, it scares the bejeezus out of me."

"The glow is because I'm sweating standing out in this heat," Mel said. "Joe's going to be home soon. You absolutely can't say a word to him about my condition. I was hoping to tell him tonight over dinner."

"Sorry, did I ruin it?" he asked.

"Yes," she said. She turned and led the way back into the house.

Peanut barked and jumped towards Steve as if he'd come over just to play with her, but he held up a hand and said, "No. These shoes are Italian and do not respond well to drool."

Peanut sat down, looking woefully disappointed. Mel rolled her eyes. "Beer?"

"Yes, please." He followed her into the kitchen. Mel thought about how much pet hair was going to get on his slick suit and she had to hide her smile. She grabbed a bottle of beer out of the refrigerator and a glass from the cupboard. She poured the beer and handed it to Steve while he took a seat at the small café table in their kitchen.

She poured herself a glass of pomegranate juice and took the seat across from his. "So, what gives?"

"I have some questions for you," Steve said. His expression became serious.

"What about?" Mel asked.

"About what you saw when you found Keogh with Dayton's body," he said.

Mel took a restorative sip of her juice. "All right, but for the record I do not like this at all."

"Relax, I'm his defense attorney," he said. "Nothing you say to me will get him in any trouble."

"Okay."

"Do you remember seeing anything, anything at all, near Dayton's body?" he asked.

"That's a bit vague," Mel said. "What are you looking for exactly?"

"I don't know. We've just gotten the medical examiner's report and it states that Dayton didn't die from multiple scorpion stings," Steve said. "In fact, they've determined that the injuries from the scorpions they found on his person were posthumous."

Mel nodded. Ray had already told her as much.

"You don't seem surprised," Steve said.

Mel shrugged. "I'd already heard that rumor."

"You might have mentioned it."

"Things have been a little crazy. So, how did Dayton die?"

"Cardiac tamponade brought on by hemopericardium," Steve said.

Mel blinked. "Translation?"

"His pericardial sac filled with blood and compressed his heart," he said.

"Whoa." Mel felt woozy. "So, that pressure effectively stopped his heart from pumping blood?"

"As far as I can understand it," he said.

"And you're looking for a weapon of some sort that might have caused it?" Mel asked.

"The medical examiner's report indicated that there was a chest trauma," Steve said. He paused to sip his beer.

"You mean like a punch to the chest?" Mel asked.

"That would have left bruising," Steve said. "This was more insidious. It appears that there were puncture marks on the left side of his chest, two of which entered the pericardial cavity."

"Meaning?" Mel asked.

"He was stabbed with something that caused his pericardial sac to fill with blood," Steve said. "Potentially, something you'd find in a kitchen?"

"This is bad, isn't it?"

Steve nodded.

Mel thought about walking into the bakery and finding Dayton on the floor. Had she seen anything, any kitchen implement, that would explain the fatal injury Dayton had suffered?

"All I can remember seeing is Dayton on the floor," Mel said. "When I went to examine him, a scorpion popped out of his sleeve and I backed away. I forced myself to return and check him, but Keogh pulled me away."

"That's what he told me, too," Steve said. He pursed his lips as he stared out the window into Mel's backyard.

"Can you think of any baking implement that is narrow and sharp enough to puncture?"

"Puncture?"

"Yes, not a knife," he said. "According the medical examiner's report it had to be something with a fine point."

Mel thought about it. "Most commercial baking equipment is cumbersome. It's bowls, mixers, cupcake pans, and pastry bags. We really don't use anything that could puncture . . . Wait."

She rose from her seat and crossed the kitchen to her drawer full of baking odds and ends. These were the items she used less often and so they were relegated to a large drawer in the bottom of the cabinet. She sorted through the equipment until she came up with the only thing she could think of that could be used to puncture.

She returned to the table and handed it to Steve. "I don't know if they had one at the bakery where Dayton's body was found, but this is the only thing I can think of that would be used in a bakery kitchen that could puncture."

"What is it?" Steve asked.

"A candy thermometer," she said. "We can check the inventory list Keogh and Tyler used when they set up their kitchen to see if they have one. Or, I guess, simply check the drawer."

Steve tapped the tip of the thermometer with his finger. "It is pointy, but could it puncture the skin?"

"I don't know. Weirdly, that's never come up before." Mel met his gaze and he sighed. "It's primarily used to check the temperature of melted chocolate or any other sugar solution," she said. "None of those require being punctured."

"Hmm." Steve handed it back to her. "I think I'm going to head out to the bakery."

Peanut abruptly burst into a frenzy of barking, over which Mel yelled, "Joe's home."

"I guess I'll stay then," Steve said. "I wouldn't want him to think you and I were—"

Mel cut him off. "He would never think that."

"Ouch," Steve said. He placed a hand over his heart but his smile assured Mel that he was kidding.

Joe entered the kitchen from the door that led to the garage. He saw Steve and his eyebrows lifted in surprise. "Mel, didn't the exterminator come by last week?"

"Obviously not, if you're still able to enter the house, DeLaura." Steve lifted his beer in a salute.

"Enough, you two," Mel interrupted before Joe could blast back. "Play nice." She turned to Joe. "Steve was following up with some questions about when Keogh and I found Dayton's body."

"Oh." Joe nodded. He didn't say anything else, and Mel knew that being an assistant district attorney put him in a weird place when it came to talking about an ongoing investigation. He leaned forward and kissed Mel on the cheek. "I take it this is why our dinner was canceled?"

"Yes," she said.

"You look amazing," he said. "Are you sure you don't want to head out on the town?"

She glanced at Steve. "Did you have any more questions?"

"No, that was it," he said. "You were a huge help."

Mel wasn't so sure. If there was no candy thermometer at the bakery but there was one on the inventory, that could be very bad for Keogh.

"Don't fret," Steve said. "We'll get it sorted out."

She nodded. "Do you think they'll be able to keep the bakery?"

"I don't know," Steve said. "But I sure hope so, for Tyler's sake."

"Tyler's sake?" Joe asked. "Is something wrong with him?"

"Yeah." Steve nodded. "It's not public information yet, so please keep it to yourselves, but Tyler is getting cut from the Scorpions."

Mel gasped. "Why?"

"His knee," Steve said. "Keogh told me that the doctors have done all they can do. The joint is shot and even aspirating the excess fluid as often as they have won't help. His career is over."

"That's a tough break," Joe said.

"Does Tyler know?" Mel asked.

"Kendall and Keogh were going to meet with him tonight," Steve said. He glanced at the Rolex on his wrist. "In a half hour, in fact."

"Keogh?" Mel asked. "He and Kendall aren't . . . ?"

"No," Steve said. Then he looked thoughtful. "At least, I don't think so. I hope not, because that won't play out well in the media. No, I think it's just the first time she's ever had to release someone from their contract and Keogh is there for moral support for them both, I expect."

Mel and Joe both nodded.

Steve drained his beer and said, "I'd better go. I have a mission."

"Wait," Mel said. "When Keogh was stung by that scorpion a few weeks ago, wasn't it Tyler who brought him to the hospital?"

"Yes," Steve said without hesitation. "He's my first line of defense that there's no way Keogh caught a bunch of scorpions and used them to kill Dayton. I mean, Tyler saw how much pain Keogh was in and can testify that Keogh would never go near them willingly."

"I'm not hearing any of this," Joe said. "But that's an excellent plan."

"Thanks," Steve said. He looked surprised by the praise.

Mel would have been pleased by their sudden shift into maturity, but she was busy trying to do a timeline in her head. If she was right, then she knew who killed Dayton and it definitely wasn't Keogh.

"Where are Keogh and Kendall going to talk to Tyler?" she asked. Her voice came out high and tight.

"The bakery," Steve said. "Keogh wanted to convince Tyler that he could be happy there."

"Tyler's never going to be happy there," Mel said. "All he wants to do is play ball. He's been very clear about that from the beginning."

"What's wrong?" Joe asked.

"We need to go there now," she said.

Joe frowned. "To the bakery? Why? What's wrong?"

"I think Keogh might be in danger," she said. She turned to Steve. "Is Mama June with him?"

"No, she didn't think Tyler wanted any witnesses to his release. Embarrassing, you know? Plus, she can't abide Kendall. She's at Keogh's house." Steve studied her face. "What's wrong, Mel? Why would Keogh be in danger?"

"Can you call Detective Rivera?" she asked. "He needs to get to the bakery right away." She looked at Joe as she grabbed her phone. "Can you drive? I'm going to try and reach Keogh."

"Mel, you're spinning, tell us what is happening," Joe said.

"No time, we can talk on the ride," she said. She looked at Steve. "Let's go."

"All of us?" he asked. "Aren't I supposed to be doing a covert op to look for the . . . er . . . implement?"

Mel waved her hand. "No, you don't have to. The thermometer is of no consequence. I know what killed Dayton."

"What?" Steve asked.

"A syringe," Mel said. "The kind you aspirate a knee with."

Twenty

Joe drove. Mel was in the passenger seat while Steve sat in back and called Detective Rivera. Mel could hear only part of the conversation as she was trying to call Keogh at the same time. He wasn't picking up.

Mercifully, rush hour traffic had cleared out and they made good time arriving a few minutes before Keogh and Kendall were about to meet with Tyler. Maybe, just maybe, they wouldn't be too late. Joe parked on the far side of the parking lot behind the delivery truck for the pool supply store on the end of the row.

Mel glanced at the bakery and sighed with relief. The cars for the employees were all gone, which made sense since the bakery was technically closed now. She had been worried that Ray and Marty and the new hires might have gotten caught in whatever was going down.

Mel reached for the door handle to get out, but Joe said, "No, I want you to stay here and wait for Detective Rivera. Where is he?" He scanned the lot. There was no sign of the detective. "Steve and I will sneak in through the back door."

Mel knew he was right. She should wait. That way she could intercept Detective Rivera and tell him her suspicions before he went inside.

"All right." She handed Joe her key to the bakery. "But if I hear anything worrisome, I'm driving right through the front door to get you out if I have to."

Joe smiled. "You would, too."

"You're a lucky man, DeLaura," Steve said.

"I know it," Joe said. He kissed Mel quick and the two men walked towards the building. She tried not to fret. She knew Joe could handle himself but there was so much more on the line now. He was going to be a father and he didn't even know it.

The shades were pulled over the newly installed large front window and front door so Mel couldn't see inside. She shifted in her seat. She had a bad feeling about this. There was still no sign of the detective. Not even a patrol car had arrived.

She put her hand on the door handle and then let go. She reached for it again but stopped. It was feeling stuffy in the car. Joe had left it running but even the air-conditioning coming out of the vents couldn't stop the trickle of sweat she felt slide down the side of her face. She wiped it away and stared at the bakery, willing the door to open so she could see inside.

Was Keogh in there? Was Kendall? Had they parked in back? Was Tyler here already? Were her suspicions correct or was she way off base? She liked Tyler. She thought about the times she'd seen him stand up for Keogh and how they called each other *brother*. What if she was wrong?

She turned off the engine and reached for the door handle but before she could unlatch it, a face popped up in the window. *Tyler!*

Mel yelped and started in her seat. She put her hand on her chest and sucked in a gulp of air.

Tyler pulled her door open and leaned down to her level. "Mel, what are you doing here?"

"I was waiting for . . . um . . . I stopped because . . . I forgot . . ." Mel stopped talking. She couldn't even formulate an excuse as to why she was sitting outside the bakery.

"You seem flustered," Tyler said. He stared at her. "Why don't you come in and get a glass of water. You're probably overheated."

Mel shivered. Had his eyes always been this cold and flat or was she just noticing now because he was probably bringing her inside to kill her?

She glanced around the parking lot. Where was Detective Rivera? She felt her heart rate speed up. She didn't want to go in there with him. If Keogh and Kendall kicked him off the team, there was no telling what he'd do. He'd already murdered two people. Her throat was dry and when he took her elbow and helped her out of the car, she didn't fight it. The only way she could save this situation was to stop Kendall from releasing Tyler from his contract.

It could buy them enough time until Detective Rivera arrived and then they could arrest him and cart him off to jail. The desert heat of the early evening blasted her as she shut the car door. Tyler let go of her arm and led the way to the bakery.

"I like your shoes," Mel said, hoping to distract him.

Tyler paused and looked down at the name-brand black sneakers he was wearing. "Thanks. I own like twenty pairs of these. All black. They're my only sponsor, so I try to do right by them."

Mel frowned. There was something about the shoes that nudged a part of her brain. But what was it?

Tyler used his key to open the front door and then gestured for Mel to lead the way. Feeling anxious, Mel stepped into the bakery and called out, "Hello? Anyone home?"

She glanced over her shoulder at Tyler and smiled. She had no idea why, probably an instinctual ploy to win him over? He didn't smile in return.

Mel walked farther into the bakery. The lights were on but the main room was empty. She wondered if Keogh and Kendall were even here. He'd never answered his phone. Maybe they'd changed their minds.

"Doesn't look as if anyone is here," Mel said. She glanced at the kitchen doors, wondering if Joe and Steve were in there. Wanting to let them know she was in the building, she yelled, "Hello!"

No answer. Tyler locked the door behind them and Mel felt her heart drop. She glanced at him and asked, "What brings you by the bakery so late?"

Tyler studied her. His face was set in harsh lines. "I got a text from Keogh asking me to meet him here. Something about buying me out of the bakery."

"Buying you out?" Mel asked. "What? Why?"

Tyler's stiff posture relaxed and the tension in his face eased. "You didn't know?"

"This is the first I'm hearing of it," Mel said. "And I'm shocked."

"Me, too." Tyler looked validated and his face resumed its usual jovial expression. "Thank you. Also, I think I owe you an apology. I know I haven't been as enthusiastic about the bakery as Keogh, but I don't want to be bought out." He glanced around the shop and there was a look of pride in his gaze. "I like it here. I like it a lot."

"Really?" Mel asked. She'd assumed he couldn't care less.

"Yeah, I like the vibe, I enjoy meeting people and eating cupcakes." He laughed. Mel felt her own tension evaporate. "Besides, between you and me, I think I might get cut from the team because of my knee, so I'm going to need something to do."

Mel's eyes went wide. She swallowed. "You think they're going to cut you?"

He gestured to his knee. "How can they not? Doc straight up said I'll be lucky to play again and never at my old level. I can't hold Keogh and the team back like that."

"You seem like you've made peace with it," she said. Oh, man, if this was true, she'd been wrong. So very wrong. If the killer wasn't Tyler, then it had to be . . .

"I haven't totally come to grips with it, but I'll get there," he said. He started to cross the room and waved for Mel to follow him. "Come on, let's get you some water."

He pushed through the kitchen door and came to an abrupt stop. Mel slammed into his back and he reached behind to steady her.

"Kendall, what are you doing?" he cried.

Mel glanced over his shoulder and immediately wished she hadn't. Kendall was standing in the middle of the kitchen, holding a gun on Keogh. *What?!*

Tyler tried to push Mel back through the door, but it was too late.

"Don't!" Kendall snapped. "Get in here, both of you, and keep your hands where I can see them."

Tyler raised his hands and strolled forward slowly. He angled his body in front of Mel, using his broad shoulders to shield Mel as much as possible. Kendall wasn't having it.

"Separate," she ordered. She shifted so the gun was pointed in their direction. Tyler and Mel took a small step away from each other. Keogh met Mel's gaze and the look in his eyes verified what she'd just realized. Tyler wasn't guilty of murder. Kendall was.

Mel quickly scanned the room but there was no sign of Joe or Steve. She breathed a small sigh of relief.

"What's going on, Kendall?" Tyler asked. "What are you doing?"

"Shut up and sit down," Kendall snapped. There was no flirty look or hair toss to go with the command. She gestured to the two stools beside Keogh.

Mel and Tyler walked around the steel table, giving Kendall and her gun a wide berth. Mel glanced at the table in front of her and blanched. There was an open tub of vanilla buttercream and several newly frosted cupcakes sitting right there. Oh, no.

"Key, what's going on, bro?" Tyler asked.

"Kendall murdered Chad and Coach and now . . . us," Keogh said. He turned to look at Mel. "I'm sorry, Mel. You shouldn't be here. You shouldn't be a part of this."

"Too bad, so sad." Kendall made a fake sobbing sound and pointed the gun right at Mel's chest. There was pure hate in her gaze and Mel felt a shiver of fear zip up her spine. But she also felt vindicated for her intense dislike of the woman from the start and wished that she could call Angie just to say, *I told you so*.

"Why kill Coach?" Tyler sounded perplexed. "I mean, killing Dayton gave you the team so where was the gain in murdering Coach?"

Mel was grateful that Tyler was asking the questions as she had to focus on mouth-breathing so as not to let the smell of the vanilla cupcakes on the table trigger her vomit response.

"Because he was going to ruin everything," Kendall said. "I had a plan. It was all going so well and then he . . ." She paused to gesture at Keogh with the gun. ". . . decides to open a bakery? A freaking bakery?!"

Kendall was dressed in a curve-hugging purple che-mise paired with stiletto sandals. She looked like she was ready for a night of clubbing, not confessions of murder.

Mel wanted to glance at the door and see if Joe and Steve were aware of the situation. She knew that they most likely were and that Joe was probably having a com-plete freak-out that Mel was inside with a gun pointed at her. She didn't hear any sirens so there was no way to know if the police had arrived yet.

"What do you care if Key opened a bakery? Why would you murder Coach over that?" Tyler asked. He still looked confused. Mel gave him a lot of credit as she was having a tough time staying upright, never mind talking.

"Because the plan was that I'd marry Chad, he'd change his will so that I inherit the team, and when he tragically dies, Keogh and I would live happily ever after as the quarterback and the owner of the Scorpions," Kendall said. "But because of this stupid place, Keogh wouldn't sign his contract and Coach Casella was going to trade him because of his lack of commitment. I couldn't allow him to do that. I had no choice."

Tyler looked at Keogh and said, "But she was framing you for the murders. How was that supposed to work?"

"Not me, bro." Keogh shook his head.

Tyler pursed his lips as he thought about it and then his eyebrows lifted. "Me? She was framing me?"

"Kendall stabbed Dayton in the heart with a needle, much like the one they used to aspirate your knee," Mel said, piecing it all together. "It caused his heart to stop, and she tossed the scorpions on top of him to make it look like the person who took Keogh to the hospital after he was stung was the same person who murdered Dayton. Also, she knew that everyone knew the code to Keogh's gun safe and that if she used Keogh's gun, you'd be implicated in Coach's murder as well."

"That's cold," Tyler gasped. "Why would you do that to me?"

"Because you are a washed-up has-been who is expendable," Kendall snapped.

"Mean." Tyler frowned. "So, that's why Dayton was in the bakery? You got him in here and killed him and then made it look like I did it."

"How'd you get in?" Mel asked.

"I stole a key at the open house," Kendall said. "How'd you think?"

"Cheri's key," Keogh said.

"That's right," Mel said. "She said she lost it."

"Do I really seem like the type to cover a person in scorpions?" Tyler asked.

"Who cares? There was a lovely metaphor to it, don't you think?" Kendall asked. "Death of the Scorpions' owner by scorpion." She laughed, and it was one of the scariest sounds Mel had ever heard.

Mel shivered. She had been witness to some unrepentant killers before but Kendall was actually terrifying in her lack of remorse.

"Okay, I can see how killing Dayton would give you the team," Tyler said. "But killing Coach over a possible trade? He was a good man. He didn't deserve that."

"He was going to ruin everything. He had to go." Kendall began to pace around the kitchen. She was looking for something. Mel wondered what. "It's unfortunate that this place doesn't have gas. It'd be so easy to send you all off into permanent dreamland."

"Are you really going to add three more murders to the two you've already committed?" Keogh asked. "You'll never get away with it."

"Won't I?" she countered. "I've set it up so that everyone will think Tyler is the murderer and that he vandalized the bakery—"

"What?" Tyler cried. "I would never. Besides, that terrible video showed the person who broke into the bakery was wearing white kicks. I only wear black. I am loyal to my sponsor to the end."

"Well, your end is about to come," Kendall said. "The vandalism of the bakery had two purposes. One: It was supposed to make you want to quit. And two: I had some rage to work out."

"You're terrifying," Tyler said.

Kendall grinned as wide as her chemically altered skin would allow her to. "Thank you. Now when I stage the scene here, the police will think you murdered Keogh and her and then killed yourself."

"What?" Mel cried. "That's mental. No one will ever believe that!"

Kendall whipped her head in Mel's direction. She raised the gun and pointed it right at Mel's face, looking like she was about to pull the trigger. Both Keogh and Tyler jumped up to try and protect her but Kendall waved them back to their seats.

"Move towards her again and I'll shoot her first," Kendall said. Mel gasped, and that was when the smell of the vanilla punched her right in the nose.

"Oh, no," she cried. She could feel her stomach lurch and saliva pooled in her mouth. "Not now, not now."

"What's wrong with you?" Kendall demanded. "Why do you look like that?"

"She's going to be sick," Keogh said. "Hand her a trash can."

Kendall turned to look at him. One perfectly sculpted eyebrow lifted mere millimeters, which was likely all she could manage, given the amount of Botox she was rocking, and she said, "Do you really think I'm going to fall for that? You're a quarterback. You'll take that bin and weaponize it to take me out. I'm not stu—"

Mel lost the battle to keep her lunch down. Like something out of a vintage horror movie, she projectile-puked across the table right onto Kendall, who dropped the gun to the floor with a clatter as she shrieked in revulsion. She waved her hands in the air, her pointy acrylic nails flashing, as if she could make the ick vanish.

The back door burst open and Joe and Steve erupted into the kitchen, making a beeline for Kendall. She raced for the gun, slipping in her high heels. Steve hesitated, but Joe did not. He took Kendall down with the precision of a linebacker making a sack. Kendall tried to fight him off and grab the gun.

Keogh jumped out of his seat and snatched the gun right before Kendall could. He yelled, "Go long!"

Tyler darted across the kitchen and Keogh lobbed the gun at him. Tyler caught it with both hands and then turned and deposited it into a tub of flour. A cloud of white filled the air, making him cough.

Steve grabbed a trash can, which he held in front of Mel while she tried to contain her retching. Keogh dropped to the floor and assisted Joe in containing Kendall, who continued to scratch and claw, desperately trying to break free.

"Nobody move," Detective Rivera said as he stepped into the open doorway with two officers behind him. He took in the scene at a glance. Joe and Keogh were on the floor, holding down Kendall; Tyler was covered in flour; and Steve held the trash can in front of Mel as she spit into it with his head turned away as if hoping she had nothing left to throw up.

"Kendall murdered Chad Dayton and Coach Casella," Keogh said. "And she was planning to murder the three of us until Joe and Steve arrived."

"Lies! You're a liar!" Kendall screamed. She kicked out at Keogh, who dodged her foot. "Tyler killed Chad and Coach and now he's trying to frame me, and they're all helping him." She sobbed but somehow it didn't have the same damsel-in-distress effect when she had vomit in her hair.

"Technically, it was Mel puking on her that stopped her," Tyler said.

"My apologies," Keogh said. "You're right. Mel really saved the day."

Detective Rivera looked at Steve. "I thought you said in your message that Ty—"

"I was wrong." Steve shrugged. "It happens."

"Can we move to the front of the shop away from the smell of vanilla?" Keogh asked. "It makes Mel sick."

"Yes, of course." Detective Rivera signaled for his two officers to take Kendall away from Joe and Tyler. "Take her outside."

"You have to listen to me," Kendall demanded. "I'm the victim here."

The officers both wrinkled their noses at the ick covering Kendall and secured her wrists behind her.

"Don't you dare believe them over me," Kendall threatened. "I'll have your badge."

Rivera rolled his eyes and Mel knew he must have heard that ridiculous threat a thousand times during his career.

"He doesn't have to believe us. I have our conversation recorded," Keogh said. He took his phone out of his pocket and held it up. The display was that of an old tape recorder, and it was clearly recording and had been for some time. He switched the app off. "She confessed to everything on there and even told us about her plan to murder the three of us."

"That's my client," Steve said with a distinct note of pride.

"Excellent, that makes my job easier," Detective Rivera said. "Save it to your cloud and then give me your phone. It's evidence now." He turned to his officers and said, "Go ahead and take her to the station. I'm going to get their statements and I'll be right behind you."

"Keogh, don't let them do this!" Kendall cried. "Don't you see? I did it all for you."

"Don't." Keogh snapped. "None of this was for me." He looked at her with a mixture of confusion and contempt as if he couldn't believe what she had done or what she had planned to do.

"Are you okay, cupcake?" Joe asked as he washed his hands in the sink. He dried them quickly and put an arm around Mel.

"I need to get out of this room," she said. She didn't know how much longer she could avoid the vanilla.

"Right, of course," he said. He led her into the main room of the bakery. Keogh, Tyler, and Steve followed as well as Detective Rivera.

Joe led Mel to a seat at one of the small café tables. "Can I get you anything?"

"No, I just need a minute," she said. She took a deep breath, relieved to be able to breathe freely.

"Are you sick?" Joe asked. His brow was creased with concern. "Why is the smell of vanilla bothering you so much? How long has this been happening?"

"Not long," Mel said. She glanced up at her husband. He looked frantic and frazzled and so full of worry for her that she knew this was the moment. It wasn't going to be the romantic hearts and flowers scene of her dreams, but that was okay. The poor guy needed to know. Now.

"Is it an allergy?" Joe asked. "Is there something you can take?"

"No." She laughed. "In fact, I'm sure it will clear up on its own."

"Cupcake, I saw what happened in there. That was not normal," Joe said. His eyes were wide as if he still couldn't believe it. "You have to find out why you're getting so sick."

"I already have," she said. She was aware of the others watching them, but she pretended it was just the two of them. She took his hand in hers and squeezed his fingers. "Joe, I wanted to tell you in a more romantic way, but I'm afraid that will never happen. The truth is . . . I'm pregnant."

Joe stared at her for a heartbeat and then another and another. He blinked. The color slowly drained out of his face and, as if someone had kicked his legs out from under him, he dropped to the floor in a dead faint.

Twenty-One

Thankfully, football players have swift reflexes, and Keogh grabbed Joe by the front of his shirt before his head bounced off the floor like a runaway cantaloupe in the produce section. Mel dropped from her chair to the floor, where Keogh carefully set Joe down.

"Someone throw some water on him!" Steve cried. Mel suspected it was more because he wanted his old rival doused than because he wanted to wake him up.

"No, he'll be fine," Mel said. She gently patted Joe's cheek. "Hey, honey, are you all right? Can you hear me?"

Joe blinked. He looked at Mel and then at the other faces staring down at him.

"You good, Joe?" Keogh asked.

Joe's gaze flitted back to Mel. He lurched up to a seated position.

"Easy," Mel said. "You just fainted. Give yourself a second."

Joe ignored her. He cupped her face in his hands and held her gaze when he asked, "Did I hear you right?"

Mel nodded. "Yeah, you did."

Joe swallowed and his eyes were damp. "We're having . . ." He stopped talking as if he was afraid he'd jinx it by saying it out loud.

"We're having a baby," Mel said. "You're going to be a father."

A fierce look passed over Joe's face and then he hauled Mel into his arms, squeezing the breath out of her. She laughed and he let her go. He cupped her face and pulled her in for a kiss. This moment, witnessing his joy, was everything Mel had hoped for. When he released her, his gaze swept over her from head to toe.

"When? How?" he asked.

"Well, if you don't know that, DeLaura . . ." Steve teased.

"Come on, you guys, let's give them a minute," Tyler said.

"Yeah, we'll be in the kitchen, putting away the vanilla cupcakes," Keogh said. "And cleaning up."

"Sorry," Mel said.

"Don't be," Keogh said. "Your baby probably saved all of our lives."

Mel and Joe watched the men leave the room. Even Rivera had the decency to give them some privacy. When the door swung shut behind them, Mel turned to her husband and asked, "Are you happy?"

"Beyond," Joe said. "I love you so much."

"I love you, too," Mel said.

Joe rose to stand, pulling Mel up with him. He wrapped his arms about her and rested his cheek against her hair. For the first time in days, Mel felt at peace. It was the perfect antidote to the terror they'd just been through. That was, right up until Joe said, "My god, we're going to be parents."

\\'\\'\\\\'\\

"Is it weird to be a full-time baker now that you and Tyler have retired?" Mel asked.

"No, I think it was always meant to be," Keogh said.

They were in the kitchen of his bakery, trying to get ahead of the mad rush that they knew was coming, while Tyler manned the front of the shop, which really suited his extrovert personality better than Keogh's.

"Knock, knock," a voice called from the swinging door into the bakery.

Mel and Keogh turned to see Cheri Spinelli standing there with Tyler.

"We have a visitor," Tyler said. He gestured for Cheri to lead the way and she walked around him and into the kitchen.

"Hi. I heard the murderer was bagged and tagged so I was wondering if you all needed any help . . ." Cheri's voice trailed off and she glanced around the kitchen, anywhere but at Mel and Keogh, as if she was bracing for rejection.

Keogh and Tyler exchanged a glance and then they both turned to Mel.

"It's your call," she said. "But I would hear her out. Good chefs are hard to find."

Jenn McKinlay

"Cheri, it's nice of you to join us," Keogh said. He pushed a chair out with his foot. "Give us a reason to give you a second chance and we'll consider it."

Tyler nodded as if he'd been thinking the same thing.

Cheri looked relieved and strode forward. Her light brown hair was held up in a clip, she was wearing a tie-dyed T-shirt dress and sandals. She slid onto the stool, keeping one foot planted on the ground as if she might have to make a run for it.

"As I mentioned, the police and I don't exactly get along," she said. "I've got some priors—drug-related stuff from when I got hooked on opioids after a car accident, but I served my time. I've been clean and sober for five years, but I still get anxious when the police are around."

Keogh nodded. "As a person who was recently considered a person of interest by the police, I can understand the reaction," he said.

"I am truly sorry for panicking and leaving you in the lurch," Cheri said. "And I should have told you about my record, but I was ashamed."

Tyler and Keogh exchanged a look of understanding.

"Works for me," Tyler said.

"You'll give me another chance?" Cheri asked.

"On one condition," Keogh agreed. "You don't run again. If a problem comes up, you come to me or Tyler and tell us, you don't just bail."

Cheri nodded. "All right, it's a bit out of my comfort zone to trust people, but I can try."

"We'll try, too," Keogh said. He held out his hand and they shook on it.

"Excellent. Now grab an apron and get to work," Tyler said. "We're getting slammed."

Cheri grinned. She dropped her shoulder bag on the counter and took an apron off the hook. When she approached the table, she looked at Mel and said, "I can take over for you. You should probably take it easy, given your condition and all."

Mel's eyes went wide. "How did you know?"

"Are you kidding?" Cheri asked. "You're giving off an expectant-mama vibe that is impossible to miss."

Mel handed Cheri the pastry bag full of frosting and took her spot on the stool. She was tired and did not mind sitting for a spell.

"So, what happened here?" Cheri asked. "I was watching the news accounts but there were these two dorky men who said you were the killer in cahoots with the dead guy's wife, and I was like 'nah, that can't be it.' Honestly, I couldn't make out what really happened."

"Well, it all started with Keogh wanting to buy a bakery," Tyler said.

The door to the bakery opened and Marty and Oz joined them.

"Oh, hey, the missing baker is back," Marty said.

"We were just catching her up," Tyler said.

"How far did you get?" Marty asked.

"They were up to buying the bakery," Mel said. She pushed a stool in Cheri's direction. "You may as well sit."

"And you should grab a cupcake or two," Oz said. "It gets crazy. You need to fortify."

Cheri's eyes went wide.

While Oz went to fetch them all cupcakes, Marty put on the coffee. By the time it had brewed, Keogh and Tyler had reached the part about Dayton being covered in scorpions. While they talked, the back door opened and Tate and Angie joined them along with Joe. Mel smiled. The gang was all here.

Joe moved to stand behind Mel. He wrapped his arms about her and whispered, "How are you doing, Mama?"

"Not bad," she said. "No vomit today as of yet."

"Good," he said. "My mother has been cooking all day, making all sorts of high-protein and high-iron meals for us to keep in the freezer."

Mel grinned. "Between Maria and Joyce, we may not have to cook for a solid nine months."

"We have the best moms," he said.

"Yes, we do," she agreed.

"Mel, this is the part where you thought Tyler was the murderer," Keogh said, calling their attention back to the conversation.

Mel cringed. She glanced at Tyler, and said, "I am so sorry."

"No need." Tyler held up his hands. "I've already accepted your apology and, on the surface, I absolutely get why you thought it might be me. Mostly."

"You really thought it was him?" Cheri asked. She was munching on a raspberry lemon cupcake from the tray that Oz had just delivered.

"It made sense at the time," Mel said. "When I learned that there was a puncture to the pericardial sac causing it to fill up with blood, I knew it had to be someone with access to an item that would puncture, and Tyler kept having to have his knee aspirated."

Cheri glanced from Mel to Tyler. "That is logical."

"Until you remember that the dead guy's wife used to be an aesthetician who is much more skilled with needles than me," Tyler said.

"Oh," Cheri said. "Is that how she did him in?"

"Stabbed him in the heart with a needle multiple times until she caused cardiac tamponade," Marty said.

"Brought on by hemopericardium," Mel said. "The sac around his heart filled with blood, essentially stopping his heart."

"That's cold," Cheri said. "What about the scorpions?"

"She did that to frame me," Tyler said. "Because I happened to be there when Keogh got stung a few weeks ago, so I knew how much pain a sting could cause."

"Okay, so how did she get Dayton into the bakery the night she murdered him?" Cheri asked. "I mean, wouldn't he have been suspicious as to why his wife wanted to go into her old boyfriend's bakery?"

"It hasn't been confirmed, but we suspect she convinced her husband that they should burn down the bakery to destroy Keogh's dream and get him to focus on the team," Joe said. "Turns out she has a lengthy criminal record as a teen, and one of her convictions was arson."

"That's why Dayton used to call her Fire Starter as a nickname," Tyler said. "He knew about her past. We thought he meant a different kind of fire, but apparently, no, he meant actual fire."

"Yikes!" Cheri said.

The back door opened and Mama June entered the kitchen. She took in the sight of her son and the rest of the bakery crew and she sighed. "It makes a mom's heart happy to see her son surrounded by good, kind people."

She was wearing an orange-and-purple-striped dress today. It had a fitted top and a flared skirt. She'd paired it with large purple earrings that dangled to her shoulders and a handbag and sandals that were also orange. Her hair had been styled in braids and she looked as if she was getting ready to do some traveling.

"You're not leaving, are you, Mama June?" Mel asked. She didn't want her new friend to go.

"I'm afraid I have to," she said. "I have three more children to mind. But don't worry, I'll be back." She looked at Keogh with one eyebrow raised. "Your sister has taken up with that banker again."

He made a face but Tyler glowered. "Kerry has taken up with who? Do you need us to go and have a chat with this guy?"

"Kerry is a grown woman," Keogh said. "It's not our business who she dates so long as they treat her right." He looked at his mother. "He *is* treating her right?"

"Of course, she wouldn't put up with anything less," Mama June said. "He's just so . . . boring."

"Why would she settle for that when she could have . . ." Tyler's voice faded and he reached for a cupcake.

Mama June smiled at him with a knowing look in her eye. "If you have an opinion about it, Tyler, don't you think you should be talking to Kerry?"

Tyler blushed a hot shade of red and stuffed the cupcake into his mouth. Mel exchanged a glance with Joe. Clearly, Tyler's feelings for Kerry Graham ran deep and not in a brotherly way.

Mama June looked at Cheri. "I don't believe we've met."

"Hi, I'm Cheri Spinelli." Cheri held out her hand, which Mama June ignored.

"The runaway baker," Mama June said. Cheri dropped her hand and looked down at her lap, clearly embarrassed.

"Well, you're here now. Everyone deserves a second chance," Mama June said. She stepped forward and hugged

Cheri. When she released her, Cheri was beaming. Mama June just had that way with people.

"Okay, to finish our discussion, I get why Kendall murdered her husband, but why the coach?" Cheri asked.

Marty poured cups of coffee and everyone helped themselves. When Mel reached for one, he intercepted her with her own mug. "Decaf."

Mel sighed. "Thanks."

Joe squeezed her shoulder.

"Coach was going to trade Keogh," Tyler said. "Which would have ruined Kendall's plan to get back together, so she shot him."

"Wasn't the gun Keogh's?" Cheri asked. "Wouldn't he have been the prime suspect and ruined her plan?"

"Yes, but she got ahead of that by playing into the fact that everyone knew the combination to Keogh's gun safe because of his previous stalker situation," Tate said. He glanced at Keogh and Tyler. "Being a celebrity must suck."

They both nodded and Tyler said, "It definitely comes with a price."

"Okay, so I can almost see where her psychotic brain was going, but there's one thing I don't get—why did she trash the bakery?" Cheri asked.

"Still trying to frame me," Tyler said. "She used my jersey to wrap her hand up when she punched through the door, but she wore the wrong shoes. I only wear my sponsor's shoes. That's how we knew it wasn't me. Mostly, she was attempting to cause a rift between me and Key by trying to convince him that I was the one who trashed the place."

"And it almost worked," Keogh said.

Tyler shook his head. "I would never."

"I know," Key said. He opened his arms and they hugged. "I'm sorry."

"It's okay," Tyler said. "I'd be lying if I didn't admit that for a nanosecond, I thought you might have killed Dayton."

"What will happen to Kendall now?" Cheri asked.

"A trial and either a lifetime in jail or worse," Joe said.

"And the Scorpions?" Cheri asked. "Who gets the team?"

"I can answer that," Ray chimed in. "The Dayton brothers will now inherit it, and I heard from a very reliable source that they're going to sell."

Tate straightened up. "You know, cupcakes and football are an awesome pairing."

Keogh looked at him. "Are you thinking what I'm thinking?"

"We could buy the team," Tate said.

Angie looked at Mel. "'There's a moment of orderly silence before a football play begins. Players are in position, linemen are frozen, and anything is possible. Then, like a traffic accident, stuff begins to randomly collide.'"

Mel recognized the movie quote immediately and said, "*The Blind Side*."

They shared a knuckle bump, then Angie turned to Tate. "We're not buying the team."

Tate shook his head as if shaking off a daydream. Then he nodded. "You're right. What was I thinking?"

"Seriously, what would you call it, the Arizona Cupcakes?" Marty asked.

Keogh and Tyler both groaned and then more suggestions were shared to a chorus of laughs and jeers.

"The Arizona Bakers," Oz offered.

"The Arizona Mixers," Angie suggested.

"The Phoenix Patissiers," Tate said.

"What's going to be on the uniform, a chef's hat?" Cheri asked. She was laughing so hard she was wheezing, and Mama June was right there with her.

While their friends continued to call out ridiculous names, Mel leaned against Joe. She turned to him and said, "These are the people who are going to fill our child's life."

Joe glanced from her to their friends and grinned. "Lucky baby."

Mel laughed. "I couldn't agree more."

Acknowledgments

It is unfathomable to me that I have written sixteen Cupcake Bakery Mysteries. Thank you so much to every reader who has enjoyed the series and asked for more. It truly is a joy to pen each and every one.

And, of course, I am so grateful to my team: Kate Seaver, Christina Hogrebe, Amanda Maurer, Kaila Mundell-Hill, Kim-Salina I, and Jessica Mangicaro. I am so fortunate to work with such a talented and dedicated group of people, both at Berkley and at JRA.

Special thanks to my assistant, Christie Conlee, who brings magic wherever she appears. And a shout-out to my fam—the McKinlays and the Orfs—your endless enthusiasm and support are much appreciated.

Recipes

Peach Cobbler Cupcakes

A dense peach cupcake topped with vanilla
buttercream and peach cobbler filling.

3 cups all-purpose flour
4 teaspoons baking powder
1 teaspoon salt
½ cup sour cream
⅔ cup whole milk
1 cup butter, softened
2 cups sugar
2 teaspoons vanilla extract
3 large eggs, room temperature
1½ cups peach cobbler filling, pureed

Cobbler Filling and Topping

> *3 15-ounce cans of peaches in light syrup*
> *½ cup sugar*
> *3 tablespoons butter*
> *2 teaspoons ground cinnamon*
> *½ teaspoon ground nutmeg*
> *1 teaspoon vanilla extract*
> *3 tablespoons cornstarch*

Preheat the oven to 325 degrees. Put paper liners in the cupcake pan. In a medium bowl, whisk the flour, baking powder, and salt. Set aside. In a small bowl, mix the sour cream into the milk and set aside. Using a large bowl, mix the butter until creamy. Add sugar, vanilla extract, and eggs until fluffy. Alternately add the dry ingredients and the milk mixture, do not overincorporate. Set aside and make the cobbler filling.

In a medium saucepan, add the peaches, sugar, butter, cinnamon, nutmeg, and vanilla extract. On medium heat, cook for 10 minutes. Once the mixture starts to bubble, add the cornstarch. When the filling has thickened, remove 1½ cups of the mixture and puree it in a blender.

Mix the pureed peach filling into the cake batter until well combined. Fill the cupcake liners half-full and bake for approximately 18 to 22 minutes until tops are golden brown. When completely cooled, frost with a swirl of buttercream. Garnish with a cooked peach slice from the cobbler filling and drizzle the sauce over the cupcakes. Makes 24.

Buttercream Frosting

½ cup (1 stick) salted butter, softened
½ cup (1 stick) unsalted butter, softened
1 teaspoon clear vanilla extract
4 cups sifted confectioners' sugar
2 tablespoons milk

In a large bowl, cream butter and vanilla. Gradually add confectioners' sugar, one cup at a time, beating well on medium speed and adding milk as needed. Scrape sides of bowl often. Beat at medium speed until light and fluffy. Pipe onto cooled cupcakes in big swirls using a pastry bag.

Watermelon Cupcakes

A vanilla cupcake topped with
watermelon buttercream and garnished with
mini chocolate chips.

1½ cups all-purpose flour
1½ teaspoons baking powder
¼ teaspoon salt
½ cup butter, softened
1 cup sugar
2 eggs, room temperature

3 teaspoons vanilla extract
¾ cup milk

Preheat oven to 350 degrees. Put paper liners (green would be ideal to add to the watermelon look) in cupcake tin. In a medium bowl, whisk together the flour, baking powder, and salt. Set aside. In a large bowl, cream together the butter, sugar, eggs, and vanilla. Alternately add the dry ingredients and the milk, mixing until smooth. Fill cupcake liners until two-thirds full. Bake for 17 to 21 minutes until a toothpick inserted in the center comes out clean. Makes 12.

Buttercream Frosting

½ cup (1 stick) salted butter, softened
½ cup (1 stick) unsalted butter, softened
4 cups sifted confectioners' sugar
2 tablespoons milk
1 packet watermelon Kool-Aid powder mix
Red food coloring
Mini chocolate chips

In a large bowl, cream butter. Gradually add confectioners' sugar, one cup at a time, beating well on medium speed and adding milk as needed. Mix watermelon Kool-Aid powder and blend until thoroughly incorporated. Add red food coloring, one drop at a time, until desired color is achieved. Scrape sides of bowl often. Beat at medium speed until light and fluffy. Pipe onto cooled cupcakes in big swirls using a pastry bag. Garnish with mini chocolate chips.

Chocolate-Pistachio Cupcakes

A half-chocolate, half-pistachio cupcake with chocolate ganache topping garnished with crushed pistachios.

Pistachio Batter

> 1½ cups all-purpose flour
> 2 teaspoons cornstarch
> 1½ teaspoons baking powder
> ¼ teaspoon salt
> ½ cup butter, softened
> ¾ cup sugar
> 3 large eggs, room temperature
> ⅔ cup milk
> ¾ cup finely ground pistachios

In a medium bowl, whisk together the flour, cornstarch, baking powder, and salt. Set aside. In a large bowl, mix together the butter and sugar until fluffy. Add the eggs one at a time. Alternately add the milk and dry ingredients until well incorporated. Lastly, mix in the ground pistachios until well blended. Set aside.

Preheat oven to 350 degrees. Put paper liners in cupcake tin.

Chocolate Batter

1½ cups all-purpose flour
¾ cup unsweetened cocoa
1½ cups sugar
1½ teaspoons baking soda
¾ teaspoon baking powder
¾ teaspoon salt
2 eggs, room temperature
¾ cup milk
3 tablespoons vegetable oil
1 teaspoon vanilla extract
¾ cup water, warm

In a large bowl, whisk together flour, cocoa, sugar, baking soda, baking powder, and salt. Add eggs, milk, oil, vanilla extract, and water. Beat on medium speed with an electric mixer until smooth, scraping the sides of the bowl as needed.

Place a spatula in the center of the cupcake liner and fill one side with pistachio batter and the other with chocolate batter until the cupcake liner is two-thirds full. Remove spatula and let the two batters merge. Repeat for each cupcake. Bake for 18 to 22 minutes until a toothpick inserted in the center comes out clean. Allow to cool completely. Makes 24.

Ganache Topping

4 ounces semisweet chocolate
½ cup heavy cream

2 tablespoons unsalted butter, room temperature
1 cup pistachios, chopped

Place the chocolate in a heat-safe bowl. In a medium saucepan, bring the heavy cream to a simmer and then pour over the chocolate. Let stand for 1 to 2 minutes. Whisk in a circular motion until the chocolate is melted, then whisk in the butter until fully incorporated. When ganache is thickened, dip the top of each cooled cupcake into the ganache and sprinkle with chopped pistachios. Allow the ganache to set.

Butter Cake Cupcakes

A rich buttery cake topped with buttery glaze
and dusted with powdered sugar.

1 cup butter, softened
2 cups sugar
4 large eggs, room temperature
1 tablespoon vanilla extract
3 cups all-purpose flour
1 teaspoon baking powder
½ teaspoon salt
1 cup buttermilk

Preheat the oven to 350 degrees. Put paper liners in a cupcake tin. In a large mixing bowl, combine all the ingredients, mixing with an electric beater on medium for 2 to 3 minutes until fully incorporated. Fill the cupcake liners until three-quarters full. Bake for 18 to 22 minutes until a toothpick inserted in the center comes out clean. Set aside to cool completely. Makes 24.

Butter Glaze

⅓ cup butter
¾ cup sugar
2 tablespoons water
2 tablespoons vanilla extract
Powdered sugar for dusting

In a small saucepan, heat the butter, sugar, water, and vanilla extract, stirring constantly until smooth. Pour a spoonful of the thickened glaze over each cupcake. Dust with powdered sugar.

Turn the page for an exclusive look at Jenn
McKinlay's next Library Lover's Mystery . . .

A MERRY LITTLE
MURDER PLOT

"*Let it snow, let it snow, let it snow . . .*" a voice sang softly.

Library director Lindsey Norris glanced up from the computer monitor where she was working. Standing in front of the reference desk was a snowperson . . . sort of.

It was actually their children's librarian, Beth Barker, who also happened to be one of Lindsey's closest friends. Beth was wearing an oversized white T-shirt with three black felt buttons going down the front; around her neck she wore a red scarf; and on her head was a white baseball cap with two large googly eyes and a pointy nose made out of a batting-stuffed cone of orange felt, which was attached to the front just above the brim. She looked adorable.

"Let me guess," Lindsey said. "It's a snow-themed story time today."

"What gave it away?" Beth scratched her head beneath the cap as if perplexed. Then she laughed and said, "We're reading *Little Fox in the Snow*, *Making a Friend*, and *A Thing Called Snow*. Then we're crafting giant sparkly paper snowflakes to hang in the window. So fun." Beth hopped up and down as if she couldn't contain her enthusiasm. No one promoted stories and reading like Beth. She was a treasure for their small public library in the shoreline village of Briar Creek, Connecticut.

"What are you working on?" Beth asked.

"I'm thinking of offering a website-building workshop, so I'm going over the possible free options because I don't want to charge patrons. I just want to give them an idea of what's available and teach them how to get started," Lindsey said. "Our volunteer Ali McMahon is a website designer, and she's offered to teach the classes if I can come up with a curriculum."

"Sweet," Beth said. "I've considered taking a class so I can design a web page where I load up all of my story time information as a resource-sharing thing, you know?"

"I do," Lindsey said. "Potentially, we could link your page to the library's website as an additional resource, assuming I can get this class going. Honestly, it's more complicated than I expected."

"You'll figure it out. And when you do, I'll be there." Beth nodded, making the felt carrot nose on her cap bob up and down.

"I appreciate your confidence." Lindsey smiled.

"Did you finish the book for our crafternoon today?" Beth asked. Thursday was their weekly crafternoon meeting, in which they discussed a book they'd read, ate lunch, and did a craft.

"Capote's *A Christmas Memory*?" Lindsey clarified. "Yes, I did. I'd read it before but there was so much I'd forgotten. It's really a wonderful story."

"I thought so, too," Beth agreed. "Who's in charge of food this week?"

"Mayor Cole."

"Excellent." Beth pumped her fist. "She always brings meatball subs as soon as the temperature drops into the thirties."

"With extra cheese." Lindsey felt her stomach rumble. She was more than ready for lunch. She glanced at the time on the top right corner of her computer monitor. Another hour to go. Ugh.

"Library Lady!" A precocious little boy ran at Beth with his mother trailing behind him, carrying an armful of picture books and his coat. "Why are you dressed like a snow library lady?"

Beth glanced at Lindsey with a grin. "I love my job."

Then she turned back to the boy. "Hello, Nate." Beth squatted down to be on his level and said, "Why do you think I'm dressed up as a snow library lady?"

Nate leaned back, squinting his right eye as he studied Beth as if she were a riddle to be solved. After a few moments, his face cleared and he said, "Because we're reading stories about snow?"

"Yes!" Beth held up her hand for a high five and Nate reached back, then slapped her palm with his, giving it his all.

"Hi, Beth, Lindsey." Lisa Bryce, Nate's mother, joined them. "He's very excited for story time today."

"So am I!" Beth cried. She held out her hand and Nate took it. As they departed for the children's section where the story time room was, Beth called over her shoulder, "See you at lunch!"

Lindsey waved and turned back to her computer. The cursor on the blank document in front of her blinked impatiently. She glanced at the notes she'd made on the legal pad beside her. Surely, writing a class description and choosing software could not be more difficult than getting her master's degree in information science, right?

She studied her notes, felt suitably daunted, and decided she needed to get up and do a walkabout in the library. Avoidance? Yes. But as the director of the library, she tried to meet and greet as many patrons as she could during her short time on the reference desk. Also, it gave her a chance to browse the new books.

She passed through the adult reference area, which was quiet, and moved to the general fiction section. Three of the study carrels were in use by local college students cramming for their fall semester finals, and several more patrons were browsing.

In the periodical area, Milton Duffy was in his usual position, standing on his head in the corner while he did his yoga practice. His eyes were shut, so Lindsey didn't interrupt him. He was one of the town's biggest advocates of the library, taught chess club every Wednesday afternoon, and was dating Mayor Cole, so Lindsey was fine with him standing on his head wherever his heart desired.

She reached the prominently displayed new bookshelves by the front door and paused. The holidays were two weeks away, and the first December snow had fallen, leaving the town blanketed in white and fully embracing the New England Christmas vibe. She wanted something to read that matched that holiday spirit.

She supposed she could revisit a classic like *Little Women*, but there was so much more going on in the novel than the holidays, and she didn't want to over-commit emotionally. She supposed she could read a thriller, but she could always just watch *Die Hard*. She picked up a Meg Langslow mystery set during Christmas by Donna Andrews. This definitely had the humor and heart she was seeking. She scanned the bookshelf for more and scored a Royal Spyness mystery by Rhys Bowen. Christmas in England with Lady Georgie. Her evening was looking up.

Lindsey left the new books and approached circulation, taking her place in line. She wanted to ask her staff person how things were going but she didn't want to cut ahead of anyone to do it. There was only one person in front of her, and Lindsey tried to identify her from the back, which wasn't easy given that, like everyone during this December cold snap, the patron was swaddled in winter gear.

From the back, she was a tall woman, almost as tall as Lindsey, with chin-length wavy dark hair. She was wear-ing a long, navy wool coat over wide-legged tweed pants and brown, thick-soled, lace-up boots. She had a Louis Vuitton handbag dangling from her elbow, and a pair of sunglasses was pushed back on her head. When she turned her head, Lindsey recognized her profile. It was Helen Reed, a new resident in Briar Creek who had only been in the library a few times. Lindsey had tried to en-gage her in conversation, but Helen had not been recep-tive. Still, Lindsey was always polite. She wanted her patrons to know that they were among friends in the library even if they wanted to keep their distance.

Paula Turner, the head of circulation, was manning the desk and assisting Helen. Paula was known for her elaborate tattoos, although they weren't visible at the moment beneath the turtleneck sweater she was wearing, and her colorful hair. Presently, it was a stunning shade of bright red, and she was wearing it in a thick braid that draped over her shoulder and was tied with a vermillion green ribbon. Very festive.

"Here you are, Ms. Reed. Have a great day." Paula pushed the short stack of books across the counter and Lindsey glanced at the pile. She didn't mean to be rude but she liked to see what the library users were checking out so she could order more of the same.

The pile was an assortment of FBI manuals. They weren't items the library currently owned, so she assumed that Helen had ordered them through the library's interlibrary loan service. Interesting.

"We'll see," Helen said to Paula. "The best predictor of the future is the past." With that, Helen scooped up the books and turned, almost bumping into Lindsey.

"Did you just quote the Mallory Quest books?" Lindsey asked. "That's one of my favorite thriller series and the protagonist Mallory always says that very phrase."

"I have no idea what you're talking about," Helen said. She didn't meet Lindsey's gaze but glanced around the library as if checking to make certain they weren't overheard.

"You must have heard of them," Lindsey insisted. "They're written by H.R. Monroe, and are always on the top of the bestseller lists. And the main character, Mallory, always says, 'The best predictor of the future is the past'—right before she cracks the case wide open."

"That sounds dreadfully predictable." Helen glanced at her watch.

"Oh, no, they're wonderful." Lindsey gestured toward the thriller section with her hand and clipped the books Helen was holding, almost sending them tumbling to the floor. Helen grappled with them and Lindsey reached out and helped to steady the thick tomes.

"Sorry!" Lindsey cried. Then she tried to lighten the awkwardness. "Doing a little light reading?" Helen didn't smile. She clutched the pile close to her chest as if she was trying to hide them. Was Helen concerned that Lindsey was judging her? Lindsey felt the need to explain her joke. "You know, because the books are so big?"

Helen lowered her sunglasses over her eyes as if they were a shield. "I got it."

"Oh, good." Lindsey suddenly felt incredibly awkward and didn't want to leave things like this. "Is there anything else we can help you with?"

Helen lifted her sunglasses and stared at Lindsey. "That depends. Are you a skilled laborer as well as a librarian? I could use some tile work done in the bathrooms of my cottage."

"Uh . . . no," Lindsey answered.

"That's a shame." Helen lowered her sunglasses again. Despite her deadpan demeanor, Lindsey sensed Helen was joking and she got a kick out of Helen's acerbic personality.

"But we do have a list of local handypersons in our files if you need some recommendations," Lindsey offered.

"I'll keep that in mind." Helen made a noise that sounded like an impressed humph.

Lindsey would take it as a win. She didn't want to press her luck, but it was the holidays and Helen was new, and she didn't want the newcomer to feel lonely.

"I don't know if you're interested, but—"

"I'm not," Helen interrupted her, but Lindsey continued undaunted.

"We have a crafternoon group that meets every Thursday," Lindsey said. Helen sighed impatiently. "We have a book discussion, share lunch, and do a craft." She could see Paula making a slashing motion across her throat behind Helen's back. Lindsey ignored her. "You're welcome to join us, if you'd like."

Helen stood still for a moment as if considering. Then she tipped her head to the side and said, "That is a very generous offer, considering I've never given you any indication that I would be even remotely interested in anything like that, so thank you but no."

With that Helen strode out the door without a backward glance.

"Lindsey, what were you thinking?" Paula hissed. "That woman is not crafternoon material."

"You don't know that," Lindsey said. "She could be aloof because she's shy."

"No." Paula shook her head. "She is not shy. She is antisocial. There's a difference."

"I think she's funny," Lindsey countered.

"Inasmuch as sharpened knives are hilarious," Paula said.

Lindsey raised her hands in surrender. She knew there

was no way Paula was ever going to agree with her about Helen.

"I'm going to keep the invitation open regardless," Lindsey said. "She's new in town and she could probably use a friend."

She felt a patron approach from behind and she moved aside so that Paula could help them. The woman was bundled in a puffy green coat with a blue and white striped knit hat on her head and a matching scarf looped about her neck.

"Do you know who you were speaking to?" the woman asked. Her voice was high-pitched with excitement as if she knew some juicy gossip and couldn't wait to share. Lindsey found that off-putting, but she didn't know how to avoid answering the question.

"She's a patron." Lindsey hoped that would end the conversation.

"She's more than that," the woman insisted, clearly not taking the hint. "Helen is H.R. Monroe, the thriller writer."

"Are you sure?" Paula asked, not bothering to mask her doubt.

"You heard her," the woman said. "She quoted her own book."

Lindsey and Paula exchanged a glance. There was no arguing with that. Lindsey frowned at the door. Helen was H.R. Monroe? Helen did check out a stack of FBI handbooks, and she had looked clearly uncomfortable when Lindsey mentioned H.R. Monroe. It certainly seemed possible. Maybe that's why Helen was so private. Perhaps she had her fill of fans and followers and tried to maintain a low profile. That made perfect sense to Lindsey.

"I'm Jackie Lewis," the woman introduced herself and placed a stack of novels on the counter. Judging by the Friends of the Library stickers on the book covers, they were from the book sale shelf that the Friends maintained by the library entrance. One dollar per book was a bargain.

"Do you know Helen personally?" Lindsey asked.

"Oh, yes, I've been her number one fan since her very first book," Jackie said.

Lindsey felt a silent alarm go off in her brain. She had dealt with a stalker of her own before and she knew how fixated they could become.

"So, you've met her and she knows you?" Lindsey clarified.

"Oh, yes, Helen knows me," Jackie said. There was something ominous in her tone that made the alarm in Lindsey's head clang even louder. Something must have shown on her face because Jackie threw back her head and laughed and added, "I mean I've read all of her books multiple times and I follow her on social media. Not that she posts much, but I saw a picture of the Thimble Islands on her feed yesterday so I knew she was here. I decided to come for a few days to stay at the Beachfront Bed and Breakfast and see if I could meet up with her."

She winked at them, and Lindsey exchanged a concerned glance with Paula. This was not good. Jackie might be harmless, but the fact that she was following Helen was worrisome.

"Did you visit with her while she was here in the library?" Paula asked.

"No." Jackie looked dejected. "I didn't want to interrupt her, but I'm certain she'll be happy to see me when we run into each other. And since Briar Creek is such a small village, it would be impossible not to."

"I don't know," Lindsey said. "Helen seems to be a very private person."

"That's okay," Jackie insisted. "I told you, I'm her number one fan. I'm sure she'll be happy to see me."

Paula took the money that Jackie handed her and counted it. "Five dollars exactly. You're all set."

"Thanks." Jackie grinned and scooped the books up in her arms. "Byeeee."

Lindsey and Paula watched her step through the automatic doors and hunch into her coat against the cold winter wind that blew in from the bay. She disappeared down the sidewalk, and Lindsey said, "We should warn Helen about her, don't you think?"

"I think we should mind our own business," Paula said. "Every time we don't, we end up in a murder investigation and it's very stressful."

"But I got a weird feeling off Jackie," Lindsey said. "You know, a stalker-like feeling."

Paula sighed. She lifted her braid and adjusted the ribbon on the end. "I did, too, but we could just be overreacting. Why don't we ask the crafternooners what they think?"

"Good idea." Lindsey nodded. "I'm certain they'll be the voice of reason and agree we should tell her."

"Or not," Paula countered.

Learn more about this book
and other titles from
New York Times Bestselling Author

JENN McKINLAY

SCAN ME
or visit
prh.com/jennmckinlay